W9-BNZ-457

Dear Readers,

Many years ago, when I was a kid, my father said to me, "Bill, it doesn't really matter what you do in life. What's important is to be the *best* William Johnstone you can be."

I've never forgotten those words. And now, many years and almost two hundred books later, I like to think that I am still trying to be the best William Johnstone I can be. Whether it's Ben Raines in the Ashes series, or Frank Morgan, the last gunfighter, or Smoke Jensen, our intrepid mountain man, or John Barrone and his hardworking crew keeping America safe from terrorist lowlifes in the Code Name series, I want to make each new book better than the last and deliver powerful storytelling.

Equally important, I try to create the kinds of believable characters that we can all identify with, real people who face tough challenges. When one of my creations blasts an enemy into the middle of next week, you can be damn sure he had a good reason.

As a storyteller, my job is to entertain you, my readers, and to make sure that you get plenty of enjoyment from my books for your hard-earned money. This is not a job I take lightly. And I greatly appreciate your feedback—you are my gold, and your opinions *do* count. So please keep the letters and e-mails coming.

Respectfully yours,

William W. Johnstone

WILLIAM W. JOHNSTONE

BLOOD BOND
GUNSMOKE AND GOLD

PINNACLE BOOKS
Kensington Publishing Corp.
http://www.kensingtonbooks.com

PINNACLE BOOKS are published by

Kensington Publishing Corp.
850 Third Avenue
New York, NY 10022

All Kensington Titles, Imprints, and Distributed Lines are available at special quantity discounts for bulk purchases for sales promotions, premiums, fund-raising, and educational or institutional use. Special book excerpts or customized printings can also be created to fit specific needs. For details, write or phone the office of the Kensington special sales manager: Kensington Publishing Corp., 850 Third Avenue, New York, NY 10022, attn: Special Sales Department, Phone: 1-800-221-2647.

Pinnacle and the P logo Reg. U.S. Pat. & TM Off.

First Pinnacle Books Printing: April 2006

10 9 8 7 6 5 4 3

Printed in the United States of America

One

"Two riders comin'," the cowboy said, knocking the dust from him with his hat. "They look like hardcases to me. Be here in about five minutes. I grabbed a look-see from the rocks and come in the back way."

The knot of men followed him inside the saloon and up to the bar. The cowboy ordered a mug of beer and drank half of it before setting the mug on the bar. He wiped his mouth with the back of his hand.

"What brands?" he was asked.

"None I ever seen before. Fine horses, though. Real fine."

"Then it's happenin'," another said. "The damn nesters and sheepmen has hired guns."

"Aw, now, hell!" another man spoke from a table. "Don't none of us here know that for a fact. Simmer down. It's probably two drifters lookin' for work."

"With tied-down guns?" the messenger asked softly.

"Some men tie 'em down, others don't," the voice of moderation said. "We'll look 'em over when they get here."

"Suppose they head over to the Plowshare?" he was asked.

"Then we'll know, won't we?"

Matt Bodine and Sam Two Wolves rode into the town, reined up at the start of the long street, and gave the town a once-over.

"We have our choice of watering holes," Sam said. "The Red Dog and the Plowshare."

"And a fine hotel," Matt replied with a grin.

"I'm more interested in a long hot bath, a shave and a haircut, and something to eat. You see a barber shop?"

"Not yet. Let's ride on in and have a beer at one of the saloons."

"The Red Dog looks like it's doing a land-office business. Want to try the Plowshare?"

"Why not? It looks quiet. Maybe for once we can have a beer without getting into trouble."

"That would be a novel experience," his blood-brother replied dryly.

They rode on in.

"I knowed it!" the cowboy said. "Swingin' down in front of that damn sheep-dip bar."

The man who had tried to calm everybody stood up and watched the strangers. The town's two saloons were located directly across the street from each other. He grunted as he watched Matt Bodine slip the hammer-thongs from his guns the moment his boots touched the ground.

"Gunhands, all right. Shorty, you'd best ride for the ranch and tell Pete it's started."

"Right, Mr. Dale. I'm on my way."

"Frisco, get to the Circle X and tell Blake."

"I'm gone, Mr. Dale."

Mr. Dale looked around for a rider from the Lightning

Arrow spread. There was nobody in the bar who worked for Hugo Raner. Well, he'd hear soon enough.

Matt turned at the batwings as the two cowboys jumped in their saddles and lit out of town like it was a double payday at the ranch.

"Curious," he muttered.

"Maybe we need a bath more than we think?" Sam said good-naturedly.

Matt laughed at his half-breed Cheyenne brother and pushed open the batwings. Sam's father had been a great and respected chief, his mother a beautiful white woman from the East. Matt and Sam had met while just children, and soon Matt was spending as much time in the Cheyenne camp as he was at home on the ranch. They grew up together and Matt was adopted into the Cheyenne tribe and became a true Human Being. Sam's father had been killed during the battle at the Little Bighorn, after he had charged Custer, alone, unarmed except for a coup stick. Matt and Sam had witnessed the slaughter—something they had never told anyone—and when they rode down from the ridges to stand over the carnage, it had affected them deeply. They decided to drift for a time, to blunt the edges of the terrible memory before they returned to their ranches along the Wyoming-Montana border.

Both were not without resources, for Sam's mother had come from a wealthy family and was fairly well-off for the time. Matt owned a huge and very profitable cattle and horse ranch—as did Sam—so while they might look like saddlebums, they certainly were not.

They were handsome and muscular young men, both in their mid-twenties; both with a wild and reckless glint in their eyes. Sam's eyes were black, Matt's were blue. Sam's hair was black, Matt's was dark brown.

Both were big men, but very agile for their size—over six feet tall and weighing about one ninety each. They could pass for full brothers and had many times. Sam had inherited his mother's white features; only his cold obsidian eyes—which could sparkle with high humor at a moment's notice—gave him away.

Medicine Horse, Sam's father, when he knew war was coming and knew he must fight, had ordered his son from their encampment and ordered him to adopt the white man's ways and to forever forget his Cheyenne blood. Medicine Horse made his son repeat the pledge, knowing that even after his death, Sam August Webster Two Wolves would not disobey.

Both young men wore the same three multicolored stones around their necks, the stones pierced by rawhide.

And both young men were highly respected when it came to gunfighting. It was not a title they sought or wanted, but they were called gunfighters. Of the two, Matt Bodine was faster, but not by much. Matt had been at it longer than Sam.

Matt had killed his first man when he was fourteen, defending his father's ranch. The man's brothers came after him when he was fifteen. They were buried that same day. At sixteen, rustlers came when Matt was nightherding. Two more graves were added. He lived with Cheyennes during his seventeenth year and then went to work riding shotgun for gold shipments. Four men died trying to rob the shipments. Later, two more called Matt out in the street. Neither man cleared leather.

After that he was a scout for the Army, when they asked him to be. He saved his money and bought land. His ranch was one of the largest in the state.

Sam Two Wolves was college-educated, while Matt

was educated at home by his mother, who was a trained schoolteacher. Matt would be considered well-educated for the time.

There were four men in the saloon, including the barkeep. Both Matt and Sam noticed how tensed-up the men became as the brothers walked across the room to the bar, spurs jingling with each step.

Matt smiled at the barkeep. "Howdy," he said. "How about a couple of beers?"

The barkeep hesitated, then nodded and pulled two mugs of beer.

"All the business seems to be across the street," Matt remarked. "What's the place have, dancing girls?"

"Mister," one of the men seated at a table said, "you sure you're in the right saloon?"

Sam smiled at the man. "Is there a right place and a wrong place to get a beer in this town?"

"There sure is," another man said. Both brothers noticed he wore low-heeled boots and had his gun stuck behind his belt instead of in a holster.

Farmer, the brothers concluded. Then the name of the saloon sank in. The Plowshare. A saloon for farmers and sheepmen, probably.

"Well," Matt smiled the word. "If we have one beer in here and the second beer across the street, we'll please everybody, right?"

A man smiled in return. "A reasonable person might think so, but around here lately, reason seems to have flown the coop."

"Was I you boys," yet another man said, "I'd have my beer and then ride on. You been marked just by coming in here."

"Marked?" Sam asked.

"Range war shapin' up around here. Cattlemen and

hands use the Red Dog. Farmers and sheepmen use this place. You was seen comin' in here. Them across the street probably think we hired you. You're marked."

"Sheep and cattle can get along, if both sides use some sense. Sheep have to be moved regular to keep from overgrazing. Hell, so do cattle." Matt took a sip of beer.

"A reasonable man," the barkeep said. "What a breath of fresh air around here."

"Are you boys lookin' for work?" the fourth man asked.

"Not really," Sam told him. "We're just drifting. Seeing some country. We both own spreads west of here."

"Cattlemen?"

"Yes," Matt answered. "There are farms all around our spreads. We get along just fine."

The farmer shook his head. "I wish that were the case here. There are three big ranches in this area. The Box H. owned by Pete Harris; the Circle V, owned by Blake Vernon; and the Lightning Arrow, owned by Hugo Raner. They control—or think they do—hundreds of thousands of acres. We came in—the homesteaders and a few sheepmen—and filed on our land legal and proper. We've stayed and proved it up according to law. Built us a school and a church. We didn't expect all the hostility we're now facing."

Sam and Matt took their beers and moved to a table by the window.

"We put up wire to protect our crops, the cattlemen tear it down. If we try to irrigate—when we need it—the cattlemen dam up the water."

"Do you share the water?" Sam asked gently.

"Absolutely. We don't want it all, just a small portion of it. This really isn't an issue of water or land—no matter what the cattlemen say. It isn't. It's a question of who is the most powerful. Raul, one of the sheepmen, petitioned the government for grazing rights, and got it, in writing. Hugo Raner told Raul he didn't give a damn what was written on some piece of paper. Said if Raul didn't move his sheep, he'd kill them, then he'd kill Raul."

"And? . . ." Matt asked.

"Raul's lost several hundred sheep. He's written for some of his relatives to come up here and join him. They'll be along any day now."

"Basque?" Sam asked.

"Yes. They're good people. Gentle people. But if they're pushed, they'll fight."

The farmers filed out, leaving the place empty except for the bartender and the brothers by the window.

"The hotel have a dining room?" Matt asked.

"Yep," the barkeep said. "Good one. Nice rooms, too. But I doubt if Mister Dale will let you boys register there."

"Mister Dale?" Sam questioned.

"Owns this town. Well . . . he don't own it outright. He settled it. He's the mayor, owns the bank and the real estate office and some other businesses. He saw to it that Jack Linwood got the sheriff's job—rigged the election. You boys heard of Jack Linwood?"

"Yeah," Matt said. "Supposed to be a fast gun."

"There ain't no supposin' to it. He's fast. I've seen him work more'n once. And his deputies is scum. Buster Phelps, Sam Keller, and Wes Fannin."

"If the situation is as tense as the farmers say it is, don't you think you're talking a bit too much?" Sam asked.

The man smiled. "Name's Chrisman. I come in here two days behind Dale. I own this place, free and clear. I also own me a little spread west of town. Run a few head of cattle."

"What is the name of this town?" Matt asked.

"Dale. What else?"

The brothers saw to their horses and walked over to the hotel, carrying their saddlebags, bedrolls, and rifles. They had no trouble checking in, although the desk clerk's eyes bugged out when he read their names. As soon as the brothers had climbed the stairs to their rooms, the clerk sent a boy running across the street to the saloon.

"Matt Smith and Sam Jones," Mister Dale said. "Yeah. I'm sure those are their real names."

"I can run them out of town," Sheriff Linwood said, leaning against the bar, sipping a whiskey. "That'd be the easiest way to handle it."

"We don't know for sure who they are, so for now we'll leave them alone," Mister Dale said. "And I mean alone. Let them clean up and have a drink and eat and I think they'll probably pull out in the morning."

"And if they don't?" Pete Harris asked.

Mister Dale shook his head.

"I don't like it, them goin' straight to that sheepcrap and nester saloon," a cowboy said. "It's like they knew what they was doin.' "

"We'll see," Mister Dale said. "If they don't pull out in the morning, we'll . . ." he paused, ". . . Take the appropriate action." He looked at Jack Linwood. "Understood?"

Jack nodded his head. He was liking this job less and less. He'd used his gun many times, but he was no cold-blooded killer. And if Dale thought that, the man was flat-out wrong.

Two

Their boots were polished by a boy in the shop. Now, bathed and shaved, the hair cut off the backs of their necks and around their ears, and smelling like dandies (it was only a dime more to get that genuine imported aftershave splashed on), the brothers dressed in their last clean sets of clothing and left the rest to be washed and ironed by a lady who lived on the edge of town—recommended by Chrisman.

They stepped into the hotel dining room. The place was about half-full of early diners. "The town's gentry, so to speak," Sam muttered, looking around him.

"Hush," Matt told him. "You'll get us thrown out of here."

"I'll leave that up to you, since you're the expert at starting trouble."

"Thank you."

The brothers took a seat, very conscious of the sly gazes being tossed their way by the young ladies in the room; and they did look dashing. Matt was dressed in a red checkered shirt and dark jeans, a black kerchief at his throat. Sam had dressed in a sparkling white shirt, a red kerchief at his throat, and dark jeans. The brothers set some feminine hearts to palpitatin'.

Outside, the wide street rumbled under the hooves of hard-ridden horses.

"It's Rusty and some of the boys from the Lightning spread," a Box H hand said. "Damn! They're headin' into the hotel. I bet Shorty cut across their range headin' to home and told 'em."

"Stop them!" Mister Dale said.

"Too late. They're in the hotel."

"Where's Linwood?"

"I dunno. I haven't seen him or any of his men in a couple of hours."

"Damn!" Mister Dale said.

"Maybe Rusty and them boys will just end it right now, a Box H hand called Coop said.

"We can always hope," Mister Dale said.

The dining room fell quiet; not even the tinkle of silverware or the rattle of coffee cups being placed in saucers sounded. Sam looked over his shoulder and grimaced.

"Why do you always get us into trouble, brother?" His dark eyes were twinkling.

"I see them. And we just got cleaned up."

"Yes. But at least we won't have to fight on a full stomach. It's not good for the digestion."

"That really makes me feel better, Sam. You sure do know how to cheer me up."

"Thank you," Sam replied modestly.

"You two slicked-up dudes yonder!" Rusty called. "Outside. I want to talk to you."

Matt was facing the archway. He sized up the cowboy. Pretty good-sized ol' boy. Late thirties, he'd guess, and all muscle and gristle and bone. The three with him were about the same size, with hard-packed muscle and callused hands from years of wrestling steers and handling rope.

"Here we go," Sam muttered, not knowing what Matt was going to do, but knowing full well he was about to irritate someone.

"Are you speaking to us, Jackass Mouth," Matt called, "or you braying at an early moon?"

About half of the men and women in the big dining room did their best to hide smiles. And that told the brothers that the big ranchers in the area were not all loved, providing these hands came from one of the Big Three, and both brothers were sure of that.

"You say that to *me?*" Rusty yelled.

"You're the only person in the room braying like a jackass," Matt told him. "As a matter of fact, you sort of resemble a jackass. In a way."

Rusty was so mad he looked like he was about to explode.

Sam turned around and stared at the red-faced foreman of the Lightning spread. He shook his head. "No, brother," he said loud enough for all to hear. "A jackass is much better looking."

Several men and women laughed out loud.

"By God!" Rusty yelled. "You people don't laugh at me. I'll tear this damn town apart."

"Oh, shut up," Matt told him. "Go away. We're trying to order supper."

Rusty marched over to the table, his men right behind him. They ringed the table. Real close. Sam smiled. "By God, saddlebum, you'll learn when a Lightning man tells you to do something, you'll do it."

"I doubt it," Matt said.

Rusty reached down, clamped a hand on Matt's good shirt, and jerked him to his boots. He tore the shirt. Bad mistake.

Matt knocked the bejesus out of the foreman. The blow sent the man stumbling across the room, crashing into tables and sending diners scrambling to get out of the way, but staying close enough to watch and enjoy the fight.

Sam rammed his chair back, knocking a puncher sprawling, and a split-second later he jammed the square-cornered table into another Lightning hand's groin. The hand dropped to his knees, his face white with pain, both hands holding his crotch, his mouth open in a silent scream. Sam came up fast and grabbed a chair, splintering it over the fourth puncher's head and knocking him to the floor.

"Get that dirty son, Tulsa," the puncher on his knees moaned as Tulsa was getting up off the floor.

Sam got set, a strange smile on his lips.

Matt had backed Rusty into a corner and was concentrating on beating the stuffing out of him. The initial blow had caught the foreman off-guard, and had been powerful enough to stun him. Now Matt was going to finish it.

Rusty swung and Matt ducked that one and the left that followed it. He grabbed the man's left forearm and slung him across the room. Rusty wiped out a row of tables as he spun out of control, Matt right behind him. Rusty hit the wall and looked confused for a moment. He wasn't used to people doing this to him. Then Matt was all over him as Sam yelled, "Hurry up, damn it. Quit showin' off."

Matt hit the foreman a combination of blows that rocked the man's head from side to side, bloodying his mouth, busting his nose, and pulping one ear. He finished the foreman with a thundering right to the man's belly. Rusty coughed up bile and slumped to the floor, out of action.

Matt screamed like a panther, and that nearly scared the women in the room out of their corsets. It frightened some of the men, too. It also startled the hell out of a Lightning hand named Buck. What really got Buck's attention was when Matt hit him in the mouth with a fist that looked about the size of a brick and was just about as hard. Pearlies flew from the man's suddenly bloody mouth. Matt hit him two more times, then clubbed him on the neck on his way down to the floor.

Sam was dealing his opponent some real misery. The man's eyes were glazed and his mouth and nose were smashed and bloody. One ear was badly swollen, and all in all, he looked like he really wished he had stayed back at the ranch. Sam hit him one more time and the man kissed the floor.

Then Matt and Sam turned on the man who had met the corner of the table. Together, as one man would later say, "Them boys beat the hell outta that Lightning hand."

Matt left Tony to Sam and looked around just as Rusty was staggering to his boots. Matt grabbed the man by the seat of his pants and his shirt collar and ran him squalling and bellering across the room, using the path Rusty had earlier cleared. Matt threw him through the window.

Rusty hit the boardwalk and kept on going. He impacted against the south end of a hitchrail, did a real nifty little flip, and landed in a horse trough.

Matt stepped through the broken window, dragged the man out of the trough, and retrieved Rusty's pokesack from his pocket. He stepped back into the dining room. Mister Dale and the others had lined up on the boardwalk in front of the Red Dog, disbelief in their eyes.

But it wasn't over yet.

Matt counted out a few bills and held them up while Sam was gathering money from the other bully-boys. "This is for my shirt, folks." He put that in his pocket. He tossed the rest onto a table. "That will pay for the expenses, along with what money we pull from these other galoots."

"Ripped my brand new trousers," Sam griped. He counted out enough for a new pair of pants and tossed the rest of the money onto the table. There was over a hundred dollars in gold and greenbacks.

The brothers looked at each other and grinned. They then proceeded to toss the other Lightning hands out the shattered window. It made quite a pile when they were through.

They returned to their table, righted it, found chairs, and sat down. "Now," Matt said. "Can we please have something to eat?"

Hugo Raner stood on his front porch and watched as his foreman and three of his top hands came riding in at sunset. They were sure sorry lookin'.

"What the hell happened?" he shouted.

Rusty dismounted carefully and painfully. "I don't know who them hombres is, boss. But they're ring-tailed-tooters. I ain't never had my ashes hauled this bad in all my life."

"For God's sake, men. How many were there?"

"Two," Tulsa said sheepishly.

"Two!" Hugo roared. "The townspeople join in with them?"

"No, sir. They just laughed and had them a good time."

Hugo Raner flushed. "Nobody laughs at my hands. That's the same as laughing at me."

His son stepped out to see what all the shouting was about. He stared at the beat-up top hands. Carl fancied himself a fast gun, and in truth he was good, very quick. He was also cocky, arrogant, and cruel to both humans and animals.

"You men see a doctor?" Hugo asked.

"Yeah, boss," Buck lisped the words through the gap where his front teeth used to be. "Nothin' broken."

"Get cleaned up. Supper's over but the cook saved you some grub. Tomorrow we'll all ride into town and see what this business is about."

"Right," Carl said, a cruel glint in his eyes.

Mister Dale walked over to the hotel and watched as workmen boarded up what was left of the big window in the dining room. He shook his head and walked into the lobby. He nodded at the desk clerk and stood under the archway, looking at the two strangers sitting in the nearly deserted dining room, having an after-supper coffee and cigar. Mister Dale decided there was only one way to get to the bottom of this. He walked over to the table.

"Gentlemen," he said with a smile. "Do you mind if I sit down?"

Matt pushed out a chair with the toe of his boot and the man sat down. He waved to a waitress and she poured him coffee.

"That was quite a fight, boys," Mister Dale said.

"So-so," Sam replied.

"Some friendly advice from an older man?" Dale was about forty, the brothers guessed.

"It's free, so go ahead," Matt told him.

"Were I you boys, I'd pull out first thing in the morning," Mister Dale said.

"We like it here," Sam said.

The mayor smiled. "Hugo Raner owns one of the biggest spreads in all of Colorado. He has about thirty hands. I'm sure he and his boys will be riding in first thing in the morning. You boys wouldn't want to endanger women and children by engaging in a gunfight on Main Street, now, would you?"

"If there *is* a gunfight," Sam said, "it won't be us who starts it. So the logical thing to do would be to ban this Hugo person and his hands from town."

Mister Dale chuckled. "Logic. Well, yes, I suppose you're right. But Hugo and his men live and work and spend their money in this town. You boys are just drifters. You'll spend a few dollars and then drift on. You catch what I mean? By the way, I'm Mayor Dale."

"I'm Matt and this is my brother, Sam."

"Smith and Jones?"

"We're half brothers," Sam told him.

The mayor nodded his head. "Boys, don't play dangerous games with me. You won a fistfight. Fine. No real damage done. The people I talked with said the Lightning crew started it. All right. No charges will be filed." His face tightened and his voice became hard. "Now let's get down to the nut-cuttin'. I own this hotel and dining room. You boys spend the night, sleep well, then get out of here come morning. You catch my drift?"

"Oh, yeah," Matt said. "We'll check out in the morning."

Mister Dale smiled. "Fine, boys. Fine."

"Is there a boardinghouse in town?" Sam asked.

The mayor sighed, losing his smile. "You don't seem to understand. I can have you arrested for vagrancy."

Matt tossed a sack of gold coins on the table. Sam did the same. Matt said, "I'd sure like to see that charge stand up in a court of law."

Mister Dale carefully opened each sack. The banker in him surfaced. His eyes glinted at the dull gold shining at him. "That's a lot of money for a couple of saddlebums to have. I just might ask the sheriff to lock you up until we can decide if that money is stolen."

"We both own ranches in Wyoming," Sam told him. "And there are papers in our saddlebags to prove it. I would imagine our spreads are as large—or larger—than those around here. Try again, Mister Mayor."

Mister Dale sugared and creamed his coffee. He sipped and added more sugar. "Two ranchers passing through," he said softly. He shook his head. "We all make mistakes. Why did you go into the Plowshare instead of the Red Dog?"

"The Red Dog looked full," Matt said. "We chose the quieter saloon."

Mister Dale chuckled. "Things are tense here, gentlemen. My apologies for the behavior of Hugo's boys, and for my ordering you out of this hotel. Stay as long as you like." He tapped one sack of gold. "I'd bank that money, boys. That's a tidy sum to be carrying around."

"We might do that," Sam told him.

The mayor stood up. "Smith and Jones," he muttered. "Why not?"

He walked out of the dining room.

Bodine and Sam looked at each other and grinned.

Hugo brought every hand he could spare into town. They made quite a show of it and succeeded in raising a dustcloud that a tornado would have been hard-pressed to match.

Mister Dale met the rancher on the boardwalk in front of the Red Dog and briefly explained the situation.

Hugo Raner shook his big head. Everything about Hugo was big. He was a bear of a man. "That don't make a damn to me, Dale," he said. "I aim to see those two horsewhipped. Now get out of my way."

"Just calm down a second," Mister Dale said. "And think about what you're planning. Smith and Jones came into town looking for a room and a meal. That's all. They are respected Wyoming ranchers and have the funds and the papers to prove it. Your men were out of line. What we don't need now is trouble that will be carried out of this area. We don't want outside authorities to catch wind of this upcoming war. Now think about that, Hugo."

The big man thought for a moment and then sighed. He removed his hat and ran thick, blunt fingers through his dark hair. "All right, Dale. All right. I see what you mean. It was a misunderstanding all the way around."

"There they are, boss." Tulsa spoke from the saddle.

Hugo looked at the two men coming out of the hotel. His experienced eyes took in Matt's two guns and the way the man walked. He shifted his gaze to Sam. "They're gunfighters, Dale. Both of them. And that one has some Injun in him. *Injun!* Jumpin' Jesus Christ, Dale, they're ranchers, all right. But I'll tell you something else: that's Matt Bodine and Sam Two Wolves!"

Three

The news spread throughout the town very quickly. Children gathered around—but not too close—to stare at the gunfighters whenever they made an appearance. Hugo sent most of his crew back to the ranch and found him a table at the Red Dog. He had sent men out to the other two ranches, calling for a meeting, and now he waited for the arrival of Pete Harris of the Box H, and Blake Vernon of the Circle V.

"I don't understand why you're doing this," Mister Dale said. "Bodine and Two Wolves don't hire their guns out."

"I know that. But they got nose trouble. They're always stickin' their noses into other folks' business. You heard about that crap they pulled down in Texas. They didn't have no business gettin' involved in that. Nose trouble."

"And you're thinking they may decide to get involved in our . . . situation?"

"I don't know. But if they do, they're meddlin' fools.

Me and Pete and Blake can mount up close to a hundred men. Dale, I aim to run them homesteaders and sheepmen out of this country. And I don't give a damn who gets hurt or killed in the process. And that includes Bodine and his damn half-breed Injun brother."

"I just wish they'd leave town peacefully."

"They won't," Hugo said, his words grimly spoken. "They'll stick their noses in this sure as shootin'."

"Pete and Blake ridin' in," a hand called through the batwings. "Got about ten men with them."

Hugo nodded. The owners of the Box H and the Circle V stomped in, ordered beer—although it was still early in the day—and joined Mister Dale and Hugo at the table. Their hands fanned out in the big room.

Dale laid the cards on the table.

"I don't like it," Blake said. "I don't think it was coincidence that Bodine and Two Wolves showed up here. I don't think that at all."

"Just steady down," Pete said. "But I will say that those two got the reputation as troublemakers."

"Well, we're in agreement on that," Hugo said. "So what do we do about it?"

"Force their hand," Frisco, the foreman of the Circle V, suggested.

Rusty, foreman of the Lightning, sure agreed with that.

"Now, just hold on," Pete Harris said. "Let's don't start shooting before we know all the facts. We'll just keep men in town and see what those two outsiders do. If they start gettin' chummy with the nesters and the sheepmen, then we'll know and we can move. I don't aim to go off half-cocked and lose a bunch of men fightin' Bodine and that breed brother of his. And boys, we would damn sure lose men. Those two won't go down easy."

"That's easy for you to say, Pete," Blake spoke up. "You don't have nesters squattin' on your land and sheepmen ruinin' the land."

"I ain't seen any land bein' ruined, Blake," the rancher countered. "And I do have sheep on my south range. But it's free range, Blake. Those sheepherders have government permission to be there. And they know what they're doin', boys. They don't let the sheep eat the grass down to the roots. They move them long before that can happen. I was out there the other day, me and Robert and Millie. Watchin' those dogs work is a pure delight. We had a good time."

"Whose side are you on here, anyways, Pete?" Hugo asked, giving the man a queer look. "Seems like to me you're suckin' up to them damn sheepmen."

Pete stared hard at the man. "Don't press me too hard, Raner. Just because I don't want to go in and start a bunch of killing don't mean I won't pull iron with you."

"Hold it!" Mister Dale slammed his hand on a table-top. "Now settle down—the both of you. I . . ."

The batwings squeaked open and Bodine and Two Wolves walked in and up to the bar.

"Beer for both of us," Bodine said.

"I ain't servin' no goddamn greasy Injun in here," the burly barkeep said.

"That's a real pity," Sam said. "And a mistake." Then he reached over the bar and dragged the man over the top, kicking and screaming and cussing.

The men in the room then noticed that Matt Bodine had his hands full—of .44's. He had drawn so fast that no one had even caught the motion.

"Stand easy, boys," Mister Dale said.

Sam adjusted the bartender's attitude three times.

Two rights to the mouth and a left to the gut. The bartender sat down on the floor, blood running out of his mouth. He tried to get up. He got as far as his hands and knees. While his big butt was up in the air, Sam reared back, kicked him on his behind, and sent him out the batwings, rolling off the boardwalk and into the dust of the street.

Sam walked back to the bar and behind it. He pulled two mugs of beer and tossed money down for the brews. Matt holstered his guns and picked up the mug. Together, the brothers walked to a table and sat down, their backs to a wall.

Pete Harris seemed amused by the entire affair. Hugo Raner looked like a thundercloud and so did Blake Vernon. Mister Dale's expression was bland, but his eyes were shiny mean.

"I'll go see about Charlie," Tulsa said. "I do know how he feels," he added.

"I figured you boys would be hangin' around over to the nester bar," Hugo said. "I sure got a whiff of sheep-shit when you walked in."

"That's probably your own underwear you're smelling," Matt told him.

"Now, by God," Hugo yelled, pointing a finger at Matt. "I warn you now, I'll take only so much of this."

"You started it," Pete spoke the words quietly. "That's one of your problems, Hugo. You like to dish it out, but you just can't take it right back."

"The hell with you all!" Hugo yelled, jumping to his feet. "Come on," he snarled to his men. They trouped out en masse, almost tearing the batwings off their hinges.

"Man has a hot temper," Matt remarked.

"He has some justification," Pete said, shifting his

chair to face the brothers. "His best water is fenced off."

"By farmers?" Sam asked.

"Yeah."

"And they fenced it off . . . when?" Matt asked.

Pete smiled. "You boys are cattlemen. I know that for a fact. You know how it started."

"Probably," Matt said. He took a swig and set the mug down. "The farmer came in and legally filed on his sections. Hugo and his men then made life miserable for the man and his family. They'd ride over the man's garden, shoot his milk cow and his pigs, scare his wife and kids half to death." Matt noticed that some of the cowboys in the bar had embarrassed looks on their faces. "Takes a big, brave man to do things like that."

Some of the cowboys looked at the barroom floor and shuffled their boots. Matt knew then that those men were not bad people. They rode for the brand and did what they were told . . . but they didn't have to like doing it.

"So finally the farmer did the only thing he could do," Matt continued. "He put up fences. I grew up different, I guess. My daddy put me behind a plow and a mule when I was about the size of a tadpole. He made me appreciate the fact that there is more in life than what can be seen from the hurricane deck of a horse. Any of you boys ever plowed an acre garden? I can tell you, it's hard work. Has anybody tried to get along with the farmers and the sheepmen?"

"I don't aim to try," Blake Vernon said. "I come here back in the fifties. I fought Injuns and outlaws and helped tame this country. It's my land, and I'll stand with a gun in my hand on it, and die and be buried in it, rather than give up any of it." He stood up, a hard man in a hard land, but also an unbending man in changing times. "Come on, boys. Smells like sheep and hogs in here."

The owner of the Circle V stomped out with his men about the time that Charlie the bartender came lurching back in. He gave Sam a baleful look but kept his mouth shut. He went behind the bar and took to polishing glasses.

"We're gonna have trouble in this region," Pete said, toying with his empty beer mug. "And good people on both sides are going to get hurt. Sad thing is, it could all be avoided."

"How?" Mister Dale said. "How, Pete? Blake and Hugo are not going to go kowtowing to the nesters and the sheepmen, hat in hand."

"The farmers and the sheepmen have gone to them to try to work something out," Pete responded. "Hugo's son dragged that one so bad he's crippled for life. And your pet puma of a sheriff didn't do one damned thing about it, didn't even investigate it— right, Dale?"

"It was his word against Carl and about fifteen other hands," the mayor said. "There wasn't even any point in bringing it to a court of law. And you know that's right, Pete."

"Of course, the publicity it might have caused had nothing to do with that decision?" Pete asked.

Mister Dale sighed audibly. "Maybe Hugo is right, Pete. Maybe you don't belong with this group. Maybe you *are* siding with the nesters and the sheepmen."

Pete stood up and the mayor tensed. "I'm not wearing a gun, Pete," he said.

"No. You never do, Dale. People like you blow off at the mouth and don't have the courage to back up your remarks with fists or guns. Hell with you, Dale. You're a mealy-mouthed coward."

He walked stiffly from the barroom, his hands following him out, protecting his back.

Matt and Sam drained their beer mugs and stood up. "Going to get real interesting around here before long," Matt said. "Might be fun to stick around. What do you think, Sam?"

"I think you're right, brother. I believe we should stick around."

"Get out of my hotel," Mister Dale said. "Pack your crap and get out."

"Sure thing, Mister Mayor," Matt said. "Bed wasn't very comfortable anyway."

After the brothers had left, the mayor looked at the bartender. "Charlie, what do you think about it?"

"You want my honest opinion, Mister Dale?"

"Yes, I do."

"Times are changin'. Cattlemen are gonna have to get along with farmers and sheepmen. And anyone who don't think that's possible is a bull-headed fool. And I think them two that just left here are poison— clear-through poison. They're gonna side with the nesters and sheepmen and you ain't got nobody on your payroll who can outgun 'em. And now you and Raner done made Pete Harris mad, and *he's* gonna side with them, too. That's what I think."

Mister Dale nodded his head. "Charlie?"

"Yes, sir."

"You're fired."

Sam and Matt checked out of the hotel—the desk clerk had told them they were no longer welcome in the dining room—and walked down to the Plowshare, carrying their possessions. Chrisman looked at them as they dumped their belongings on a table. There were several tables full of men, farmers and sheepmen and a few locals.

"Tossed you boys out of the hotel, did he?" Chrisman asked.

"That he did," Sam said.

"And being the law-abiding and gentle folk that we are," Matt added with a smile, "we obeyed meekly."

One of the locals laughed at that. He had been one of the diners when the Lightning hands had jumped the brothers.

Charlie walked out of the storeroom, an apron tied around his waist and a broom in his hand. He walked up to Sam and stuck out his hand. "I got my walkin' papers too. Sorry about that remark of mine."

Sam smiled and shook the hand. "Sure. Forget it. Glad to see you got a job so soon."

Charlie grinned. "I got a wife and two kids to support. Mister Chrisman hired me right off. Looks like the farmers and sheepmen got another local on their side—me!" He turned and then stopped and once more faced the brothers. "Say, I just remembered: I got a shack right on the edge of town. It's got a stable, of sorts, right in the back, and the roof to the house don't leak. The kitchen pump works and there's a cookstove. You boys wanna use it?"

"That'd be great," Matt said. "We'll rent it on a weekly basis." Charlie opened his mouth to protest and Matt waved him silent. "We won't have it any other way. We'll pay you the same thing we were paying for the rooms at the hotel. You toss in pillows and sheets—deal?"

"You got a deal."

"There's a Mex cantina and café right behind here," Chrisman said. "They serve up good grub. Lots of folks have a drink or two here and walk right out the back to eat. I recommend the place. Juan and Anita run the café."

"Thanks," Sam said.

Chrisman introduced the brothers to the men in the room. There was Simmons, who owned the general store. Walters ran the saddle and gun shop. McClary was the blacksmith and owned the livery stable. Of the farmers having an afternoon beer were Rich Ansel, a big Swede; Paul Dennis—the first man in the area to farm, and the spokesman for the area farmers, and a quiet man named Reed.

"He don't say much," Simmons said. "Kentucky man. Has four sons: Jake, John, Jesse, and Joe."

"Pleased," the Kentucky man said, and returned to his beer and his Bible reading.

"You, ah, always read a Bible in a saloon?" Sam asked.

"Ain't no better place in the world for it. Think about it."

Matt and Sam looked at each other and grinned. The man did have a point. They picked up their gear and looked over at Charlie.

"Last house on the right, headin' out of town," he told them. "Thataway," he added, pointing. "You can't miss it."

"See you boys later," Chrisman said. "And . . . thanks for sticking around."

The brothers smiled at the man and headed for their new home. They spent the rest of the afternoon sweeping and dusting and cleaning what windows remained intact. They found hammer and nails and boarded up the broken ones. Matt walked the short distance to the general store and bought a few essentials like coffee and sugar and flour and several boxes of . 44's.

Simmons tossed in a free box. "I think there's gonna be a run on ammunition," he said.

Matt looked at him to see if the man was joking.

He wasn't.

Four

Someone out back was playing a guitar and singing a sad song in Spanish when the brothers entered the Mexican café just as twilight was fading into the velvet of Western Colorado night. They found a table and ordered tequila before looking at the supper menu.

A lovely Spanish girl brought them their drinks and smiled at Sam. He smiled back. She lingered. Sam began to sweat. Matt began to feel like a dog that had just wandered into a party for cats.

"Victoria," her mother called from the kitchen, "you have other diners."

"*Sí, Madre,*" she said, her voice soft.

Sam began to look like a calf that had just lost its mother.

"This is pitiful," Matt said.

"Ummm?" Sam asked, without taking his eyes from the young lady.

"I said you have a piece of straw sticking out of your ear."

"That's nice," Sam said dreamily.

"Victoria!" the call came from the kitchen. *"De prisa, por favor."*

"Your mother wants you to hurry up, Victoria," Matt said. He spoke enough Spanish to know that much.

She shook her head and looked at him. "Sir?"

"Your mother is calling from the kitchen."

"Victoria!" a man's voice shouted.

"Sí, Papa!" she called, and left the table at a fast walk.

Sam rocked back in his chair and watched her walk away, stars in his eyes at the sight of her swaying hips.

Matt grinned and stuck his boot under Sam's chair and jerked. Sam toppled over backward and lay on his back on the floor. He cut his eyes to Matt, grinning down at him. "I'll get you for this, Matt."

Matt lifted his glass of tequila. *"Salud!"*

Victoria came rushing over to see if Sam was hurt and to help him to his boots. Juan and Anita came running out of the kitchen to join in. Matt sat in his chair, sipping his tequila and enjoying the spectacle.

"Señor!" Juan said, brushing at Sam's clothing. "Are you hurt?"

"No, but he's going to be in about an hour." He pointed at Matt.

"What'd I do?" Matt asked. "I can't help it if you can't hold your booze." He looked at Anita. "He has this . . . ah, drinking problem."

"I do not!" Sam huffed.

Momma and Poppa caught on immediately and both grinned. Victoria looked confused.

Matt was going to milk the moment for all it was worth. But before he could heap more insults on Sam's head, a noisy group of cowboys came stomping into the café/cantina. One of them had a very bad mouth on him.

"Lightning Arrow bunch," Juan said, disgust in his voice.

"Call the sheriff and have them tossed out," Sam suggested.

Juan smiled sadly. "You do not yet understand the situation in this town. I would be laughed at if I did that . . . by the sheriff. All we can do is cope with them and hope they don't break too much."

"Do they come in here often?" Sam asked, the tipped over chair and verbal insults from his brother forgotten—for the moment.

"Only to make trouble," Anita said. "And to see if there are any farmers or sheepmen and their families here. They make fun of them. Humiliate them. Try to make them fight. They are not fighters."

"Don't bet on that," Matt said, remembering the Bible-reading Kentucky man with the four sons. "They just haven't been pushed enough."

"Git on over here, greaser!" one man hollered. "We want some damn service."

Matt stood up, shoulder to shoulder with Sam. The Lightning hands saw them and fell silent. Matt and Sam walked to the center of the big dining area. People got out of the line of fire quickly.

"Your show, Sam," Matt said quietly.

"How do you figure?"

"You're the one making goo-goo eyes at the girl."

"Goo-goo eyes," Sam muttered. "Oh, all right." He raised his voice. "Brand new set of rules have just gone into effect for this establishment, boys. No loud noise, and absolutely no profanity will be allowed."

"And who's gonna enforce them rules?" a man asked.

"Me," Sam said quietly.

"Well, why don't you come over here and git to en-
forcin', then?" he challenged.

"I have a much better idea, loudmouth."

"Well, tell me, Injun boy."

"Why don't you shut your damn mouth and fill your
hand?"

And there it was. Harassing people was one thing; a
fist fight got you some sore hands, some cuts and
bumps and bruises. But this changed the whole game.

"Easy, Clint," one of his friends cautioned. He
glanced at Sam. "This ain't no shootin' deal, mister.
The sheriff don't mind us doin' this, so I 'spect you just
better back off."

Sheriff Jack Linwood pushed his way through the
knot of unwashed by the door. "You want to go to jail,
Injun?"

"His name is Sam," Matt said. "And if you think
you're hoss enough to put him there, deal yourself in
this game. You're pretty good, Linwood; but I'm better.
Now you either enforce the law, fair and equally for
everybody, or drag iron!"

"That's it!" Mister Dale yelled from just outside the
door. "Get out of the way, damn it! Move!" He stepped
into the café, shoving Lightning riders out of his way.
"What the hell's going on here?"

"Very simple," Sam said. "These loudmouth hands
came in cussing and insulting people. I ordered them to
leave. They refused. That one in particular." He pointed
with his left hand. "Then your pet sheriff comes in and
threatens to take me to jail instead of ejecting the troublemakers. Tell me something, Dale: when are you going
to wean him?"

"Why, you god . . ." Linwood started to lunge at
Sam.

Dale pulled him back. "You boys are pushing," he said to Sam and Matt. "You're pushing hard."

"No harder than your side pushes," Matt reminded him. "What's the matter, Mister Mayor, don't you believe in equal justice for all?"

Dale stared at Bodine. He pursed his lips and sighed. "No more trouble in here, Jack. Troublemakers get the same treatment. Understood?"

"You mean to tell me . . ."

"Yes, damn it!" the mayor yelled. "That's exactly what I mean." He grabbed the sheriff's arm and pulled him outside. "Look, Jack. We play it close and safe. If nothing happens, those two will leave sooner rather than later. You understand what I'm saying?"

Linwood nodded his head. "All right. Suits me."

"You gave in real quick, Jack. What's the matter, are you developing a conscience?"

Jack Linwood walked away without replying. He really didn't want to lose this job. Best job he'd ever had.

Mister Dale stepped back inside the café. "Break it up," he ordered the Lightning crew. "If you can't control your cursing, leave."

"We'll leave," one said.

"Fine. There is to be no more trouble in here. You have my apologies, Mister Garcia."

"Thank you, Mister Dale," Anita said. Juan said nothing; but his eyes shone hate and distrust at the man.

The mayor stepped back into the night and the patrons of the popular café settled down and resumed their eating. Sam and Matt returned to their table. Juan came over and pointed to a chair.

"Sure. Sit down," Matt said.

"Don't trust Mister Dale too far," the man spoke softly. "And be careful of the townspeople you might decide to trust. Even some of those you see eating here this night are in truth his friends and supporters; they listen and spy and report to him. This is a town filled with suspicion and fear. I tell you this because you took our side and stood up to those troublemakers. And," he said with a smile, looking at Sam, "I think my daughter likes you very much."

"She is a beautiful girl," Sam said. "You and your wife should be proud."

"Oh, we are," Juan replied. "We are." He sobered. "Be careful, boys. The night holds few friends. The sheriff is not a bad man, I think. I have seen a streak of decency in him. But I also think Mister Dale is playing a waiting game. He does not want trouble while you are here. He wants very much for the two of you to become bored and leave. Then he will strike." He stood up. "Enjoy your meal, boys. It is, as the saying goes, on the house."

The food was delicious, the plates held plenty of it, and the café did a brisk business. The brothers lingered over coffee and watched the café slowly empty of patrons. It was eight-thirty when Juan hung up the Closed sign and pulled down the blinds.

"I think," he said to the brothers, "it would be wise for you two to leave by the side door. I was just told that the front and back is watched."

"By Linwood and the deputies?" Sam asked.

"No. By riders from the Circle V and the Lightning. Keep this in mind: more than one or two people have been dragged by those men. One was killed and another badly crippled. You walk among snakes, boys. Be careful where you put your feet."

He led them through a storeroom, then blew out the

lamp, plunging the room into darkness. Matt and Sam removed their spurs. Juan opened a door that swung on well-oiled and soundless hinges. *"Vaya con Dios,"* he whispered, as Matt and Sam stepped out into the darkness.

They spoke with Cheyenne hand signals. Sam went one way and Matt the other, the brothers hugging the outside wall of the café/cantina. Men were posted front and back. The brothers swung around them in the darkness and slipped away from their watchers, coming out through an alley that ran alongside the Red Dog.

"Care for a drink before bedtime?" Matt asked.

"But of course," Sam replied.

The brothers stepped into the Red Dog, startling several riders from the Circle V and the Lightning. They ordered whiskey and took their drinks to a table, sitting down with their backs to a wall.

"One of you boys needs to go fetch your buddies over by the café," Matt said to no one in particular. "They're probably getting scared standing out there in the dark; the boogeyman might get them. They sure aren't very attentive."

A hand cursed and stomped out of the saloon.

"It's just a game to you boys, ain't it?" a Circle V hand asked.

"Staying alive can hardly be called a game," Sam said. "Actually, it's rather nerve-racking."

"Then why don't you move on? You're not welcome in this town."

"We've probably read too much about Robin Hood," Sam replied. He pointed to Matt. "He's the hood."

"What the hell does that mean?" the cowboy asked.

"Forget it," Sam told him. "It would take entirely too long to explain."

The small town of Dale was settling in for the night;

few homes still had lamp or candlelight in the windows. The night was void of moonlight, the sky heavy with dark clouds that threatened rain.

Those inside the Red Dog were silent, one group sullen and ill-tempered as they stared with open hostility at the blood brothers. Boots sounded on the boardwalk as those who had been watching the café entered the saloon and took seats, ordering drinks.

"Maybe they left slidin' on their bellies like snakes," one said, staring directly at the brothers.

Matt and Sam stared back and made no comment.

"Stinks in here," a Lightning hand remarked. "Smells like sheepdip and dirty Injuns."

A drummer who had ridden the stage in that day and who was leaving the next day looked nervously around him. He wanted to leave, but had to pass directly between the two factions. He decided not to chance it. But he sure wished he had taken the afternoon stage instead of laying over.

Jack Linwood and his deputies walked in and sized up the situation.

"Knock it off, boys," Jack ordered. "You'd best be ridin' if you're gonna miss the rain."

The hands took the hint and trouped out. The drummer left his unfinished drink and got the hell gone from the Red Dog.

Jack's deputies stayed at the bar. Jack walked to the table and pulled out a chair, sitting down.

"Do sit down," Sam said.

When Jack spoke, his voice was low. "I don't know why you boys are stickin' your noses in this town's troubles, but I'm gonna give you some free advice: saddle up and ride. Maybe you boys are quick on the shoot. I don't know. I've never seen you in action. But you can't fight sixty or seventy top hands and expect to win. There is a range war shapin' up here. And they're ugly things to behold. I 'magine you've both seen what happens."

"We've seen it," Matt replied, his eyes studying Jack Linwood. The man was in his late thirties, Matt guessed. Solidly built. But like most men who depended on their guns to earn their living, Jack was going to fat around the middle. His hands looked soft; like he hadn't done any real work in a long time. But Matt wasn't going to underestimate the man. Jack Linwood was tough and dangerous.

"I'm not goin' to nursemaid you boys," Jack said. "Me and the deputies was makin' our night rounds when we come in here. That's the only thing that saved your bacon this time. Them ol' boys you was facin' would have et you up and spit you out in chunks and pieces."

"It's been said that we don't chew so good," Sam told him. "Meat's too tough. Unpalatable."

"Whatever that means," Jack said. "You got a smart mouth for a damn breed, you know that?"

"And you're wearing a gun," Sam spoke the words very softly. "Would you like to stand up and we'll settle this?"

Matt knew the insulting 'Injun' and 'breed' business was beginning to stick in Sam's craw. Sam, by nature, was not a pushy person or a trouble-hunter. But neither was he the type of man to do much backing up.

Linwood's face held a strange expression, as did his eyes. Matt misread it, thinking that Linwood wanted desperately to stand up and see who was the better gunhand. Matt already knew. Linwood, if he chose to drag iron, was in for a shock.

Linwood cut his eyes for a heartbeat. The new bartender, Bert, his back to the trio, was out of earshot, polishing glasses. The three of them were alone. No one knew of this except them. There would be no loss of face.

Linwood slowly exhaled and placed his hands on the table. "No, I don't think so. Not just yet, anyways."

"Yeah, run along, Linwood," Sam told him, with a mean smile on his lips. "I would imagine you have to go tuck Mayor Dale into bed and empty out his chamberpot."

Linwood's face mottled with rage. He whirled around and stalked out of the saloon, slamming open the batwings.

Matt leaned back in his chair. "We're not exactly winning friends in this town."

Sam shook his head. "This place is bringing out the worse in me, brother."

"Oh, I don't know," Matt said cheerfully. "I thought you looked fairly natural all sprawled out on the café floor."

Sam smiled at him. Matt had not seen him ease his boot under the chair. He jerked his foot and Matt hit the floor. Sam lifted his drink and said, *"Salud!"* He downed his drink and walked to the batwings and stepped out onto the boardwalk.

Four fast shots cut the night.

Five

Bert the bartender hit the floor and Matt was on his boots and running toward the batwings, both hands filled with .44's. "Sam!" he yelled.

"I'm all right," Sam called. "Stay behind the wall. One of them slipped in the mud just as he lifted his pistol. I heard the sound and jumped. The shots came from right across the street. In the alley."

"You got a good position?"

"Behind a horse trough."

"I wonder if they have the back covered?"

"Probably."

"I think I'll take a look." He ran to the bar and grabbed the sawed off shotgun off the rack. He broke it open. Full. He put the small sack of shells into his pocket and told the bartender, "Stay down."

"Don't you worry about that, mister. I ain't leavin' this floor."

Matt slipped into the dark storeroom and made his way to the back door. The rain was coming down hard, hammering on the roof. Matt found a large, empty wooden box and eased the door open. He kicked the box out the door. Muzzle flashes licked the night as guns roared from a few feet away from the back door. Matt stepped into the doorway and pulled both triggers of the shotgun. The express gun roared and bucked in his hands, spewing flames out the barrels like a cannon, and also hurling out rusty nails, buckshot, ball bearings, and whatever else whoever loaded the shells could find to stick in there.

Someone screamed horribly in the stormy evening. Lightning lanced the night and Matt could see one man down, his belly torn open and his lifeless eyes filling up with rain, and another man trying to pull himself away with his hands. The leg he had left was bloody and mangled.

"What the hell's goin' on in there?" Jack Linwood yelled from the barroom.

Matt reloaded the ten-gauge and snapped it closed. "Ambush, Sheriff. Come on in and see for yourself."

"Yeah," Jack said, coming cautiously into the storeroom. "I know. Bert backs that up. But damn it, there wasn't supposed to be any of this, Mister . . ." He shut his mouth.

"Mister Dale said that if nothing happened, we'd get bored and leave," Matt finished it.

Linwood's silence confirmed that.

Matt pointed to the open door and the storm-ravaged night. "You know these boys?"

Linwood took a look when lightning flared. He grunted. "I hate a shotgun. I hate them." He turned to Matt. "Will you tell Bert to fetch Doc Lemmon?"

"Sure." Matt relayed the request and sat down at a table. Sam joined him.

"You got one?"

"One dead and another with one leg blowed off; he probably wishes he was dead."

The brothers sat in silence as the barroom began filling up with men in various dress, or undress. Mayor Dale bulled his way in. He looked at the blood-bonded brothers with open disgust in his eyes and on his face.

"I want you two out of this town," he ordered. "Now, by God. Move!"

"We didn't start this thing," Matt told him. "And Bert over there has already told the sheriff that. There is no law anywhere west of the Mississippi that says a man can't defend himself."

Doc Lemmon came back in, dressed in a slicker, rain dripping from the brim of his hat. They're both gone. That shotgun cut one almost in two, and the other one bled to death. They were a couple of Hugo Raner's Lightning riders." He shook his head. "They'll be hell to pay now." He looked at the brothers. "You men all right?"

"Fine," Sam told him.

Doc Lemmon was not much over thirty, but there was age in his eyes. He looked at Mayor Dale. "Why in the devil can't you people get along with each other?"

He walked out before the mayor could reply—if he intended to reply.

The undertaker and a helper came in, toting stretchers. "Some of you boys help me," he said. "I got dressed as soon as I heard the shots—or when there wasn't no more of them, I should say. How many dead?"

"Two," Jack Linwood told him.

"They got any money?" the undertaker asked bluntly.

"Just haul them off and get them ready!" Mayor Dale snapped peevishly.

The undertaker glared at him. Then he smiled. "Don't

get uppity with me, Dale. Just bear in mind that some-day I'll work on you, too."

Mayor Dale shuddered.

Matt and Sam stood up and faced Sheriff Jack Linwood. "You got any questions for us?" Matt asked.

The sheriff shook his head. "Nope. Right 'fore he died, Doc Lemmon heard that one with the blowed-off leg say it was a deliberate ambush. You had a right to defend yourselves. I just wish to hell you'd both leave town."

The brothers walked out of the saloon and trudged through the rain to their rented house.

It had stopped raining before dawn, but the skies were angry-looking when the brothers saddled up the next morning and rode the short distance to the café for breakfast. They planned to ride out into the country that day, to check around.

Many of the townspeople were friendly to them, waving and speaking. Others stared hate at them. It was easy to see where the battle lines were drawn.

The café was filling up when the brothers stepped inside, savoring the rich smells coming from the kitchen. Victoria took their orders while openly flirting with Sam. Doctor Lemmon came in and walked up to the table.

"May I join you?" he asked.

"Sure," Matt said, pulling out a chair.

Victoria took his order and brought them all coffee.

"Just in case you're curious," the doctor said, "I'm not new to the West. I'm Colorado-born and -reared. But I don't support the cattlemen in this fight."

"No one with any sense would," Sam replied. "It isn't really a question of right or wrong; it's a question of power."

"Exactly. The cattlemen know that responsible handling of sheep won't harm the range. Vernon and Raner are just too hardheaded to admit to that." He took a sip of coffee. "Teal—that's the one who was alive in the alley when I got there last evening—told me about somebody coming in. He said Raley was coming in. That mean anything to you men?"

"Red Raley," Matt told him. "Hired gun out of New Mexico. If he's coming in, someone paid big money to hire him and his boys."

"It's not just a single gunfighter, then?" Doc Lemmon asked.

"No," Sam picked it up. "It's a gang. And they're as vicious as pirates."

"You read about the Chester County range wars?" Matt asked.

"Oh, yes. A terrible thing down in Texas."

"Red and his boys did most of the killing. The Rangers finally came in and ran them out. Red doesn't dare show his face in Texas. They'll hang him for sure. We were down there a couple of months ago. A ranger name of Josiah Finch told us all about the Raley gang."

"How many men in his gang?"

Sam shrugged. "It might be ten or twelve, it might be twenty-five or thirty. No way of knowing until he shows up."

"And you men intend to do what?"

Matt smiled at the doctor. "Sticking around for a while. You have a nice, peaceful, friendly little town here."

The doctor returned the smile, then sobered. "Before this range war is over, somebody will rename this place and call it Hell."

* * *

The brothers rode out into the country and it was a beautiful part of the state. This area of Colorado had it all, from placid, lush valleys, where cattle could walk belly-deep in grass, and crystal clear and cold streams, to towering mountains. Lakes dotted the region and many gold mines were working, miners also panning the streams and running placers.

"Beautiful country," Sam remarked.

"Almost as pretty as Wyoming," Matt replied. He pointed to a blaze of slow-moving white against the green grass on a gentle slope. "Sheep. Let's go pay a visit."

"Let's also be careful," Sam cautioned. "Those sheepmen might be quick on the shoot."

"With good reason," Matt added.

But the word had spread quickly among the farmers and sheepmen and the man tending the herd—that they could see—greeted the brothers warmly, inviting them into the camp for coffee.

Few cowboys ever turned down coffee.

Squatting around the fire, Sam said, "You better stock up on ammo. Word we got this morning is that Red Raley and his gang of cutthroats have been hired to come in here."

"I am not familiar with that name," Raul said.

"You will be," Matt told him. "Where is the Box H ranch house from here?"

"Straight north, over that ridge a few miles. Pete Harris is a fair man. He's caused us no trouble since he learned that we do not intend to destroy the range. I will not say that we are friends, but I can truthfully say that we are not enemies." He shook his head. "I cannot say the same thing about Hugo Raner and Blake Vernon."

"Hugo Raner strikes me as being a very unreasonable man in just about any situation you could put him in," Matt said. "Either do it his way, or you're wrong."

"That is a very accurate statement, Mister Bodine."

"Matt. Just Matt will do." He watched as one dog came into camp and another dog went out. He grinned. "Just like regular hands. One takes a break and another takes his place. I'll be darned."

Raul's face turned grim. "Hugo and Blake had both threatened to kill our dogs. That would be a very serious thing for them to do. These dogs are not only highly trained and intelligent animals, they are our friends. I would kill a man who tried to do harm to my dogs."

"I don't blame you," Sam said. "Many Indian tribes revere the dog and would not lift a hand to help someone who did harm to a dog."

"You're Indian?" Raul inquired.

"My father was Medicine Horse, a chief of the Cheyenne. He was killed in battle." Sam had learned the hard way not to say where.

"I'm sorry."

Sam shrugged it off. "It was his choice. That is something I had to accept."

"Do you sell the sheep for meat?" Matt asked, changing the subject.

"No. These are woolers. Some of the finest wool in all the world comes from these animals. And believe it or not, some of the sheep are just as much a friend to us as our dogs. You get to know them after a time. Poor foolish creatures. They must be protected at all times."

Matt refilled his coffee cup. "I was told in town that you've lost sheep."

Raul's look was serious and his eyes were flint hard. "Several hundred. But I will lose no more. Several of my people have arrived." He stood up and shouted words in a language that neither man had ever heard before.

But both heard the snicking of levers working rounds into rifles. Neither Matt nor Sam moved.

"It is all right, my new friends," Raul said. "They know you are friendly to us. If they did not think that, they would have blown you out of the saddles with those Sharps .52's and Remington .45-caliber buffalo rifles."

"Impressive," Matt said. "What language was that?"

"Basque. Some call it Euskara." He smiled. "But I also speak Spanish, French, and of course, English. Would you like something to eat, my friends?"

"No, no," Sam said. "We had plenty back at Juan and Anita's."

Raul smiled. "Of food, or mischief with the ladies?"

Sam blushed and shook his head. "You have quite a grapevine, Raul."

"In the business we are in, we must have spies, or we would die. But I am telling you nothing that you both do not know. You are gunfighters, like the legendary Smoke Jensen."

Matt grunted. "Lord, I'm not in his class. But from what all I can gather, he's a fair man. Be interesting if he was to show up around here, wouldn't it?"

"Now that, brother, would be just too much to hope for," Sam said. "Why don't you wish for Louis Longmont while you're at it?"

Raul whistled. "While we are dreaming, why don't we wish for Charlie Starr?"

The three men chuckled and put such thoughts out of their minds. Raul was thanked for the coffee, and with a promise to stop by whenever they could, the brothers rode away.

Jean, Ramon, and Pierre came down from the slopes

to sit by the fire and have a cup of coffee. "How did you find the men?" Jean asked.

"I like them both. I think they are sincere in their help. And I think they are going to stay until it's over."

Good. We need all the friends we can find. What was all that chuckling about?"

Raul told them.

"Oh, sure!" Pierre said. "Smoke Jensen, Louis Longmont, and Charlie Starr. I have heard about them in France! I would settle for just one of them to show up."

"Well, it was just a dream."

The gambler left Denver riding in his own custom-built and luxurious coach pulled by four huge black horses. His valet, his cook, and Mike, his enormous bodyguard, rode in the custom coach behind his. The second coach was also pulled by four huge black horses. The gambler had tired of Denver. He'd gotten restless. Denver was just too damn tame. He wanted some action. He leaned back against the cushions and sipped his glass of wine. Maybe he'd find it on this trip, over in the gold country of northwestern Colorado. And then, too, he had to see about some investments of his in the Dale area. He'd just invested heavily in a project. He hoped it would pay off; not that he needed the money.

The gambler's name was Louis Longmont.

The man carefully put out his fire and buried it. He wiped all traces of his camp away before swinging into the saddle and heading out, the sun to his back. He was in his late fifties, and his jacket was old and his jeans patched. His hat had seen better days, too. Like his clothes, his Colts might be old, but they were clean.

His face was burned dark by the sun and his wrists were thick, his hands big and scarred and calloused. His eyes were cold and constantly moving, missing nothing. Charlie Starr had stayed alive for fifty-odd years living by his wits and a fast gun. He wasn't about to change now. He was heading for a little town on the Colorado, a place he'd never been and where nobody—he hoped—would know him. He might be able to find work pushing cows around, riding for some spread.

Charlie was going to find work, but it wasn't going to be pushing cows around.

Six

The brothers stopped at the gate to the main house. It was closed, and neither of them wanted to open it without permission. They waited. Within moments, a rider loped out to meet them. He was a friendly-looking and handsome young man, about twenty, wearing an easy smile.

"You have to be Matt Bodine and Sam Two Wolves," he said, leaning down and opening the gate. "I'm Robert Harris. Pete is my father."

"Would it be all right for us to ride in and see him?"

"Oh, sure. Dad's nothing like Hugo Raner and Blake Vernon. He doesn't want a war and has no intention of moving against the sheepmen or the farmers. Dinner'll be ready in about an hour. So you'll have to stay or insult the cook."

"Well, let's not insult the cook," Sam said, returning the young man's smile. "You folks might have to live with that for a long time."

Pete Harris was standing on the long front porch when the brothers swung down from the saddle and started to hand the reins of their horses to a hand, to be led off to the barn. Both men noticed that the elder Harris had stationed men, in a casual manner, at both ends of the porch and behind them. Matt unbuckled and untied and looped his gun belt over the saddlehorn, Sam doing the same.

Pete and son smiled at that, Pete saying, "You men go on back to work," he said to his hands. He looked at the brothers. "And you boys get your guns. You can hang the belts from a peg in the house. Let's sit here on the porch 'til dinner is ready. We're havin' fried chicken and mashed potatoes and gravy. That sound good to you boys?"

"Great," Matt said, sitting down in a wood-and-hide chair.

"Millie," the father called. "Bring us some coffee, will you, honey?" To the brothers: "That's my youngest. She's nineteen. And gettin' hard to handle," he added.

"Oh, Dad," Robert said. "She's just lonesome. We need to have a dance and box supper and have folks over to socialize. Millie . . ."

The words hung up in his throat when his sister appeared on the porch, carrying a tray with coffeepot and cups and sugar and milk.

Millie was wearing men's jeans and they didn't leave any doubt as to her gender.

"Great Jumpin' Jehoshaphat!" her father thundered, half rising from his chair. "Where in the hell did you get them britches, girl?"

Millie set the tray on a table. "I got them from town and did some taking in and tucking and so forth. Don't you like them, Poppa?"

"Hell, no!"

Matt looked like he'd been kicked in the head by a

mule. Robert took off his hat and held it over his face. Sam looked embarrassed.

"Get outta them britches and get into a dress, girl!" Pete yelled. "That's indecent."

Millie unbuckled her belt and Pete jumped to his feet, standing between his rebellious daughter and the others. "Not here, for Lord's sake, girl. Mother!" he roared. "You come out here and do something with this daughter of yours!"

"I like jeans, and I intend to wear jeans," Millie said, standing her ground. "So get used to it, Poppa. And that's my final word. Are you going to introduce me to our guests or just stand there with your mouth open?"

Pete sighed and sank back into the chair. "I give up. I just give up. I can't do nothin' with you, girl. I don't know where you get this unholy streak. Don't come from my side of the family." He waved a hand. "Matt Bodine and Sam Two Wolves. Set two more plates for dinner, girl."

Millie did a mock curtsy at the brothers. "I'm so pleased. I hope you plan to spend the day. We're so isolated out here I'm dying to get caught up on all the gossip."

Matt stared at her. Heart-shaped lovely face, light brown hair, worn very short for the times, and a complexion that needed no make-up. "Uh . . . well . . . I . . ." he stammered.

"He's a little on the slow side," Sam said, getting back at Matt for the other night at the café. "Not quite retarded, but . . ." He waggled his hand from side to side. ". . . Close."

Matt gave him a dirty look and stood up, hat in hand. "My brother was kicked in the head by a horse when he was a child. He's been a child ever since. I'm very pleased to meet you, Miss Harris."

"Millie, for heaven's sake." She stuck out her hand like a man and Matt looked at it, then awkwardly shook the small hand.

A very pretty woman pushed open the door and stepped out onto the porch. Pete stood up. "This is my wife, Rebecca. Becky, for short. Becky, please do something about your daughter. She looks disgraceful."

"I'll try," the woman said. "But I'll make no promises. By the way, you asked me what Millie was burning out back this morning? Her sidesaddle."

Pete looked at his daughter. "Why would you do . . ." He bit that off and shook his head, realizing why she did it. "I ain't a-gonna have you ridin' astride, girl. I ain't a-gonna have it. That's my final word."

Millie laughed at him and ran skipping across the yard toward the barn.

"Lord have pity on a man who has to raise a daughter," Pete said, sitting back down as his wife poured them coffee and then took a seat beside her husband.

"You want me to do *what?*" a hand yelled from the barn. "The boss'd skin me alive, girl!"

"Hang in there, Don," Pete muttered.

Becky smiled and asked, "You boys planning on staying in this area long?"

"We'll stay until this, ah, situation is resolved," Matt told her.

"What situation?" she asked, her eyes twinkling. "Millie?"

"I'm gonna cut me a limb," Pete said. "I'll settle that situation. Tan her butt so's she can't sit a saddle."

"You'll do no such thing," his wife said. "She's only doing what Denise Raner is doing."

"Denise Raner is an eighteen-year-old spoiled brat," Pete replied. "And she doesn't have good sense, either."

"Yee-haw," came the shout from the barn, and Millie came barreling out on a paint pony that looked like it could fly. She galloped past the house, waved and yelled again, and headed for the hills on a horse that just naturally loved to run. And Millie was sitting the saddle astride.

"Lord have mercy," Pete muttered.

Don came running up. "I didn't saddle that hoss, boss," he panted. "She done it herself."

"It's all right, Don. Nobody's blamin' you," Pete told the hand.

"Yee-haw!" came the faint yell.

Millie was back in time for dinner, and much to the relief of her father, she said she would freshen up and then change into a dress. She did, in a manner of speaking. She changed into a bright-colored Navaho skirt that fell just below her shapely knees, and a low-cut blouse with a silver conched belt that accented her figure.

"I reckon that's sort of an improvement," Pete muttered. "Pass the chicken around, girl." And don't lean over, he silently prayed.

"What do you think would happen if we called on the Lightning spread and the Circle V?" Sam asked.

"I think either man would probably shoot you on sight," Pete was blunt with them. "I got word about the ambush early this morning. I don't hold with that sort of thing and I aim to tell Blake and Hugo that. We can settle this thing without any blood being spilled—any more blood, that is—if they'd just listen to reason. But neither one of them will do that. They're stubborn and bull-headed, and they think only one way is the right way, and that's their way. They can't see that times are changing and they've got to change with them. But I think they'll die before that happens."

"Eat up, boys," Becky urged them. "We love company and so does the cook."

Neither Sam nor Matt really needed much urging, for their appetites were healthy.

"Save some room for pie," Millie said. "I made them this morning."

"She can cook," her father said. "I'll give her that. Her mother taught her."

"And ride, Poppa," she said.

"Yeah, that too, I reckon. Come by that natural. Practically born on a horse." He glanced over at Matt and Sam and their heaping plates. He smiled. "How often you boys eat, once a week?"

The brothers left the ranch after promising they would be back whenever they could. They also got the word from Pete that he had no intention of joining Hugo and Blake in any damn war against the farmers and sheepmen.

He warned them about Hugo's son, Carl, and about the sons of Blake Vernon, Lane, Dewey, and the nutty one called Hubby.

"He's not right in the head," Pete warned. "But he's not as goofy as he'd like people to think. He's a dangerous young man. Watch him. And this is Ute country, boys," he added. "We got most other tribes on the reservations—God help them—but the Utes are still fighting. So watch it. We got a small detachment of

Army up on the White River. But they don't do us much good down here. Ride with your eyes open."

The boys did not tell Pete about the Basques who had arrived to strengthen the sheepmen's force. He told them after they admitted they'd had coffee at one of their camps.

"Raul's got some hard-eyed ol' boys packing long-distance rifles," Pete said with a smile. "Yeah. He told me. Raul's all right. If all the sheepmen was like him . . ." He shook his head. "No, even that wouldn't do for men like Blake and Hugo. They hate all farmers and all sheepmen."

"And you don't think anything will soften their views?" Sam had asked.

"Only the grave," Pete said quietly.

The brothers visited several farmers that afternoon and one other sheepman, tending his flocks with his brothers. They did not encounter one hostile eye during the entire day. They didn't miss the sensation, knowing they would encounter plenty of hostility as soon as they rode back into town.

Their horses were tired, so they walked them, letting the animals pick their own pace on the road back to Dale, Colorado.

"I think Millie has her eyes on you, brother," Sam said with a laugh, as he reached over and poked his blood brother in the ribs.

Matt reined his horse out of the way of the poking finger and said, "And Victoria flusters up and gets orders mixed when you're around."

"And about a hundred people are trying to kill us," Sam added. "Or at least it seems that way."

"It can only get worse."

"True."

"Just think, if you were to marry Victoria, I could get my meals free."

Sam said a very ugly word in Cheyenne. He looked at Matt. "Marry? *Wagh!* You'll marry long before I will."

"To tell the truth, I don't think either one of us is a very good candidate for the ring and bit."

"Oh? Personally, I consider myself quite handsome and dashing."

"Yeah, yeah. You're a real Romeo, all right. But that wasn't what I was talking about."

"Oh? Please elucidate."

Matt reached over and pulled Sam's hat down around his ears. "Speak American, you heathen."

"Explain yourself, you cretin."

"The number of people who would like to see us stretched out with a lily in our hands."

"Ah. You're right." He was thoughtful for a moment. "Why lilies?"

"Huh?"

"Why are lilies so often associated with funerals?"

"Hell, I don't *know!* Where do you come up with these strange questions? Sam? You smell the dust?"

"Yes. I thought it was my imagination. Around that bend by those rocks up ahead would be a dandy place for an ambush."

"You're reading my mind. How do you want to play it?"

"We'll have about a hundred yards of cover when we enter those trees. Cut to the right and swing in around behind them. If it isn't our imagination."

"Like right now?"

"Let's do it."

The brothers cut off the road and into the thick stand of timber. They ground-reined their horses, removed their spurs, shucked rifles out of saddle boots, and made their way through the lush silence to the timber's edge.

When conversation was needed, they talked with Cheyenne hand signals. Sam signed: "I see two."

Matt replied: "I see them. Two more high up."

The ambushers all held rifles. Neither of the brothers could see their horses. If they could spot their horses, it would be fun to cut them loose and make the hands hoof it back to town. That beat killing any day.

The brothers worked closer to the rocks, circling now, staying in the timber that curved around the up-thrusting of rock. They finally spotted the horses, but there was no way they could get to them without exposing themselves.

Sam signed: "Now what?"

Matt grinned and made the Cheyenne sign for dust, lifting his rifle as he said it.

Sam returned the smile and the brothers separated, finding good positions from which to lay down some fire. They were less than a hundred yards from the ambushers, and from their positions, the crew of Lightning and Circle V hands were fully exposed.

Matt lifted his rifle, sighted in, and pulled the trigger just as Sam fired. Matt's slug hit the rifle's receiver and tore the weapon from the man's hands, numbing the ambusher's arms all the way up to the elbows. Sam's .44 slug slammed into the magazine tube and tore it loose from the barrel; the rifle clattered on the rocks. Matt's second shot lifted the hat from a man's head and sent him diving for scanty cover. Sam blew the heel off a cowboy boot; that brought a yelp of pain and a lot of cussing from the wearer.

The brothers started peppering the rocks with lead, being careful not to hit anyone. The ambushers scrambled for their horses and fled from that area, heading for town.

The brothers picked up all their brass and Sam buried the hulls, then smoothed the earth. Back at their horses, the brothers carefully cleaned their weapons, for both had a hunch what the ambushers were going to tell the sheriff.

"This just might get us a night in jail," Sam cautioned.

"Not if we play it right. You're a natural-born ham, so lay on the hoke when, or if, we're accused."

"A ham! Me? I'll have you know I was chosen for the lead every time a play was presented in college."

"What'd you play, the noble red man?"

"Bah!! I'm in the company of a fool."

"Come on. Let's get this over with."

They rode into town, and as they suspected, the sheriff was waiting for them.

"This time, by God," Linwood said, pointing a finger at them, "I got the goods on you boys. Get off them horses. You're under arrest."

Seven

"What's the charge?" Matt asked, stepping down.

"Attempted murder," Jack told them.

A large crowd had gathered around, friendly and unfriendly faces about equally divided.

"That's nonsense," Sam said. "We've been riding around the country all day, visiting people. We had dinner at the Box H. You can ask Pete Harris and family."

"That don't cut no ice," Linwood said. "This happened about an hour ago; two, three miles west of town. You ambushed some Lightning and Circle V hands at them rocks."

"We most certainly did not," Matt said. He drew his Colts so fast the sheriff was startled, the crowd gasped, and Mayor Dale ducked behind Linwood. Matt handed his pistols, butt-first, to the sheriff. "Check them; they haven't been fired."

Jack sniffed the barrels of the Colts, then checked Sam's pistol. "Shore haven't," he muttered.

"They was usin' rifles!" a Lightning hand called Dixon yelled. "Check them rifles."

The rifles were checked and found to be clean and powder free. "The rifles ain't been fired either," the sheriff said with a strange half-smile.

"Come on!" a Circle V man yelled. "We'll take you right to the spot and show you. They musta fired thirty or forty rounds."

"Suits me," Sam said.

"Me, too," Matt said. "I want to show you all that these men are damn liars."

A Lightning hand cussed and lunged for Matt, and the sheriff pushed him back. "Just get in the saddle and come on. Let's get this settled."

Half the town's citizens, including the mayor, made the trip out to the rocks. They found two busted rifles in the rocks, but not one bit of brass was found in the timber. Not a heelprint or a sign of disturbed brush.

"I told you they were lying," Matt said. "Are you satisfied now?"

"No, I'm not," Linwood said. "But I can't charge you 'cause there ain't no proof you two done anything."

"Do you get the impression that we're being hassled, brother?" Sam asked.

"I sure do. I think it's time we found us a lawyer and laid this in his lap."

Mayor Dale grinned. "There are no lawyers in Dale."

"But there is in the next town down the road, I bet," Matt said with a smile.

Mayor Dale's smile vanished. "Why would you want to see an attorney?"

"To sue the town, the mayor, and the sheriff," Sam said.

"Now wait a minute!" Mayor Dale yelled.

"And we'd win, too," Matt said.

"How do you figure that?" the sheriff asked, again with that strange smile.

"Because you're harassing us," Sam picked it up. "You took the word of a bunch of no-count bums, that bunch over there . . ." He pointed at the Lightning and Circle V hands; one of them gave him an obscene gesture. ". . . And placed us under arrest even after we—two prominent Wyoming cattle ranchers—protested our innocence. You have maligned our good names . . ." Sam was really getting into it now, raising his voice and waving his arms. ". . . Insulted our parentage, accused us of being low-down, dirty, filthy scum-of-the-earth ambushers, like that murderous pack of hyenas over there." Again he pointed to the Lightning and Circle V bunch.

Two of the Circle V boys were holding back another hand who was red-faced and ready to fight at that insult.

"And we're not going to take it anymore," Sam wound down. "We'll see how a court of law views these terrible grievances." He put on his best Indian face and glared stony-eyed down at the mayor.

"Now wait a minute!" Mayor Dale yelled. "We don't need a bunch of lawyers in on this." Lawyers were the last thing he needed in town. "We apologize for, ah, doing whatever it is you think we did. Don't we, Sheriff?"

Linwood mumbled something under his breath.

"What was that?" Matt leaned closer. "I couldn't hear that. Was that an apology?"

"Yes, yes!" Linwood shouted. "Sorry."

"And I want an apology from those snakes over there," Sam said, looking at the ambushers.

"You'll play hell gettin' one!" a Lightning hand called Ned yelled.

"You ain't heard the last from us, neither!" a Circle V hand yelled. "You gonna be sorry you ever lied on us."

Matt started to call out the nursery rhyme about sticks and stones, but he decided he'd pushed enough for one day. It was the same one who'd given them an obscene gesture moments earlier, so Matt returned it, waving the finger in the air.

"Stop that!" Mayor Dale said. "There are ladies present."

That evening at the café, Juan and family and staff were all smiles. Matt and Sam could pay for nothing. News of their visiting around the area had spread fast. The brothers ate until they could hold no more, then returned to their shack and turned in for the night.

About three days' ride from the town an old gunfighter was cooking his bacon and heating his coffee. He speared the strips of bacon and dumped in a cut-up potato and stirred the spuds around a bit. He added a bit of wild onion he'd pulled earlier and leaned back against his saddle. He listened to the wind that was rapidly closing in with the night. Charlie Starr was a contented man. He really had very little—his guns, his good horse, a saddle, and a few articles of clothing—but he'd never wanted for much. He sipped his coffee and stirred the potatoes and smiled. All in all, he'd had a good life, he reckoned. Not that he was figurin' on cashin' in his chips anytime soon, he was quick to think. But . . . he just didn't have anything to complain about. Charlie filled his plate and went to eating.

Not too many miles away, Louis Longmont sat in his

tent and enjoyed a fine wine with his meal, served on expensive china and eaten with silver utensils. The millionaire adventurer/industrialist/gambler/gunfighter could have been staying in Monte Carlo, or his suite in New York City, or in any one of a dozen elegant places; but Louis enjoyed the rough-and-tumble ways of the American West. The rest of the world was becoming just too tame for his liking.

Louis craved excitement, challenge. He thrived on it. And his advisers had warned him that investing in sheep in the West was a risky business. That was enough to sway Louis. The sheep were on their way; Louis was just looking for a good spot for them. He'd heard the area around Dale was just right.

The brothers stepped out to a fine day, the sky blue, the sun warming the earth, and at first glance, everything looked just dandy.

Then they looked up the street and saw the hitchrails in front of the Red Dog lined with horses.

"Wonderful," Sam muttered. "And I woke up in such a good humor."

"For a change," Matt replied.

"I *always* arise in a good humor."

"If that's the case, I'd hate to see you in a bad mood."

The brothers stood for a moment on the dirt path in front of their rented shack, staring toward the town.

"I'm hungry," Matt said. "If that pack of no-goods tries to keep me from breakfast, there's going to be trouble." He started walking toward the main street, Sam beside him. Matt had noticed that Sam had taken his second gunbelt from his saddlebags and was now wearing it. Both young men wore their guns loose in leather.

The horses at the hitchrails were from the Lightning and Circle V ranches. There were none from the Box H. But there was one horse with a brand that neither of them recognized.

"Think that's part of the Raley gang?" Sam asked.

"I doubt it. I don't think they'd be that open. From what I hear, most of those boys are wanted." He shrugged his shoulders. "But . . . who knows? I've sure never seen that brand before."

The brand was a grinning death's head. Macabre even for the wild and wooly West.

"Wait a second," Sam said, pausing to stare at the brand. "Sure. You remember that cowboy who rode along with us for a few days several months back? What was that he said about that French-speaking gunfighter?"

"Yeah! LaBarre—a French Canadian. The Mounties were looking for him. Rode a horse with a death's-head-brand. Supposed to be one of the top guns around. Some say he's better than Smoke Jensen. I guess that's his horse."

"He's supposed to be a top-money gunfighter."

"Well, if he braces me before breakfast, he'll damn sure earn it," Matt said.

But no one stepped out of the saloon as the brothers walked to the Mexican café. The place was crowded but strangely quiet for so many people.

"Is there a funeral this morning?" Sam asked Victoria when she came over, without her usual smile, to take their orders.

"The town has been tense ever since those men rode in before dawn," she told them. "Poppa says they haven't set one foot outside the saloon."

"So maybe it's payday and they're getting tanked up?" Matt suggested.

She shook her head. "The word is they're planning to kill the both of you today."

Matt grinned up at her. "Don't worry, Victoria. That's been tried by better men than that pack of saddle-bums over at the Red Dog. We're still here."

But the worry did not leave her eyes. "Be most careful today," she cautioned. "Don't be so flippant. Raul sent word in late last night that the Raley gang has ridden in. They're camped on Lightning range."

"That news does make one tend to be a bit more cautious," Sam said. "But not just us. That gang of no-goods are in here to make trouble for the sheepmen and the farmers. Have they been warned?"

"Sí. They are frightened."

"They better stay that way," Matt said. "And they better be willing to shoot first and ask questions later."

Victoria shook her head. "You know they will not—at least, not many of them. They are peaceful people for the most part."

She left them, taking their orders to the kitchen. The brothers sipped their coffee and kept one eye on the door.

"That's got to be him," Sam said softly, cutting his eyes to the door.

Matt turned. A man dressed all in black was entering the café. He was clean-shaven and neatly dressed. He even took off his hat once inside and hung it on a peg. His hair was dark and slicked back. His twin .45's were pearl-handled, the leather tied down. He walked directly to their table and sat down without being asked.

The man looked at the blood-brothers. "You are, of course, Matt Bodine and Sam Two Wolves?"

"Is that a question or a statement?" Sam asked.

The man ignored that and said, "I am LaBarre."

"Big deal," Matt replied.

LaBarre smiled. "You're very impudent."

"Nope. I'm just hungry. What do you want, LaBarre?"

"Breakfast. Some conversation. A chance to meet and get to know my enemies."

"We're not your enemies," Sam told him.

"Ah, *je vous demande pardon,* but you most certainly are. You stand in the way of my employers. So therefore you must either ride on, or be removed forcibly."

Matt studied the gunfighter. LaBarre was not a young man; he guessed him to be around forty. But he was rugged looking and appeared to be in very good physical shape.

"I hope whoever is paying you pays you well," Matt told the man, meeting his eyes. " 'Cause if you brace me, I'm going to get lead in you, LaBarre. Count on that. Unless, of course, you're a back-shooter."

The Frenchman's eyes narrowed at that. "When the time comes, my impudent and arrogant young foe, I will meet you face to face. And you can count on that."

Matt sighed and put down his coffee cup. "It always happens right when I'm about to eat. Did you ever notice that, Sam?"

Sam returned the sigh. "Do you have to do this before breakfast, brother?"

"Do what?" LaBarre asked.

"This," Matt said, and busted the man in the mouth with a hard right fist.

Matt didn't want any shooting in the crowded café. But he did want to put the gunfighter out of commission for a time. And Matt didn't believe in waiting around. LaBarre's butt hit the floor, blood streaming from his busted lips, and Sam reached down with both hands and literally ripped the man's gunbelt from him.

"I'll just keep this for a time," he said, smiling at LaBarre. "I wouldn't want anything to happen to the tools of your trade. I'm such a considerate fellow, aren't I?"

With a curse, LaBarre jumped to his feet and took a swing at Matt. Matt sidestepped, ducked, faked the man with a left, and then snapped a right to LaBarre's head. LaBarre took it flush on his honker. The hard-thrown punch broke the nose and backed the gun-fighter up, blood leaking from his bent blower. He screamed in rage and kicked up with a right boot.

Matt grabbed the foot and twisted, sending the man crashing to the floor. LaBarre was very quick; he rolled away and jumped to his boots, his face dark with anger. He backed up and raised his clenched fists. He said something in French that Matt figured was nothing complimentary.

The crowd had left their tables, most of them taking their plates with them, and backed up next to the walls, eating and enjoying the fight.

"Come on, LaBarre," Matt taunted the man. "Let's see how good you are without your guns."

LaBarre flicked a left that Matt pushed out of the way and the Canadian came boring in with a right that jarred Matt down to his boots. Matt backed up and took a vicious left on his shoulder. It hurt; it would have floored him if it had connected with his jaw.

Matt shuffled out of the way and shook his head to clear away the roaring and worked his left arm to un-kink the muscle. LaBarre pressed and got sloppy for an instant. Matt knocked the crap out of the man with a right and left that twisted LaBarre's head and sent blood flying.

Matt hit him in the belly and whoosed the air from LaBarre. The Canadian backed up, sucking in great lungfuls of air. His face was white from the sudden shock of losing all his wind.

The breakfast diners were quiet now, their eyes riveted on the combatants. Sheriff Linwood and Mayor Dale had entered the café, along with Hugo Raner and Blake Vernon and some of their hands. They stood along the wall and made no move to interfere. What they might do after the fight was anybody's guess, but for now, they let the two men slug it out.

LaBarre was wary now; he'd experienced the power in Matt's big, hard fists, and knew he could not afford to risk a clench to rest. He had to keep moving, always moving, darting in, striking, and getting out.

Matt pressed the man, never taking his eyes from the eyes of his opponent. He flicked a left at LaBarre, but the man didn't take the bait. He ducked the punch and kept his balled fists in a protective position. Matt kicked at the man's knee and LaBarre danced back. Matt spun, jumped, and showed the gunfighter some Indian wrestling moves. He got his legs around LaBarre's legs in a scissor-lock and twisted, bringing them both to the floor. Matt rolled over quickly, came to his knees, and hammered at the man's face with both fists.

LaBarre's eyes were glazing over and he was mumbling incoherently and spraying blood with each exhalation when Matt hauled him to his boots and turned him around. With one hand on the seat of his tailored pants and the other on the collar of his expensive shirt, Matt tossed him out the door. The paid gunhand landed on his belly in the alley, slid for a few feet, then lay there moaning and cussing. Matt jerked LaBarre's hat from the peg and sailed it out to him. It was heavy, the hatband adorned with silver dollars. Unfortunately, the hat landed in a big mud puddle and sank up to its pinch.

Sam had unloaded LaBarre's guns and replaced them in leather. He walked to the doorway and held them out for Matt. Matt took aim and hurled the rig out into the alley just as LaBarre was slowly getting to his knees. The heavy double rig caught him on the back of the noggin and knocked him flat on his face. This time, LaBarre did not move.

"You may wash up back here, Senor Bodine," Juan said with a huge grin. He pointed. "And your breakfast will be ready in a moment."

Mayor Dale, Hugo, Blake, and hands left sullen and red-faced to the sound of everybody in the place applauding Matt's just-concluded actions with LaBarre.

Jack Linwood was smiling.

Eight

Sam stood by the door, just in case some of the hands broke from the crowd just leaving and came back in trouble-hunting. He watched as LaBarre was lifted out of the dirt and half-dragged, half-carried to the boardwalk, a hand following along, shaking the muddy water from the gunfighter's fancy hat. The hand looked back at the café and spotted Sam. He said something, but he was too far away for Sam to make out the words. It was probably the distance that saved the hand's life, for Sam was in no mood for any more insults.

Matt reentered the café and the brothers enjoyed a quiet breakfast.

"So what's on for today?" Sam asked.

"Staying close to town. I got an itchy feeling in the middle of my back. I don't think a ride in the country is wise."

"I agree. I'd like to know what's being discussed over in the Red Dog."

"Killing us, probably."

"How's your hands?"

"A little stiff. I think I'll buy some salts and soak them for a couple of hours."

"At least doing that will keep you out of trouble," Sam remarked.

A larger crowd of hands had gathered at the saloon by midmorning, and by midafternoon, it appeared that every hand on the Circle V and Lightning payroll was in town. And they were getting rowdy. A small boy appeared at the door carrying a tray of food and a note from Juan. The man had wisely decided to close his café early and not reopen until the next day. He had gotten word that there was to be much trouble that night.

Matt had soaked his hands several times during the day and what stiffness had been in them was gone. The evening shadows were lengthening when Matt buttoned up his shirt and swung his gunbelt around his hips.

"I'm not a prisoner, and damned if I'll behave as one," he said. "I'm going to the Plowshare for a beer."

Sam pulled on his boots and buckled on his iron. "I thought you'd never suggest it."

They checked on their horses, making sure they had plenty of water and hay, then began the short walk to the gathering place of farmers, sheepmen, and local townspeople who had no desire to rub elbows with the riders of Hugo Raner and Blake Vernon.

Just as they were leaving the shack, two fast shots split the evening air. Both men quickly stepped into the shadows and waited. But it was only a drunken cowboy firing toward the sky. They walked on.

"If it doesn't blow wide open tonight," Sam said, "I'll be surprised."

But Matt wasn't all that convinced. "I don't think

Raner and Vernon will let it come to that. They're both bull-headed fools, but I'm betting they know a full-scale riot in the streets would only work against them. Look over there," he said, pointing.

A group of townspeople had gathered, all of them armed with rifles and shotguns, and now were fanning out for the rooftops. In front of the Red Dog, a cowboy watched it and stepped back inside. A moment later, Hugo and Blake stepped out and appraised the situation. They stood for a few moments, then walked back inside the saloon.

The brothers walked on through the night and stepped up on the boardwalk. The batwings of the Red Dog slammed open and a cowboy lurched out, spotting Matt and Sam.

"Bodine!" he yelled. "You just hold up right there."

Matt stopped, turning to face the man across the wide street.

The cowboy cussed Matt in a drunken voice. "I'm callin' your hand, you damn nester-lover!"

"Back off," Matt said. "Just ease up, go back to the bunkhouse, and sober up."

The cowboy cussed him, swaying in his drunkenness.

"Hugo!" Bodine yelled. Vernon! Get out here."

The ranchers stepped out onto the boardwalk.

"I don't know which brand this puncher rides for, but I don't want to drag iron against a drunk," Bodine called. "Now get your man out of here and sober him up."

"Do it," Mayor Dale called from in front of the hotel. "The man's so drunk he can hardly stand. Bodine's right." The last was said with no small amount of bitterness.

"You're yellow, Bodine," the cowboy sneered.

"You know better than that, cowboy," Matt called. "Go sober up. If you want to do this thing in the morning, I'll be right here in town."

"Come on, Jody," Blake said. "Back off. That's an order. Now do it!"

Hugo lifted his eyes. A townsman was squatting on top of the Plowshare, a rifle aimed directly at the rancher.

The Circle V hand lurched back into the saloon, still cussing Bodine.

"All right, people," Hugo shouted to the night. "You've shown us how you feel this night. You've all taken sides against us and lined up behind them damn sheepmen and nesters. We know who you are and we won't forget it. From now on you'll not get a dime's worth of business from any of us. By God, you'll see who supports this town."

"That's not true, Hugo," Simmons, the owner of the general store, called from his position on the roof of his store. "But if you want to take your business elsewhere, that's fine with me. The nearest town is forty miles north or fifty miles west. Take your choice."

"If you're not against us, what the hell are you doing up there with a rifle in your hands?" Blake shouted across the street.

"To keep your damn rowdy hands from going on a rampage," Simmons shouted. "If it's any of your business."

"Little man," Blake said, pointing a finger at the store owner. "You don't talk to me like that."

Simmons shucked a round into the chamber and leveled the rifle, the sound carrying ominousness through the night air. Blake quickly stepped back into the Red Dog.

Hugo leaned against a support post and looked up at the man's dim outline on the rooftop. "A lot of hard feelin's is gonna come from this night's actions, Simmons. A lot of things is gonna happen that can't never be changed. You real sure you want to do this?"

"What's right is right, Hugo," Simmons called, and a murmur of voices from the other rooftops agreed with him. "Those farmers and sheep people ain't causin' no harm to anybody . . ."

"You lie!" Hugo yelled, throwing his cigar down into the dirt of the street. "Them sheep is ruinin' the range and them damn nesters is cuttin' me off from my water."

"That's not true, Hugo," Walters of the saddle and gun shop called from the night. "A river runs right through your range. You don't want to share, is the problem."

"I've bought my last saddle and gun from you, Walters," Hugo's words were bitter.

"Suit yourself," the man called. "I'll get by."

"And none of my men will trade with you, either."

"If that's the way you want it."

"It's coming apart," Jack Linwood said to Mayor Dale. The men stood in front of the hotel. "Bodine's done shoved some steel up their backbones."

"I'm afraid you're right. And since I own half the businesses in this town, guess which side that puts me on?"

The sheriff looked at him. "Suits me, Dale."

"I'm a businessman, Jack," Mister Dale cut him off. "I have to know which side my bread is buttered on. I have no choice in the matter."

With a short laugh, Jack turned to walk away. Mayor Dale's voice stopped him.

"And you'd better learn very quickly which side to take, Sheriff."

Jack returned to the mayor's side. In a low voice, he asked, "Now what the hell does that mean?"

"It means that you start being a real sheriff and enforcing the law . . . whoever breaks it."

"I said it suits me."

"Believe it. You've had it easy up to now, Jack. Now you have to start being a real sheriff. You treat everybody the same, Jack. And you'd better make that clear to your deputies."

"Fine with me, but the boys will never stand for that, Dale. They won't."

"Then tell them to turn in their badges. It's just that simple."

"What happens when Hugo and Blake bust this range wide open? And you know they will."

"You're the sheriff of this county, Jack. A regular judge swore you in. If you can't do the job, he can order you out and replace you with somebody who *will* do the job." The mayor wasn't real sure a judge could do that, but he was betting Linwood didn't know that.

Jack wasn't sure about that either. He walked away.

Mayor Dale heard footsteps on the boardwalk. He turned and looked into the smiling face of Chrisman. "If you really mean that," Chrisman said, "stop both factions right now."

"It's only delaying what is sure to happen," Mayor Dale replied.

"It'll buy us time, Dale."

"All right," he said softly. "Jack," Mayor Dale stopped Linwood again. The sheriff turned around.

"Yes, sir?"

"Order the men from the rooftops and order Hugo and Blake and their men out of town. Take your deputies and do it."

"And if they want to make a fight of it?"

"You're the law, Jack."

Jack Linwood shook his head and walked slowly toward his office, mumbling about sheepdip and mule turds. Chrisman walked back to his saloon.

Matt and Sam slipped into the Plowshare and took a table after ordering beer. The place was nearly empty, with only a handful of men sitting at the tables. Paul Dennis was one of them, sitting with Chrisman. The bar owner got up and walked over to Matt and Sam and took a chair.

"It's a start, at least," he said.

"It's a good start," Sam agreed. "Maybe when those men get home and start thinking about the whole town being against them, they'll wise up a little."

"I'd like to think that's what will happen," Chrisman said. "But I know those men well. They'll brood about this for a time, then they'll start spilling blood. The good hands will leave, the troublemakers will stay, and both the Circle V and Lightning will hire gunhands and the war will be on."

Matt slowly shook his head. "There's got to be more to this than meets the eyes."

Sam looked at him. "What do you mean?"

"There are maybe a dozen farmers and three flocks of sheep in this entire region. They're not taking up enough room or water to amount to anything. There is something we're missing in this thing."

Chrisman looked puzzled. "I don't see what else it could be. Cattlemen been fightin' farmers and sheep for years, all over the West."

"Yeah, but Pete has the same suspicions I do. He started to say something about it a couple of times—I think—but changed his mind before he could complete his thought."

"Where was I when all this was going on?" Sam asked.

"In the privy."

"He didn't say what he thought it might be?" Chrisman asked.

"No. But he was sure mulling something over in his mind; worrying at it."

"Hell with all of you in this damn town!" Hugo Raner yelled from the saddle. "Damn every one of you."

"I'll strangle this town dry!" Blake boasted. "I'll turn this place into a ghost town!"

The men thundered out of town, firing their guns into the air as they rode.

When the street had settled down, Sam asked, "Can they do that?"

"Strangle the town?" Chrisman asked. "No. There are a dozen smaller spreads out around. What with those and the miners and travelers and farmers, there won't be much of a loss. There is talk the railroad will be through here in a year or so—or at least a feeder line. Oh, they'll hurt by pulling their business out; but we'll make it."

"Since it appears likely that we'll never be allowed on Circle V or Lightning range, and I know that cattle prices are down, tell me something," Matt said. "How do you suppose Blake and Hugo are fixed for cash money?"

"Oh, they're all right. Dale loans them money from time to time. But Dale would be the last person in the state to want to see this town dry up. Hell, he *owns* a big chunk of it. And he's always traveling somewheres to drum up more people to move in. And he sure wouldn't want to see two big ranchers fail. He'd lose money in the long run."

"Oh, I wasn't thinking about Dale being up to something underhanded. I'm just trying to make some sense out of all of this."

Sam looked at him. "Don't try to think, brother. You know it makes your head hurt."

Chrisman left the table with a smile on his lips, leaving the two brothers hurling insults at one another. All in all, Chrisman thought, things were working out very nicely.

Nine

"There's no need for you boys to stick around now," Jack Linwood told the brothers the next day.

They were enjoying breakfast at the café when the sheriff walked in and took a seat at their table—uninvited. He ordered a full breakfast for himself and a fresh pot of coffee for them all.

"How do you figure?" Matt asked.

Linwood shrugged his shoulders. "It's over, that's why. Blake and Hugo will stomp around for a few days and make a lot of threats, but in the end, that's all there'll be to it. They're not goin' to ride fifty miles for a drink or make a three-, four-day wagon trip for supplies. That'd be stupid, and neither one of them is that dumb."

Neither brother had anything to say about that, although both of them thought it was a crock.

"Sure surprised me when Mister Dale give in so easy last night, though," Linwood said.

"Why do you suppose he did it?" Sam asked.

"I guess he was willin' to risk losin' a lot of money

to keep a range war from happenin'. It was a chancy move on his part. Took ever'body by suprise. Me, 'specially."

"What'd Hugo and Blake do when you ordered them out of town?" Matt asked.

"Blustered up some. But me and my men were totin' sawed-off shotguns. Nobody in their right mind wants to go up agin a sawed-off up close." He looked at first one, then the other. "I'll be flat-out level with you two: I ain't got no use for either one of you; I just don't like you. I think them hands was layin' in ambush for you the other day and you turned it around on them. Cute. But chancy. I think you swept the area and hid your casin's, then made a big deal out of your not knowin' nothin' about it to make them boys look like fools. Which about half of them is," he admitted.

Linwood sighed. "Damn it, I don't know which side I'm supposed to be on. It's confusin'. First I'm told one thing, then I'm told another. I feel like a mule that's been told to gee-haw; don't know which way to turn."

Sam chuckled. "Why don't you just enforce the law equally for all, and come the next election, you might win honestly. Wouldn't that be something?"

Jack Linwood grunted. "Sure would." He smiled. "I've been a lot of things in my life. Marshal here and there. But to be elected, by the people . . . ?" He shook his head. "That would be something, for sure."

Their food came and the men ate in silence, Linwood finishing first. He stood up and looked down at the brothers. "Maybe you two ain't so bad after all. I don't know. I got some heavy thinkin' to do. See you around." He paid for his meal and left the café.

"You don't suppose . . ." Matt said.

"Could be. A lot of good lawmen have checkered pasts. Linwood just might be seeing right and wrong clearly for the first time in his life. For sure, he's torn up inside about what to do. His deputies are another matter."

Jack Linwood walked to his office and called his deputies in. "We play it straight from now on," he told them. "You take orders from me, and no one else. Not from Mayor Dale, not from none of the big three ranchers, not from nobody but me. We enforce the law, we don't hassle, and we don't take no crap from nobody. Is that clear?"

The deputies looked at one another. "What the hell's goin' on, Jack? You know what we was hired to do well as we do."

"All that's changed. No more threatenin' protection money from the merchants. We're lawmen and we're gonna be good ones. It's about time we done something good in our lives."

Three badges hit the desk.

"Git gone," Linwood told the men. "Clear gone out of the town. I won't have you in here. You got one hour to git your possibles together and clear out."

"And if we don't?" Buster Phelps sneered at him.

Jack laid a cosh up side of Buster's head, knocking the man to the office floor. Before the other two could drag iron, Jack's left hand was filled with a six-gun and his eyes were very cold and very steady as they bored into the men.

"Easy, Jack," Sam Keller said. "We're gone." He pointed to the moaning Buster. "What about him?"

"Drag him out of here and get out of town!"

"We're gone," Wes Fannin said.

Matt and Sam watched the trio leave the sheriff's office, Wes and Keller dragging the moaning Buster.

"They aren't wearing badges," Matt pointed out.

"Now it gets interesting," Sam said. "Let's wander

over and sit on the bench outside the sheriff's office. The mayor might have something to say about this."

They walked over and sat down, waiting for the fun to start.

Mayor Dale brushed by them with a curt nod of his head. He closed the door to the sheriff's office. But a window was open and the brothers could hear every word that was said.

"You want to tell me what's going on here, Jack?" Dale demanded.

"I cleaned house," Linwood said. "Now I'm lookin' for a couple of new deputies."

"You fool! Don't you know the town council could replace you in a heartbeat?"

Jack smiled. "I wired the judge this morning—first thing." He waved a telegraph reply. "The people put me in office, the people have to put me out. The town council ain't got a damn thing to say about county business."

Mayor Dale sat down and returned the smile. "All right, Jack. Good. You're right and I'm wrong. I'll work with you all the way." He stuck out his hand and Jack Linwood shook it. "Now, how about deputies? You have anyone in mind?"

"Jimmy Byrant comes to mind. He's young, but he's a good boy. And I think he'd stand if push comes to shove."

"Agreed. Who else?"

"I don't have anyone else in mind. I'll just have to wait and see. I'm gonna ride out to the Bryant spread and talk to Jimmy right now. They've been goin' through some tough times and could use the extra money, I'm thinkin'."

Mayor Dale stared at the man. "I have to ask this, Jack: why the sudden change of heart?"

"I don't know," Jack spoke the words softly. "It come up on me sudden—last evenin', after I ordered Raner and Blake out of town. They bulled up on me and told me I was supposed to be their man—bought and paid for. I didn't like that. Didn't get much sleep last night; tossed and turned most of the night. I haven't been much most of my life. Time for a change, and by God, I can do it and I'm *gonna* do it."

"Good man," Dale said, getting up and patting the man on the arm. "I'm proud of you."

Matt and Sam looked at each other. "This is getting more and more interesting with each day," Sam said.

Matt agreed. "Linwood's sure to need some help when the pot boils over."

"And since we are both so very civic minded, that help is in the form of . . . ?"

Matt smiled and pointed first at Sam, then at himself.

"Right! Tell you what, brother, when Buster and his buddies leave town, let's you and I sort of trail along behind them; see where they go."

"Straight to either the Circle V or the Lightning spread."

"That's my thinking."

"Let's saddle up."

They stood up just as the mayor exited the sheriff's office, all smiles. "Going to be great things happening in this town, boys," he said. "People all over are having a change of heart. Me included. You boys are welcome to come back to the hotel anytime you like." He patted both of them on the arm and walked on.

Jack Linwood stepped out of his office, closing the door behind him. He looked at the blood-brothers. "I still don't have much use for you, but I won't hassle you none. But if you break the law, I'll put you in jail. And that's a promise."

"Fair enough," Matt said.

Jack swung into the saddle and headed out, searching for new deputies.

The brothers saddled up, and as soon as the three ex-deputies rode out, they waited a couple of minutes and then headed out after them. At the crossroads just outside of town, the three men took the northern turn, heading for the Lightning range. Matt and Sam tailed along behind them. When they rode onto Lightning range, the brothers reined up.

"Now what?" Sam asked.

"Let's go see Pete and tell him the news. Maybe he'll spit out what's on his mind."

"Naturally, Millie has nothing whatsoever to do with this visit?"

"Naturally. She's just a child."

Sam spurred his horse and was still laughing at that when Matt rode up and took a swing at him. He missed.

"I don't know, boys," Pete Harris said over coffee on the front porch. "But it don't surprise me. Dale's gonna play on the winnin' side, every time. I reckon he seen the writin' on the wall, as the sayin' goes, and stepped over the line."

"Do you trust him, Pete?"

"Now that's an interestin' question, son. Yes, and no. Let me put it this way: I trust a rattlesnake as long as he's out of strikin' distance and I can see him. Dale is gonna make money. Period. I ain't never known him to lose any. At least, not to amount to much. I keep money in his bank, but I don't borrow none from him. 'Course, I don't really trust Chrisman, neither. Oh, he comes on like a fine fellow—and maybe he is. But there's something about him I just don't trust."

"He said he came out here about the same time as Dale," Sam recalled.

"That's right. But me and Hugo and Blake come out here years before they did. Man, this country was wild. Indians and outlaws and old sore-toothed mountain men and grizzly bears. I don't know what happened to Blake and Hugo. They went power-crazy, I reckon. Nothin' would satisfy them. They had to have the finest houses, the finest horses, the best of everything for their kids; and there ain't neither one of them got a kid that's worth a damn for anything." He paused to refill their coffee cups. "Got any more news?" he asked with a smile.

Sam told him about Jack Linwood.

"I've seen it happen before. A man takes the wrong road and takes him years to find the right turn to get back on the straight and narrow. Jack's hell with a short gun, boys, don't sell him short on that. But I always thought I seen a streak of good in him. And those no-count deputies quit and rode off toward the Lightning range, eh?"

"That's the way they were heading."

"Hugo'll hire 'em. Him and Blake brought in the Raley gang—so I heard. Robert told me. I knew a break was comin' between us when they proposed doin' that. I was against it from the start. I got me fifteen good hands, most of them men who've been with me for years. There isn't a fast gun in the bunch, but they're dead shots and there isn't a one who wouldn't charge the gates of Hell with a bucket of water. If Hugo and Raner want to take me on—and it might come to that—they'll find the Box H hands will give ten times more than they get." He grinned. "You boys want to stay for dinner?"

The grins he got back told him the answer to that.

"Oughtta just put you on the payroll," Pete grumbled good-naturedly.

Dinner that day was a thick, hearty stew, with hot, fresh-baked bread covered with butter. And there was a huge platter of doughnuts that Millie had baked. The brothers had a hard time keeping their eyes off the bear sign.

"After dinner, boys," Becky told them.

"Do the hands eat this well?" Sam asked.

"Sure. Except on brandin' and roundups. We take turns cookin' then or hire a trail cook if one can be found. The grub is one of the reasons my hands don't hardly ever quit me."

Just as the brothers were swinging up into the saddle, Millie came up with a cloth sack. "For after supper," she told them with a smile.

The sack was filled with doughnuts. "We'll keep it a secret," Sam told her. "I've known of shootings to occur when doughnuts are involved."

And he wasn't kidding. Cowboys had been known to ride fifty or more miles for a sack of doughnuts.

Pete stepped out on the porch. "You boys ride loose. Hugo and Blake won't let last night's slight die easy. They'll be like rattlers in the spring: they'll strike at anything around them. I'll see you boys in town tomorrow. It's supply day." He grinned. "Way you boys eat, I figure I'd better double the order."

Laughing, the blood-bonded brothers hit the trail, with Matt arguing with Sam over who was going to carry the doughnuts back to town.

"I will," Sam told him. "You'd have them eaten up before we got a mile. The sack, too, probably."

"What's that in your mouth? Get your hand outta that sack!"

"Oh, shut up!"

* * *

"That's quite a pair, Dad," Robert said, stepping out to stand by his father.

"Listenin' to them and talkin' with them, you'd never figure they were two of the top gunhands in the country."

"I think Matt Bodine is the most handsome man I have ever seen," Millie said, watching them ride off.

"Oh, Lord!" Pete said.

"He would certainly be a fine catch for any young lady," Becky said, drying her hands on her apron.

"Now, wait a damn minute!" Pete said.

"I can see it now," Robert said, after winking at his mother. "Millie getting married—a fancy church wedding and all that—and moving off to Wyoming. The house sure would be a much quieter place with her gone."

"Married!" Pete thundered. "Hell's fire, she just met the man a couple of days ago!"

Millie was under no delusions about Matt Bodine. He was a drifter and she knew it. But she could dream. "Millie and Matt," she said, enjoying agitating her father. "That sure has a nice sound to it."

Pete got it through his head that his family was having a fine time sticking the needle to him. He laughed. "All right, all right," he said. He looked at his daughter. "But, girl . . . you could do a heck of a lot worse."

Ten

They were five miles from the Box H when both brothers began to get a tingling feeling in the middle of their backs.

And that was something they always paid attention to.

"Now!" Matt yelled, and he and Sam sent their horses scrambling off the road and into a stand of timber. The word had just left his mouth when the rifle boomed. The slug came so close to Sam he could feel the heat of it slamming past his ear.

"Don't drop the doughnuts!" Matt yelled.

They rode into the timber and jumped off their horses, shucking their rifles from the boots. The brothers made their way to timber's edge and crouched down.

"That slope right over there," Sam said. "In that jumble of rocks."

"That was no .44 or .44-.40," Matt said. "That was a Sharps or a Spencer."

"I agree. Or an old Springfield. I've seen people

make shots at a thousand yards with one of those. Somebody is bringing out the heavy artillery. Any of those slugs would tear your head off. My father used to say that the Springfield was the one rifle the Indians feared the most . . . until the Henry came along."

"I know what your father used to say. I was there, remember? Where's the bear sign?"

"In my saddlebags."

"They'll get all crushed. I'll go get them."

Sam hauled him back by the seat of his pants. "Will you stop worrying about doughnuts and concentrate on us getting out of this mess."

"I had a hunger pang."

"Wonderful. Since we might be pinned down here for several hours, I think we'll keep the bear sign in reserve."

"Good thinking. I'll just get them out of the saddlebag before my horse figures out how to get to them and eats them."

Before Sam could put a good cussing on his brother, a slug howled over their heads and slammed into the tree behind them. Matt dug out the slug and looked at it. He whistled, holding it out for Sam to see.

"Springfield .45," Matt said.

"Far out of range for these Winchesters we've got." Sam looked around him. They were not in a good position for getting out safely. The thick timber they were in covered about five acres. To the left of them lay a rocky flat, to the right and behind them, a vast meadow, all within easy reach of the big single-shot Springfield rifle.

"Well," Matt said, putting the doughnuts out of his mind for the time being, "I think we're stuck."

"Oh, that's good, brother."

"How would you size up our situation?"

Sam thought about that for a few seconds. He grinned and said, "Stuck."

Only a few more shots were fired from the sniper hidden in the rocks above them during the next hour. And they were chance shots, since Matt and Sam were well hidden and well protected. No one came down the road and the brothers hoped no one would, for they suspected the killer above them would not hesitate to kill anyone who wandered into his field of fire.

'Who did we tell we were going out to the Box H?" Sam asked.

Matt thought for a moment. "No one. So we had to have been followed. When the sniper reached this place, he just holed up and waited for us to return."

The sniper fired again, but the slug went far wide of their position. He was searching now.

A small stray dog came walking up the road.

"Oh, hell," Matt said.

Sam's face was grim.

The sniper fired and the little dog was dead.

Matt cussed and Sam's face tightened. Both Matt and Sam had been indoctrinated into the Cheyenne's Dog Warrior society, and both loved dogs and despised anyone who was cruel to them.

"When we catch up with this scum," Sam said, "he is mine."

Matt nodded his head, his eyes on the little dog lying in a pool of blood in the road, a little dog who had meant no harm to anyone. Who wanted only to be man's friend. "If I don't get him first."

"You won't," Sam assured him.

Another hour passed. The sounds of hooves reached the brothers, the horseman coming from the direction of the Box H. Matt and Sam started yelling.

"Stay back!" they shouted as loud as they could. "Stay back. Sniper in the rocks."

The horseman veered quickly off the road to the north side and dismounted, grabbing his rifle from the boot. He concealed his horse and took up a position behind rocks. "Bodine and Two Wolves?" he shouted.

"Yeah," Matt returned the shout. "He's had us pinned down here for several hours."

"Who killed the dog?"

"Whoever that is up in the rocks," Sam shouted.

"Why'd he shoot the pup?"

"No reason. He just wanted to kill something, I reckon," Matt yelled.

The man cussed. "I hate a son of a bitch who'd do something like that."

"He's mine," Sam called. "Someday."

"Not if I find him first. Name's Cooper. Call me Coop. I ride for the Box H. I seen you boys the other day."

"We got a sackful of bear sign we'll share if we can get shut of that gunman up yonder," Matt yelled.

"Millie make 'em?"

"Yeah."

"We'll get shut of him," Coop shouted. "They's two more hands from the Spur comin' up behind me."

"Where's the Spur?" Sam called.

"Little spread on the west side of the Parachute. Good people."

That seemed to do it for the sniper. A moment later, he was riding off, putting the spurs to his horse. But the massive upthrusting of rock preventing anyone from getting a glimpse at him or taking a shot. The men gathered in the road and shook hands.

"I'll bury the dog," Matt said. "Sam, check up yonder for brass, will you?"

Coop went into the coolness of timber and dug a hole with his hands in the softer earth. Matt picked up the little pooch and carried him into the timber.

"Reminds me of a dog I had when I was kid," Coop said.

Neither man said anything else for a moment. Both of them were thinking that no decent person kills a domesticated animal for pleasure. Only people who are perverted and darkly twisted.

The dog buried, the men got their horses and waited for Sam to come down from the rocks.

".45 Springfield," Sam said. "The man's got a V-shaped cut on the sole of his right boot. And he's right-handed."

Two more cowboys rode up and swung down. Dickie and Waldo from the Spur.

"This is gettin' out of hand," Dickie said. He pointed to the dark stain on the dirt road. "Who got hit?" After Matt explained, Dickie hotly, bluntly, and with considerable passion compared the man's character to a certain part of the anatomy. And what comes out of it.

Sam said, "We'll report this to Sheriff Linwood."

Waldo looked at him. "Are you serious?"

Sam explained briefly what all had taken place in Dale.

"Well, now," Waldo mused. "That's good news, but it don't make no sense. I never figured Mister Dale would switch sides like that."

"Does that man have a first name?" Sam asked.

If he did, none of the hands had ever heard it.

They mounted up and rode into town. The hands went to the Red Dog, Matt and Sam to the sheriff's office.

Linwood listened to their story, sent his brand new deputy, Jimmy, over to the saloon to talk to the Box H and Spur men, and looked at the brass Sam had picked up.

"Only people around here who have Springfields is the Reed family, farmers. But they'd have no reason to shoot you boys. Thank you for reportin' this. Maybe I was hasty in my dislikin' you." He wore a half-smile. "Tell me something: did you two turn the tables on those hands . . . about that ambush the other day?"

Matt and Sam grinned and Linwood returned it honestly. "I thought so," the sheriff said. "You boys are pretty good actors." He looked at Sam. "But you're a ham."

Louis Longmont sent one of his men into town to check on the deed to his property, filed under a corporate name, and set up his camp on his property.

Charlie Starr rode slowly into town and swung down in front of the Red Dog. He beat the dust of the trail from his clothing with his hat and stepped inside. LaBarre was standing at the bar, his face bruised and swollen from the beating he'd received at the hands of Matt Bodine. He was in a ugly mood and ready to strike at anyone, for any reason, real or imagined.

Young Deputy Jimmy Bryant was having a sandwich and a beer at a table across the room. LaBarre made him nervous, but the kid was game, with no back-up in him. He was good with a gun, although by no means in LaBarre's class.

Sheriff Linwood was out by the rocks, trying to pick up the trail of the ambusher. But after twenty-four hours, he didn't give that much hope.

Charlie Starr ordered a rye and a beer, then made himself a sandwich from the table and took a seat a couple of tables away from the young deputy. Just a kid, Charlie thought. And that hand all in black with the beat-up face was LaBarre. That was no guess on

Charlie's part. He'd seen his likeness only a few days back. He wondered if LaBarre knew there were fresh wanted posters out on him. One thousand dollars. He'd killed a man over in Nebraska, and a judge had ruled it murder.

Well, Charlie mused, he had a few dollars in his pockets and he wasn't hunting trouble.

But LaBarre was.

"Hey!" LaBarre called. "You, the punk kid with the star on your shirt. Look at me when I talk to you, little baby boy!"

Charlie drank his rye down neat, chased it with a swallow of beer, and took a bite of sandwich. He liked the look of the young deputy; he sort of reminded Charlie of his kid brother, before a trouble-hunter like LaBarre had killed him. The trouble-hunter went down under the guns of Charlie Starr.

"I think I'll come over there and rip that tin star off your shirt and shove it up your nose, baby-face."

Charlie sized up the situation with wise eyes. The kid had both hands on the table and the leather thong was over the hammer of his pistol. If the kid moved a hand, LaBarre would kill him.

"Deputy," Charlie said. "Do you have the power to deputize citizens in time of need?"

"I, ah, think so, sir," Jimmy replied.

"Then deputize me."

"How do I do that?"

"Just say I'm a deputy."

Jimmy laughed nervously. "Ah, well, gee, you're a deputy of this county."

"Thank you." Charlie stood up. He knew his guns were loose in leather. From years of habit. He looked at LaBarre, watching the older man with a puzzled look on his beat-up face.

Charlie said, "Pretend I'm wearing that star and come over here and rip it off my shirt, you son-of-a-bitch."

LaBarre's mouth dropped open. This old geezer had to be at least sixty. LaBarre closed his mouth and cleared his throat. "What . . . did you call me, you old horse turd?"

"I called you a son-of-a-bitch. What's the matter with you, are you deaf as well as ugly?"

Pete Harris was in the saloon, having a beer and a sandwich over in a darkened corner, and his foreman, Shorty, was with him. Robert was seeing to the loading of the supply wagon and Becky and Millie were shopping and gossiping.

If this old hard-bitten rider didn't intercede, Pete had made up his mind to shoot LaBarre down himself. The tough old bird looked familiar to Pete, but he couldn't place him. Lean-waisted, but with a lot of muscle still in his upper torso. The man's wrists were thick and his hands big and callused.

"Do you have such a wish to die, old man?" LaBarre asked.

"I'll die someday," Charlie said. "That's something we all have to face. But I won't die at your hands, LaBarre."

"Oh, you have heard of me?"

"How else would I have known your name? Damn if you ain't an ignorant feller."

LaBarre looked at Jimmy with a sneer on his lips. "Are you going to let this poor old ragged man do your fighting for you, little baby?"

"Look at me!" Charlie roared.

Angry to the core, LaBarre turned to face Charlie. "I think, old man, you need to be taught a lesson in manners."

"You don't have the time, LaBarre. You were pushin' hard at the kid, knowing you're a slicker gun-handler than him. But you ain't slicker than me. I don't usually stick my nose in other's folks' affairs, but I'm makin' an exception this time. From the looks of you, somebody done whupped your head proper. Now you want to strike out at anybody." Charlie stepped away from the table. "Well, here I am, LaBarre. Will Charlie Starr do?"

Pete chuckled, then laughed out loud. "Why, you old tumbleweed," he said. "I ain't seen you in twenty-five years."

Charlie never took his eyes off LaBarre. "Who you be, mister?"

"Pete Harris, you old gray wolf. You get done with this tinhorn here, I'll buy you a drink."

LaBarre was shaken to his boots. *Charlie Starr!*

Some say Starr was the very first fast gun.*

LaBarre had backed himself into a corner and knew it. Now his honor was at stake. And his life, he reminded his monumental ego.

"Come on, LaBarre," Charlie said. "Drag iron agin this poor old ragged man." He sneered the last words. "I don't think you got the sand to do it."

"What's your stake in this, Starr?" LaBarre asked in a soft voice.

"I like the kid."

LaBarre's hands dropped to the butts of his guns.

---

*Others say Cullen Baker was, but Cullen was nothing but a two-bit killer and thief, who was conscripted into the Confederate Army, deserted, then joined the Union army. He deserted them and returned to a life of killing and looting poor farmers. After he hanged a crippled schoolteacher whose wife Cullen coveted, a posse tracked him down and killed him.

Charlie drilled him twice, the old Colts seeming to jump into his hard hands. LaBarre backed up against the bar, a very peculiar expression on his face. He managed to get one pistol clear of leather and cock it. Charlie shot him again, the hammer blow exploding against his chest, seeming to blow all the wind from his lungs.

"Damn you!" LaBarre told Charlie. He thought he lifted his pistol. He did pull the trigger. The slug blew a hole in the floor and almost hit his foot.

His pistol fell from numbed fingers to clatter on the floor. LaBarre hung on to the edge of the bar. "I'm dead because you liked the . . . kid?"

"Yep," Charlie told him.

"What a stupid thing to die over." LaBarre whispered the words.

"Yep," Charlie agreed.

LaBarre slumped to the floor to sit spraddle-legged for a moment. He toppled over and tried to reach his pistol. Matt Bodine and Sam Two Wolves stepped inside, curious as to what all the shooting was about. Sam kicked the pistol away.

LaBarre looked up. "Goddamn breed," he said.

Sam met his eyes. "Do the world a favor, LaBarre, and just go ahead and die."

He did.

Eleven

Charlie looked over at Jimmy. "I didn't mean no disrespect toward you by hornin' in on your play, son. But you'd never have taken LaBarre. He was a bad one."

"I thank you for my life, sir," Jimmy said.

"Knock off the sir, deputy. My name's Charlie."

"Yes, sir—Charlie."

"You quittin' your job now, Charlie?" Pete called, as LaBarre was being dragged out to the boardwalk. The swamper had been sent to fetch the undertaker.

"What job?" Charlie asked, after taking a bite of his sandwich and a sip of beer.

"Under the laws of this brand new state and the laws of this county, you're a deputy sheriff now. I was a witness."

Chrisman and Dale had both gone inside the Red Dog, stepping back to allow LaBarre's body room to be dragged out. It was dumped on the boardwalk just as a group of ladies walked up.

"Get that disgusting thing off the boardwalk!" one shrieked. "And do it now!"

"Yes, ma'am," Bert the bartender said. He rolled LaBarre off into the dirt, between boardwalk and hitchrail.

"Is that Charlie Starr?" Dale asked.

"Sure is," Pete told him. "And I'm going to speak to the sheriff as soon as he gets back about making Charlie a full deputy."

"I'm against it," Chrisman surprised everyone by saying.

"Me, too," Dale agreed.

"That's the first time those two have agreed on anything in ten years," Shorty said.

"Twelve," Dale corrected.

"LaBarre's got a thousand-dollar bounty on his head," Charlie said. "See that I get it, will you, deputy?"

"I sure will, Charlie."

"That ought to be enough for you to ride on out, then," Dale said. "Come over to the bank as soon as that reward amount is confirmed and I'll let you have the money. Then you can ride out."

"I think that's a good idea," Chrisman said.

Matt and Sam and Pete gave one another curious glances at this strange exchange of agreements between two men who were supposed to hate each other.

"Jimmy," Charlie said. "Go strip LaBarre's guns from him. They're yours. You and me got some working out to do."

"Yes, *sir!*" Jimmy said.

Charlie looked at Matt and Sam, taking in the stone necklaces both wore. "You boys'd be Bodine and Two Wolves. Me and some other old boys was jawin' about you two not long ago."

The men shook hands and Pete moved them all to a bigger table. Dale and Chrisman left the saloon.

"Now what do you make of those two?" Sam asked Pete.

"Durned if I know, boys. Some strange goin's-on in this town."

"How come them two wanted me gone from here so sudden?" Charlie asked. "I took a bath in a crick just this mornin'. I know it ain't that."

The men laughed and Pete said, "I don't know the answer to that neither, Charlie." He slapped the man on the knee. "But it's good to see you again. Man, I didn't recognize you when you first walked in."

'Well," Charlie drawled, "I reckon the years ain't been real kind to me. Lord knows, I never wanted the name of gunfighter. But it got hung on me anyways. Takes a toll on a man. A terrible toll."

Charlie looked at Matt and Sam. "You boys ought to head right back to Wyoming and hang them guns up—right now, while you still got a chance. Another two, three more years and you ain't gonna never shake loose from them. No matter how hard you try. Look at me, boys, I'm fifty-nine, I think. But I'm still draggin' iron. Still got to move like I'm ridin' the hoot-owl trail. Always lookin' over my shoulder."

"No more, Charlie," Pete said. "No more. You can either take the deputy's job, or go to work for me. I just signed papers with the government for a lot more acres. I need someone to run it. I heard about you helpin' out over in the other part of the state, you and Louis Longmont and Monte Carson and Luke Nations. I was sorry to hear about Luke catching the bullet."

"Punk kid, damn tinhorn little craphead name of Lester Morgan—shot Luke in the back. Smoke slapped him around a bit, then shot one ear off. So's people would know him wherever he went. I hope that no-good lives a long time, duckin' and hidin' and livin' like a poor old stray dog. I'm tired, Pete. I'll take either job. But from the way you people talk, seems to me like I'd be best suited—for a time—totin' a star."

"I'd sure like to see you wearin' one," Pete agreed.

Jimmy came back in and laid LaBarre's rig on the table. He had wiped it free of blood. "That's sure some fancy rig," the young man said.

"It ain't the rig that matters so much as the man carryin' it," Charlie said. "If you're gonna tote a badge, and I've toted a lot of them, there's some things you've got to learn. I'll teach you." He smiled sadly. "Maybe I can teach you enough to keep you alive."

Sheriff Jack Linwood rode in late that afternoon and was clearly stunned when he learned that the grizzled gray-haired man who had killed LaBarre was the legendary Charlie Starr, and very pleased that the gun-handler would consent to wear a badge. He swore him in formally and gave him a badge. Jimmy and Charlie would share a room back of the sheriff's office.

Linwood had spoken with the hands from the Spur ranch and also with Coop about the ambush, but he had lost the hours'-old trail of the unknown ambusher.

And Linwood showed he was a changed man when he said, "Jimmy, tomorrow you ride out to the Reed farm and speak to the father and his boys. They've all got Springfield rifles. Be polite but firm with them. Ask to see their rifles and tell them why you're doin' it. If any of them get nervous about it, well, just act like nothin' has happened and come on back and tell me. But I don't think they had anything to do with it. Still and all, we've got to check it out."

The sheriff looked at Charlie. "Charlie, you ride out to the Circle V and I'll ride out to the Lightning spread and nose around. It's not going to do us any good, but by God, they'll know we're not going to back up from them. Both you boys ride easy. That sniper is on somebody's payroll, and we got to figure that somebody don't like us no more than he likes Matt or Sam." He shook his head. "Place is gettin' weirder and weirder."

Matt and Sam had an early supper at Juan's and hit their blankets early.

Sam was asleep within minutes, but sleep came hard for Matt. Something was nagging at his brain and he could not pin it down. It darted and ducked and hid in the shadows. And it was the answer to the strange behavior of Dale, Chrisman, and the two holdout ranchers. But it remained a mystery as sleep finally took Bodine.

Bodine's eyes popped open and every sense was working overtime. He had no way of knowing what time it was, but he figured it was very late, after midnight. What had pulled him out of a deep sleep? He didn't know, but he sensed danger.

Bodine eased from his blankets and silently reached for his guns. Sam slept on. Bodine stood in the center of the room in his longhandles, a pistol in each hand. Something whispered against the side of the house. Bodine turned to face the west window, the top half of the window boarded up. A shadow fell, a movement followed silently. Matt caught the glint of light off a gun barrel and moved away from the center of the room. He watched as the unknown gunman lifted the weapon. It was a double-barreled sawed-off shotgun. The gunman pointed the twin muzzles toward the sleeping Sam.

Matt lifted his guns, cocking them, and fired, the slugs striking the assassin in the face and throwing him back. The shotgun roared, discharging its lethal load into the night skies. Sam was rolling out of bed, grabbing for his guns.

"Stay down," Matt urged. "And keep your eyes on the back. I'm going out the front."

Jack, Jimmy, and Charlie were out of their beds and running down the street toward the sounds of shooting, all only partly dressed, but all with their hats on and each hand gripping a six-shooter.

"Be careful!" Matt called from his crouch near the rotting front porch. The dewy grass was cool under his bare feet and the cold draft reminded him that one very essential button was gone from the rear flap of his underwear.

"Did you get him?" Jack called.

"I got him," Matt said. "But I doubt he came alone."

"I'll swing around back," Charlie said. "Cover that area."

But before he could move, a rifle report smashed the night air and a slug tore into a support post about two inches from Matt's head. Matt fired at the same time Sam cut loose. There was a choked-off cry and the sound of a body thudding to the ground.

"Coming up behind you," Jack said. He hurried to Matt in a doubled-over run and squatted down beside him. "You need to get you some needle and thread," he said. "You got a half-moon shinin' back here."

"Believe me, the breeze reminded me before you did."

Jack chuckled. "Charlie, you in position?"

"The back of the house is clear," Charlie called.

"I'm coming out," Sam said. "Using the back door."

"It's clear over here," Jimmy called. He had worked his way to the vacant meadow on the west side of the shack.

"Get some lamps," Jack ordered.

Lamplight shone on the faces of the dead men. The twin .44's had made an unpleasant mess out of the face of the shotgun toter, the slugs taking him under one eye and in the center of his forehead.

"I never saw either one of these men in my life," Jack said. "Jimmy, you were born around here; you know them?"

"No, sir. Never saw them before this night."

"What the Sam Hill's going on?" Mayor Dale asked, panting after the run from his place over the bank.

"You know these men, Mayor?" Jack asked, pointing to the dead assassins.

Dale peered at them. "Never saw them before in my life. You know them?"

Linwood shook his head. "Let's find their horses. Maybe they got something in their saddlebags."

Dale looked at Bodine. "You need to do something about that backflap, boy."

The men got dressed and went over to the sheriff's office to go through the contents of the dead men's saddlebags. It was already four o'clock in the morning, so more sleep was out of the question.

The contents of the saddlebags at first offered no further clues. They each contained a box of shells, a change of clothing, a few dollars in coin and greenbacks, a spare six-gun, and the usual odds and ends a cowboy or a drifter might carry: a length of rawhide, some blank sheets of folded paper and a stub of a pencil, a tintype of a gray-haired lady, spare socks.

"Damn!" Linwood said, walking to the potbellied stove and pouring a fresh cup of coffee.

It was Jimmy who found the first clue toward unraveling the mystery. "Look here," he said, pointing to a slit along the inside lip of the saddlebags.

Sam pulled out a small piece of folded paper. "Meet R. and D. at . . ." That word was smudged and unreadable. ". . . For payoff and inst."

"R. and D.?" Jack said. "Raner and Dale?"

"Could be," Matt said. "But I bet there's two dozen people within walking distance whose names begin with R. and D."

"Let's say it is Dale," Charlie said. "Why'd he want to kill you boys?"

Matt and Sam shrugged. "No reason," Sam said for both of them.

Matt said, "He welcomed us back to the hotel, wanted us to deposit some money in his bank, and apparently wants peace in this region. Dale being involved doesn't make sense."

"I-n-s-t must mean instructions," Jimmy said. "So maybe that means the killing wasn't going to stop with you two."

"That's right," Jack said. He looked at the men gathered in his office. "No Springfield rifle was in either saddle boot, so this R. and D. is probably paying the sniper. So I got this to think about: I wonder who's next on the list?"

The would-be assassins were buried within hours in unmarked graves on the edge of the town's cemetery while the sheriff and his deputies rode out into the county to question people. Matt and Sam decided to do some prowling on their own.

"Let's find the Raley gang," Matt suggested.

"What do we do with them if we find them?" Sam asked thoughtfully.

Matt grinned. "I bet we can think of something."

Sam swung into the saddle. He looked at his brother and grinned. "I bet you're right."

They took provisions for three days, heading straight for Lightning range. Two miles out of town, they stopped and watched a slow-moving wagon come toward them. It was driven by a boy of no more than ten or eleven years old with a bloody bandage around his head. The brothers rode up to the wagon. The boy, with dried tear-streaks having lined grooves on his sooty face, looked up at them.

"Big brave cowboys," he said, his voice surprisingly strong. "Well, I ain't got no gun, so you can shoot me like you done them back there last night and then go somewheres and brag about it." He jerked a thumb toward the wagon bed.

"What do you mean, son?" Matt asked. "What about those in the back?"

"My ma, my pa, and my sis. Box H riders hit us last night. Burned us out and left me for dead. But I fooled 'em. I put my family in this wagon before dawn this morning."

Matt rode up to the bed of the wagon for a look before it dawned on him what the boy had said. *Box H riders.* Couldn't be. He looked at the bullet-riddled bodies in the bed and gritted his teeth. This was needless and brutal and vicious. The man and woman and girl had been shot to rags. Each one had to have been shot twenty times or more.

"How do you know they were Pete Harris's hands?" Sam asked.

"Seen the brand."

"Son, we're awful sorry about your family. I'm Sam Two Wolves and this is my brother, Matt Bodine. We had nothing to do with this, and I'll bet you that Pete Harris didn't either . . ."

He let that trail off. The boy's eyes had gone blank. The lad suddenly dropped the reins, fell over backward, and landed on his father's dead body.

Matt stepped from his horse and gingerly climbed into the bed of the wagon, trying not to step on any bodies. He quickly checked the boy. "He's alive. His eyes are open. But he doesn't seem to be seeing anything."

"He's probably in shock. Is his skin sort of clammy to the touch?"

"Yes, and his breathing is all fouled up."

"Wrap him up in a blanket and hand him to me. I'll head fast for town and you bring the wagon, okay?"

Matt wrapped the boy—he appeared so thin as to be malnourished—in his own blanket and handed him over to Sam. "See you in town, brother. Sam! Have someone head out and find Linwood, get him back to town as quick as possible."

"For a fact," Sam said. "This could blow the lid off this bubbling pot."

"You know it. Take off, I'll be along."

Sam left at a gallop, holding the boy tightly against him. Matt tied the reins of his horse to the rear of the wagon and climbed onto the seat. He picked up the reins. One horse looked back at him, uncomfortable with this stranger. "Come on, team," he said. "I don't like this any better than you do."

Twelve

A crowd met him, and most were appalled at the sight of the bodies. Matt saw a few smirks among the crowd, glad to be rid of a nester family, but not many. He memorized those few faces.

He handed the reins to Simmons and the store owner shook his head in sorrow. "Terrible. What's wrong with people? Why can't we all live in peace?"

But Matt had no answer to that. He led his horse over to the doctor's office and stepped inside. The doctor was in his outer office, talking with Sam.

"How's the boy?" Matt asked.

"As stable as I can make him," Doc Lemmon replied. "We don't know much about shock yet. He will not respond to salts, and I've elevated his legs and have him warm. That's about all that modern medicine can do at this point."

"Do people die from it?"

"Oh, yes. Not often, but it happens. We just don't know how many types of shock there are. The boy has experienced a terrible mental blow. He might come out of it not remembering a thing. The mind, the brain . . . well, there again, we don't know much about that either." He looked apologetic. "The pastor's wife is in there with him. Perhaps God will take over where medicine fails."

Matt jerked a thumb toward the street. "I know what's going to take over out yonder on the range."

"What?" the doctor looked puzzled.

".44's and .45's."

The brothers walked to the sheriff's office, stoked up the stove, made a fresh pot of coffee, and sat down, waiting for Linwood.

"Something awful funny about this," Linwood said. "It stinks."

"Yeah," Matt said. "The boy said they thought they'd killed him. I think they left him alive deliberately."

"That's my thinkin', too," the sheriff said. "I'd bet my last dollar that Pete Harris had nothin' to do with this. Hell, I'd bet my *life* on it."

"So would we," Sam said. "Those night riders left that lad alive so he would tell just what he told us. The Box H brand on those horses is just a little too obvious."

"Right. That's the way I see it. Hellfire, boys, Raner and Vernon could hide a whole *army* on their spreads; much less a dozen or so horses, and nobody could find them."

"If it *was* Raner and Vernon," Matt said gently.

Sam and Jack looked at him. Sam asked, "What do you mean, brother?"

"Something is not adding up. I don't know what. It's just something that is roaming around in my head and I can't pin it down. Look, boys, we got people switching sides here like a cook flippin' flapjacks. First Dale hates me and Sam's guts, then he welcomes us with open arms. First Dale is on the side of the big three ranchers and then he throws them out of town. Chris-man has hated Dale—or so everyone thought—for ten or twelve years, now he's in cahoots with him. The rumor gets spread that the Raley gang is in this area, hired by Vernon and Raner. It was probably the Raley gang that killed that family last night, but that don't necessarily mean they were hired by Hugo and Blake. And D. and R. don't have to mean Dale and Raner. But it could. Dale could have ordered Raner out of town to make it look like there was a big split between them."

"This is makin' my head hurt," Jack said, moving toward the coffeepot. "This is like tryin' to track a cow over a stampede trail."

The men talked and waited for Charlie and Jimmy to return. But they all knew they were no closer to solving the puzzle; knew the puzzle was becoming more complicated. They finally just dropped the topic and talked about horses.

Jimmy returned from the Reed farm and said the family had been very helpful and polite. They all had Springfield rifles and showed no hesitation in producing them. The men all wore flat-heeled boots or shoes; the sniper had worn high-heeled cowboy boots. As far as Jimmy was concerned, and the sheriff agreed, the Reed family was dropped from the list of suspects.

Charlie rode in about half an hour behind Jimmy. He poured a cup of coffee and sat down. "That damn Hugo Raner is a smart-mouth, arrogant son, I'll say that first off. And if he crowds me, I'll put lead in him. But I'll add this: I don't think he or his bunch had anything to do with that sniper. Nothin' firm to back that up. Just a hunch. Both him and that Blake Vernon was coffeein' on the porch when I got there. They stayed together whilst I talked with them. A puncher come foggin' in with the news about that farm family bein' slaughtered. I don't think they had anything to do with that, either. They was both stunned over the news and they wasn't play-actin'? And both of 'em said the same thing about Pete Harris: 'He didn't do it.' "

"How about a Springfield rifle?" Jimmy asked.

Charlie shook his head. "The men said they've owned Springfields before, but that they don't no more. I don't like neither one of them men, but I believed them."

"All that's left is to talk with Pete Harris," Linwood said.

The words had not stopped echoing before Pete and his son and Shorty the foreman rode into town and reined up in front of the office. Pete stepped into the office, his face flushed.

"Boys," he said, taking off his hat. "I got the news about that farm family and come straight into town. It's a terrible thing that's happened. The word I got is that the boy is blamin' me. But I didn't have nothin' to do with that—nothin', I tell you!"

"Relax, Pete," Linwood said. "We don't think you had anything to do with it. Have some coffee and sit down. Let's all do some jawin'."

But Pete was upset and angry and frustrated. Coffee was not what he had in mind. "I'll pay for that boy's medical care and upbringin'," the rancher said. "I'll do anything I can to help that boy."

Charlie got up and put his arm around the man's shoulders. "Take it easy, Pete. Just calm down some, old hoss. Anybody who knows you *knows* you wouldn't do something like was done to that family. There ain't nobody—includin' Blake and Hugo—who thinks you had anything to do with it. So just put your mind to rest about it."

"But *somebody* did it!" the rancher said. "Somebody ridin' horses with the Box H brand. Somebody destroyed that little boy's life and besmirched my good name. I better not find nobody ridin' a Box H horse without sale papers. If I do, there's gonna be a killin'. I warn you all of that right now!" He stormed out of the room.

"Pete!" Charlie called. "Where are you goin', man?"

"To see about that little boy," Pete called over his shoulder, never breaking stride as he stomped down the boardwalk.

Sam stood up and stretched. "Somebody wants to throw blame onto Pete, and get any suspicions off of them. But we don't have any real suspects. Now if it isn't Raner or Blake, who is it?"

But nobody had an answer.

The night riders struck again that night. A group of about twenty-five men riding Lightning Arrow brand horses hit a sheepman and his herd and killed two shepherds, and their dogs and ran most of the sheep off a cliff, killing them. A third shepherd dragged himself to his horse and made it to a farmer's house. The farmer put the basque into a wagon and brought him into town, arriving just at dawn. He lived long enough to tell his story and died as the doctor was probing for the bullet in his chest.

Jack Linwood, Charlie Starr, and Jimmy Bryant looked at each other and walked out of the doctor's office. Matt and Sam were just stepping up onto the boardwalk.

"You two are now officially deputized," Jack told them. "Come to the office and get swore in and badged. And I don't wanna hear no argument about it."

Fifteen minutes later, with badges pinned to their shirts, Matt and Sam stood shoulder to shoulder with Charlie and Jimmy as Jack said, "Jimmy, you and Sam stay close to town. Charlie, Matt, and me will ride out to the killin' site and start trackin'. Three days' provisions, boys. Get supplied at Simmons and charge it to the county. Get plenty of ammo. Let's go."

Stopping at a creek to water their horses, Matt said, "First it was Box H, now it's Lightning. If the next one isn't Circle V . . . ?"

"Yeah, I been thinkin' on that, too. And I'll bet you it won't be. But I'll also bet that Blake is innocent."

"But the farmers and sheepmen won't," Charlie said.

"Right," Jack said, his words soft. "Whoever is doin' this is smart. Real smart. They've given this a lot of thought. But *why* are they doin' it? Who in the hell has what to gain by doin' it? That's what's got me stumped."

"Jack, has the mother lode been found in this county yet?" Matt asked.

"No. Lots of small strikes. Been a lot of gold taken out. But it's been a lot of smaller strikes. Why?"

"Just curious."

"You think gold might be the reason behind these attacks?" Charlie asked.

"Something is. Has any gold been found on any of the big three ranches?"

"Not that I know of," Jack replied. "But gold is the one thing I haven't thought of. Maybe you're right. Maybe somebody is trying to stir up trouble so's the big three will have at each other's throats. It's sure something to ponder on. But who is it?"

"R. and D."

"Whoever that might be," the sheriff said glumly.

The scene at the murder sight was horrible, and the stench of dead sheep didn't help any. Charlie knelt down by one of the sheepdogs.

"Hell of a price to pay for bein' hard-workin' and loyal," the famed gunfighter said, touching the head of the sheepdog. "It's like shootin' a man's horse. It'd take a sorry son to do this. Man'll do this don't deserve nothin' but a rope or a bullet."

The men dug holes and buried the sheepmen and their dogs side by side, the men figuring that's the way the sheepmen would have wanted it. Charlie got a tattered Bible from his saddlebags and read a few words.

He closed the Bible and sighed.

Jack settled his hat on his head and hitched at his double rig gunbelt. "Let's ride."

The tracks were easy to follow, unlike those of the raiders who had attacked the farmer, which had petered out after a few miles. But these were easy to read, and they led right toward the Circle V range.

"You know what they're gonna do," Charlie said. "They're gonna get with a herd and push them along, then one by one leave out."

Jack nodded his head. "Sure. As long as we trail them to Circle V range, they're thinkin' that's all it'll take to stir things up. And maybe they're right. We got to put out this fuse, boys. And we got to do it right quick."

"I figure just one more farmer gets killed, the farmers are gonna band together and start some night-ridin' of their own," Charlie said. "I seen it happen before. And don't nobody sell them sodbusters short. You crowd 'em hard enough and they'll shove back."

They spotted two punchers riding toward them just as they crossed the creek that signaled the east boundaries of the Circle V range.

"Mac and Jody," Linwood said. "Comin' from the west, probably wonderin' what happened to the herd that was grazin' here."

"What'd you boys want?" Jody said, his eyes riveted on Bodine, and on the badge he wore on his shirt.

"Some sheepmen was killed last night, their sheep stampeded over a cliff and their dogs shot. One lived long enough to tell me the raiders was on Circle V horses. We trailed them here."

The punchers exchanged looks, Jody saying, "Now that just breaks my heart about them stinkin' sheepmen and their sheep and their goddamned dogs. But we didn't have nothin' to do with it." He looked at Charlie. "Kinda old to be totin' a badge, ain't you, dad?"

"That's what LaBarre thought, too," Charlie told the mouthy puncher.

"Huh? What about LaBarre?"

"He's dead."

"Who killed him?" Mac asked.

"I did," Charlie said.

"I don't believe that!" Jody said, his hand dropping to the butt of his gun. "You're a liar."

"What he is is Charlie Starr," Matt said.

The color drained out of Jody's face. Very slowly, he removed his hand from the butt of his gun. "Pleased to meet you, Mister Starr," he said.

"It ain't for me," Charlie told him. "I just ain't got no use for smart-mouthed, pushy people."

"You got no call to talk to me like that," Jody said sullenly.

"I just helped bury two good men and their hard-workin' dogs. I killed LaBarre 'cause I took a likin' to a young deputy right off. I have always liked dogs. And I don't like you and probably never will. The reason for my sayin' that is simple: if you get mouthy with me again, you ain't gonna have the time left you for me to make up my mind one way or the other. Do you understand all that?"

"Yes, sir," Jody said, very humbly.

"Fine," Charlie said.

"We don't think you boys had anything to do with killin' them sheepmen," Jack stepped in. Charlie was on the prod and Jack knew why. Charlie was a famed gunslick, but he was also a decent man. And no decent man would kill another man's good horse or dog, any more than he would kill a woman or a child. For all his rowdy past, Jack Linwood had always had a clear streak of decency in him. But he was tough and quick and hard, just like the times.

"I swear to you, Jack," Mac said. "No Circle V hand had anything to do with no raid last night. Nor that other raid that kilt them farmers. I'll swear on a Bible and on my mother's picture."

"That's good enough for me, Mac. Let's ride single file, you two on the west side of these cow tracks, and see if we can't pick up where those raiders broke loose."

They had gone only a short distance before Mac called out. "Here's where one cut loose, but he took about a dozen steers with him."

"Here's another," Matt called from the point. "Same story."

"And here's a piece of sackin'," Charlie called. "They tied sacks around their horses' hooves. Or they were goin' to when they left them beeves they're trailin'."

The men reined up. They knew there was no point in continuing their hunt. The raiders would leave the cows at some point where nothing could be found. And after so long a time, any grass that was bent down would be springing back up.

"Thanks for your help, boys," Jack told the hands. "And don't be doin' no travelin' at night. These farmers and sheepmen are gettin' edgy and just might blow you out of the saddle."

"I'd like to see one try!" Jody blustered up. "No sod-buster's gonna get the drop on me."

Charlie snorted and swung his horse, putting his back to the man. "Damn fool," he muttered.

Jack gave the hand a long, hard look. "I'll be goin' to your funeral 'fore this is over, Jody." He turned his horse and headed back to town, catching up with Charlie.

Matt lingered, facing the two punchers. Jody's eyes burned hate at him. "Why don't we all work to bring peace to this area, boys?"

"Why don't you and your damned half-breed Injun brother both go to hell, Bodine?" Jody replied.

"Nice talking to you boys," Matt said, and turned his horse. As he rode to catch up with Jack and Charlie, he muttered, "I'll have to deal with him someday."

Thirteen

The raiders struck again that night, at two locations, killing all but one of a farm family, burning down house and barn, and killing all the livestock, and killing three sheepmen, stampeding their flocks, and destroying the dogs.

The night riders rode horses with the Box H and Circle V brands.

"That's their plan," Matt said to the sheriff and the deputies. "We were right. The only brand that isn't obvious is Hugo Raner's Lightning Arrow."

"So the other ranchers will turn on Raner. And the farmers, the sheepmen, and the townspeople," Sam finished it.

"That's the way I see it," Matt said.

"Damnest thing I ever heard of," Linwood said. "But I see the logic behind it."

"We're looking at a war here," Jimmy said. "And we'd better be darn careful to stay neutral."

"You got that right, son," Charlie told him. He cocked his head. "Who's that comin' in?"

The lawmen moved to the boardwalk and watched as Hugo Raner and a number of his hands rode slowly into town. The men were all heavily armed and grim-faced. Three of the hands rode belly-down over their saddles, tied in place. Others had bloody bandages on arms and face and legs. The riders reined up in front of the four lawmen.

"Damn nesters and sheepmen hit me early this morning, Linwood," Hugo said. "A sneak attack on my ranch. You see what happened. I didn't bury my boys right off 'cause I wanted you to see yourself. I ain't had nothing to do with these night-riding incidents . . . up to now."

"How do you know it was farmers and sheepmen who attacked you?" Charlie asked. "Did you get any of them?"

"No," Hugo said bitterly. "But who the hell else *could* it have been? They was ridin' mules and plugs and nags. That pretty well tells it, don't it?"

"Not necessarily," Jack said. "Someone is trying to start a war here, Hugo. And we don't believe it's you or Blake or Pete that's behind it. I'll tell you the same thing I told the others: just calm down and let us handle it. We'll get to the bottom of this."

"The hell you say!" Hugo's son, Carl said. "You people couldn't catch a cold. We'll take care of it our way."

"You'll go to jail if we catch you night-ridin', Carl," Jack warned the young man. "And that includes any rancher or punchers in this county."

A cowboy came fogging up the street, from the east. He reined up in a cloud of dust. "Sheep!" he hollered. "Thousands of them. They're about ten miles outside of town. They come in by train to tracks'-end and are being herded over here. I never seen so goddamned many sheep in all my days."

"Damn!" Mayor Dale said to Chrisman, as the men stood in front of the bank.

"Yeah," Chrisman replied glumly.

A lone man came riding in on a beautiful, high-stepping midnight black with stocking feet. The man was dressed in expensive and tailored clothing, his boots highly polished and costing more than the average cowhand made in six months. The man wore two guns made especially for him, hand-tooled and engraved .45's.

Charlie chuckled softly.

"You find something funny about this, Starr?" Hugo snarled at the gunfighter.

"Oh, yeah, Mister Bigshot Rancher. I sure do. He told me just a few months back that he was goin' into business in this part of the state."

"Who told you?" Carl yelled at him.

"Watch your mouth, boy," Charlie told him, " 'fore I take a notion to slap it off your face."

"Why, you . . ."

"Shut up!" his father told him. "You're outclassed, boy." He looked at Charlie. "You know that duded-up feller?"

"Shore do." Charlie turned to walk up the boardwalk toward the stranger stepping down from the saddle in front of Simmons' General Store.

"Well, who is he?" Hugo called.

Charlie turned around, a smile on his face. "That, boys, is one of the richest men in the U-nited States, one of the best gamblers in the world, and one of the fastest guns. He owns railroads, factories, huge cattle ranches, and no tellin' what else. That, boys, is Louis Longmont."

Mayor Dale almost swallowed his cigar and Chrisman's knees got so weak he had to sit down.

"And the sheep coming in belong to him," Jack Linwood said softly.

"Lord have mercy on us all if anyone messes with his sheep," Jimmy said.

"He don't look like much to me," Carl Raner said, a sneer on his face.

"Boy," his father told him. "Shut your damned mouth and get the hell back to the ranch!"

"So I take it the situation around here is very volatile," Louis said.

"Quite," Sam said. "And it's imperative that we all act with as much restraint as possible in order to avert a very calamitous end."

"What the hell did he say?" Jimmy asked Jack.

The sheriff shook his head. "Don't ask me. Sounds like his mouth hurts him."

So as not to appear to be taking sides in anything, the men had decided not to frequent either the saloon or the hotel dining room or Juan's place. They met in the sheriff's office.

"Well," Louis said, "I have done an exhaustive study on sheep ranching and know for a fact that if properly handled, sheep do no harm to the range. I have sheep on my ranch in Montana and other than a few isolated incidents, the cattlemen in that area have left me alone."

"What happened to them that didn't?" Linwood asked.

"My people buried them," Louis said.

"Get off this range," a Box H hand told a Lightning puncher. "You boys is causin' all this grief to folks, so just get off this range."

"We got strays over here," the hand stood his ground. "And we aim to get them and push them back onto Raner's ground. And you can go right straight to hell, cowboy."

"You're the one who's goin' to hell, slick," the Box H man said, and jerked iron.

Both men got iron out and both men fired, wounding each other, although not seriously. Both took their stories back to home range, each one saying the other drew first.

"Now just settle down," Pete told the hand. "This is what them behind the night-ridin' wants. They want us to kill off each other. Just settle down."

"Let's go get them boys," Blake Vernon's sons said to their father. The goofy one, Hubby, nodded his head and slobbered on his shirt, his eyes shining with a madness-induced viciousness. Hubby liked to kill. Made him feel good. He'd killed a lot of people in his life, although no one knew about it 'ceptin' his father and his brother Lane, and they covered it up. Dewey was kept out of it 'cause he was kind of goody-goody. So Hubby felt like he had a license to kill.

And Hubby wasn't nearly as goofy as he liked people to think. But he had learned early on that the goofier he acted, the less work he had to do around the ranch and the more mischief he could get into without fear of punishment. As a child that mischief was the tormenting of animals; as he grew older, it turned into the killing of drifting cowboys, and the burning down of houses, especially when someone was in them, sleeping—Hubby liked to hear people scream in pain—and rape.

Hubby could read and write and figure. Hubby could think and Hubby could reason. Hubby was a cold-blooded killer who knew exactly what he was doing and enjoyed every moment of it.

"I'll think on it," Blake said. "As a matter of fact, it's my notion that Pete Harris is behind this whole damn night-ridin' business, tryin' to get me and Hugo at each other's throats. How's Harry?"

"He's fine. It was just a nick," Lane told him.

"Get some of the boys together," Blake said, getting madder by the minute. "We're riding over to see Pete."

But before they could get saddled up, a hand came busting up, fresh from talking to a Circle V supporter from town. "Boss!" he yelled. "They's about ten thousand sheep just a few miles outside of town, comin' in from tracks'-end . . ."

Blake threw his hat on the ground and cussed. Hubby jumped up and down in excitement. He liked to kill sheep. They were so stupid they just stood there and looked at you while you blowed their brains out.

". . . But that's just half the story, boss," the hand panted. "The sheep is owned by Louis Longmont and he's in town."

"*Louis Longmont!*" Blake yelled.

"Right, boss. Himself in person."

Blake picked up his hat and leaned against a corral post. It was beginning to come together now. Sure. Bodine and Sam had been stopping by over to Pete's regular, ever since they rode into this area. Pete brought them in. Had to be. Then Charlie Starr just accidentally shows up. Crap! That was no accident; Pete sent for him. Now Louis Longmont shows up with thousands of sheep. And there was all that free range just north of Pete's place and Pete had just filed for it, and got it. That no-good . . .

Blake calmed himself. "Rocky, saddle my horse.

Couple of you boys come with me. I've got to palaver some with Hugo. Rest of you boys break out the ammo from the house. Clean up your guns and fill any empty loops in your belts."

"We ridin' tonight, boss?" Frisco, the foreman asked.

Blake nodded his head. "Probably. But it'll be late. So get some rest. Come on, Kirk, Rich—let's ride."

They didn't get two miles from the house before the long-distance shooter with the Springfield knocked Blake off his horse. If Blake had not turned his head at the last possible second, the big slug would have blown his brains out. As it was, Blake had a graze on his noggin and a whale of a headache.

"Get him!" he roared from the ground, holding a bandanna to his head.

Kirk and Rich didn't get him, but they got close enough to recognize the horse and the vest on the man. They rode back to their boss.

"It was Coop," Rich said. "We both recognized his horse and that fancy vest of his. No doubt about it."

Blake cussed. "Kirk, ride for the Lightning. Tell Hugo about this and tell him I had it figured it was Pete. Tell him to get his boys together and ride for my spread. We hit Pete tonight."

"I'm gone, boss!"

Pete had moved his herds to a more protected area, an area where two or three good punchers could contain them for a week or more. Pete stood on his front porch and stared out over that part of his holdings that he could see. He had a funny feeling in his guts. Last time he'd had this feeling, his place had been hit, and hit hard, by Utes.

Millie came to his side. "What's wrong, Dad?"

"I don't know. I just got a bad feelin', is all. Where's your brother?"

"He's been gone all day. Said he had to check over in Devil's Canyon for strays."

"Girl, go fetch Shorty for me. Move, girl. Hurry."

She could sense the urgency in her father's voice and she ran toward the foreman's quarters. Shorty came running.

"What's up, boss?"

"Shorty, you've been with me a long time. You remember the last time them Utes came at us?"

"I sure do. That was a heck of a fight."

"I had this same feelin' that afternoon, Shorty. Get the hands gathered. Millie, you and your ma break out the rifles and load them up. Get all the ammo from the chest and get ready to pass it out to the boys. Then you and your ma get to makin' sandwiches. A lot of them. And lots of coffee."

"Right, Dad."

The hands gathered, Pete said, "I'm hopin' I'm wrong, boys, but I got a gut hunch they's trouble on the wind. And it's comin' straight for us. We've done this before, so you all know where you're supposed to be. Get ammo and sandwiches from inside the house and start gettin' into position. Put the horses in the barn and cut the others loose. We can round them up in the mornin'."

"Boss," a hand named Forest said. "There ain't been no sign of hostiles around here."

"Oh, I think we've been surrounded by them for a long time and just didn't know it," Pete replied. "Now get some food and water and get into position."

*   *   *

Matt and Sam stepped out of their shack on the edge of town and looked up at the deserted main street. Not one horse was tied to a hitchrail. The afternoon stage had come and gone; no one got off, no one got on.

"I don't like it," Sam said. "There's always some hand from the Box H in town, having a drink or buying some tobacco, or just hanging around talking. Something's wrong."

"Have you been consulting the bones again?" Matt needled him with a smile.

"The only bone I'm going to consult is when I put my fist up against your head," Sam fired back.

"You'd just break your hand."

"Point made," Sam scored one. "Brother, what we talked about this morning . . . were you serious?"

"It has to be considered."

"It would be a terrible thing. Matt, you have no proof."

"I know it. It's just something that I'm going to check on. For now, let's keep it between us."

"And tomorrow we do a little snooping?"

Tomorrow we do a lot of snooping."

Sam nodded his agreement. "You talked last with Louis Longmont. What's his position in all this?"

"He says he won't get involved unless his camp or his sheep are attacked. Then he said, somebody will pay the piper."

"Did you take a good look at that bodyguard of his when he drove the wagon in for supplies?"

"Yeah. I'd hate for him to hit me. I think that's one of the biggest men I've ever seen."

Dusk was settling over the land. The brothers walked up to the sheriff's office, where they had their meals sent from one of the two eating places, always alternating so as not to show partiality.

Simmons had closed his store. The Red Dog and the Plowshare were open, but had no customers. Impending trouble seemed to hang thick in the air. The brothers stepped into the sheriff's office and took in the grim looks on the faces of Linwood, Charlie, and Jimmy.

"I take it that we are not alone in our feeling that something is terribly wrong," Sam said, pouring a mug of coffee. He handed that to Matt and poured one for himself.

"I ain't usually wrong in my hunches," Charlie said. "And I got a bad feelin' about this night."

A lone horseman came riding slowly into town. The men in the sheriff's office watched him dismount at the Red Dog.

"That's Grove from the Lightning spread," Linwood said. "And he's ridin' with his saddlebags full and bedroll tied on. Come on. Let's find out what's goin' on."

"I quit Raner," the puncher explained. "That's what's goin' on. That damn sniper tried to kill Blake Vernon today; grazed his head. He says it was Coop from Pete's place. I don't believe that. Coop couldn't hit a bull in the butt with a bass fiddle. Worse shot I ever seen. And I've known Coop for ten years. He ain't got no damn Springfield long rifle."

"You're not ridin' for the brand anymore, Grove. What's up for tonight?"

Grove hesitated for a moment. He sighed. "They're gonna hit the Box H tonight. Blake and Raner is convinced Pete and his hands is behind all this night-ridin'."

"And you?" Charlie asked.

"I don't believe it. Pete's always been the peace-maker. He's always the one who says wait and cool off before you act. But I'll tell you who's been actin' queer of late, and if it's repeated, it didn't come from me.

That damn Dewey Vernon is doin' a lot of lonesome ridin'. I been seein' him from the north end of Devil's Canyon clear up toward the South Fork. Something is goin' on that he don't want his pa to know about."

The lawmen exchanged glances, each one thinking: that could be the D. But who is the R.?

"I got me a job offer workin' on a spread down on the Gunnison," Grove said. "I'm havin' me a drink and pullin' out. Good luck to you boys." He stepped into the saloon and bellied up to the bar

"Let's ride," Jack said. "We might get there in time to head this off." He consulted his pocket watch. "But I doubt it," he added.

Fourteen

The Circle V and Lightning men hit the Box H ranch an hour after dark. Almost sixty hands struck the ranch hard, coming at the defenders from all sides.

But Pete had had plenty of time to station his men. When the call came that riders were coming hard, Pete's men lit torches that had been positioned around the yard and then ran back to cover. The first volley from the Box H hands emptied five saddles; two of those who hit the ground did not move. One of the other three tried to limp away into the darkness. Rifle fire hammered him to the ground. He did not move.

Coop was on the front porch of the ranch house, with Pete. Robert had returned and was stationed at the back of the house. Coop was using a shotgun and was taking a dreadful toll on the raiders. He wasn't much good with a rifle or short gun, but he could play all kinds of hell with a shotgun, and this night he did just that.

Becky and Millie were frontier women, not a pair of shrinking violets. They both had rifles and knew how to use them. Both had experienced Indian attacks and outlaw attacks. They stood their positions and calmly picked their targets amid the wind-whipped torchlight and the swirling dust.

The ranch defenders broke the initial attack, sending the night-riders back out of rifle range. The Circle V and Lightning crews left five dead on the grounds of the Box H and several more wounded. They were gearing up for another charge when Sheriff Jack Linwood and his deputies rode up.

"That's it!" Jack shouted. "This is the law talkin'. The first man on either side to fire another shot gets arrested for attempted murder of a peace officer, and by God I'll see that man put in prison for the rest of his life."

"Them stinkin' skunks in the ranchhouse tried to kill me today," Blake shouted through the night and the settling dust. "Pete sent Coop to bushwhack me."

"You're a damn liar, Blake!" Pete Harris yelled. "And if I was gonna send somebody, it sure as hell wouldn't be Coop."

"He's right about that, boss," Frisco, the Circle V foreman, said. "I forgot that Coop couldn't hit a barn if he was standin' inside it."

"You want to file charges, Pete?" Jack yelled.

"No. Just get these polecats off my range and order them to stay off. Now and forever."

"We got wounded and dead," Raner hollered.

"Then drag 'em out of here and get gone, God damn you!" Pete shouted.

"Back your men off," Jack yelled. "I want to hear them ride out. Blake and Raner, you and your foremen and a couple of hands stay and gather up your wounded and dead. Everybody lay down your rifles and shove iron back into leather. Now do it!"

The Circle V and Lightning hands backed off and

rode out. Linwood and his men rode in. Raner and Blake and their sons and their foremen came in and began gathering up horses and loading the dead and wounded. The Box H hands held their positions and waited.

"It ain't over," Hugo Raner promised. "All you done this night, Linwood, was put the showdown off for another day."

"I ain't got nothin' to gain by makin' war on you or nobody else, you damn fool," Pete yelled from the porch. "Now think about that on the ride back home."

"You want it all!" Blake said from his saddle. "We know all about you sendin' for Bodine and Two Wolves. We know you sent for Longmont and them damn stinkin' sheep."

"You're crazy!" Pete said. "Crazy as a lizard!"

"Where'd you hear that crap?" Bodine asked from the saddle. "And that's what it is, crap!"

"Are you callin' me a liar, Bodine?" Blake asked.

"No, I'm not," Bodine eased the tension some. "What I am saying is that whoever told you that Pete sent for me and Sam doesn't know what in the hell they're talking about. And Louis Longmont can't be bought. He's already a millionaire ten times over."

"Now think about this," Sam said. "If neither of you are behind the night-riders, and Pete isn't . . . who is? And why?" Sam looked at Dewey, standing beside his father. "And why have you been doing so much lonesome riding?"

"What—what?" his father sputtered. "What do you mean by that? What are you accusin' my boy of here, anyway?"

"I'm not accusing him of anything. But he's been spotted—more than once—ranging miles from his home base, and at some unusual hours, too." Sam wasn't sure about that, but he thought he'd toss it in for spice.

Blake stepped down from the saddle. "Is that true, boy?"

The young man shuffled his boots in the dirt and refused to answer.

"I asked you a question, boy. I expect some sort of answer."

"Yeah, I been doin' some ridin', Pa. I got me a girl."

"A girl! Well, why in tarnation don't you bring her to the house so's everybody can meet her?"

" 'Cause, damn it, she's a nester's daughter!" Dewey faced his dad. "And I love her, Pa. We're gonna be married."

"You took up with nester trash?" Blake asked.

"She ain't trash, Pa. And don't you call her that. I'm warnin' you, don't do it."

"You're . . . warnin' *me?*" Blake said, his voice small.

"That's right, Pa."

Blake hit his son, a sneaky punch that came out of the darkness and flattened the young man. He jerked his son's gun from leather and shoved it behind his belt. "My son don't date no damn nester's whore."

Dewey hooked one boot around his father's ankle and brought the man down. "Maggie ain't no whore!" the young man said, getting to his knees and knocking the crap out of his father.

Blake fell to one side and Dewey got to his boots. "Don't you never call Maggie that again, Pa."

Blake got to his feet, blood running from his mouth. "Damn nester whore!"

Down he went. Hubby stepped in to bust his brother's head with a rifle butt and Lane pulled him back. "Let 'em fight it out, Hubby. They gotta settle it sometime."

Father and son stood toe to toe for a moment, slugging it out, both of them taking some hard licks. Blake scored a good one and his son's butt hit the ground. Father tried to kick son and Dewey grabbed his boot and twisted, throwing the man to the ground. He jumped on top of him and laid left and right to his dad's jaw.

Frisco stepped in and pulled the young man off. "He's out, boy," the foreman said. "He's had it. Now lay off."

Lane and Hubby pulled their nearly unconscious dad to his feet and held him there. Pete brought a basin of water and a cloth from the kitchen.

"Here, Blake," he said, holding the basin out.

"Hell with you!" Blake said, slurring the words through his busted and bleeding mouth. "I don't need your damn sympathy."

"I'm not offering any sympathy," Pete said. "I'm just tryin' to help a man who used to be my friend."

Blake smashed the basin out of Pete's hands. "You're no friend of mine, Pete. All right, so you didn't order that shot at me. But you still side with the nesters and the sheepmen. And that makes you my enemy . . ."

"And mine," Raner said.

Hubby giggled and slobbered and cut his eyes to Millie, standing on the porch. He sure would like to get her all alone.

Blake turned to Dewey. "I'll have all your gear packed. I don't want you on my range. Not as long as you see that nester . . ." He bit back the word, not wanting his very powerful son to bust him in the mouth again. ". . . Girl. Now where do you want your crap sent?"

"Why don't you send it into town?" Linwood suggested. "You're gonna need a job, Dewey. You ever thought about deputy sheriffin'?"

"You offering me a job, Sheriff?"

"Sure am. And I'll let you have time off to see your girl."

"You just hired a deputy."

Blake snorted his contempt at that and staggered off toward his horse. The dead and wounded were collected and the men rode off.

"Mother," Pete called. "Would you please draw another basin of water and get some cloth so's we can patch up Dewey here? Millie, pour us all some coffee and lay out them sandwiches. A good fight always makes me hungry!"

Matt and Sam kept their badges, but with the addition of Dewey Vernon, their services would not be needed as often for official business. Charlie started working with both Jimmy and Dewey, showing them the tricks of the gun-handling business. Both young men proved to be quick learners.

Blake Vernon sent his son's belongings into town in a wagon, the young man's three horses tied to the back of the wagon. The hand refused to lift a finger to help unload the gear. Linwood, Charlie, and Dewey unloaded the wagon.

"Your pa said to tell you this, Dewey: Your name's been tooken out of the family Bible. You ain't his son no more. Don't never set foot on Circle V range."

Jack Linwood pointed a finger at the man. "You take a message back to Blake, from me. This man, Dewey Vernon, is a deputy sheriff of this county. Anytime we have official business to take care of, he goes where he damn well pleases, and that includes Circle V range. Blake or any of you interferes, I'll have warrants swore out on you and put your butts in jail . . . or kill you. Can you remember all that?"

"Shore can, Jack. I'll give him your message." The hand clucked the team into movement and rattled out of town.

Matt and Sam had walked up, to stand listening. Matt said, "Takes a bull-headed man to disown his son."

"Or a damn stupid one," Sam added.

"What you boys plannin' for the rest of this day?" Jack asked.

"Prowl around. We got three days' rations and are just gettin' ready to head out. Anybody seen Louis Longmont?"

"Not hide nor hair. He's stayin' out at that fancy camp of his."

"Since it turns out that Dewey here ain't the D. we thought he was," Charlie said, "do either of you boys have any idea who we're lookin' for?"

Matt and Sam shook their heads, Matt saying, "I thought I did. But it turned out wrong. I'm stumped." Actually, that was not entirely true. Matt did have some ideas, but they were so fuzzy in his mind he had told only Sam. He hoped to brush away some of that fuzziness on this trip . . . provided he and Sam didn't get shot while attempting it.

"You boys take care," Jack told the brothers as they swung into the saddle. "And pin them badges on your shirts for some added protection."

'When the sunlight hits them, they also make good targets," Sam said.

"For a fact," Jack admitted. "For a fact."

The brothers rode out of town, conscious of both friendly and unfriendly eyes on them as they left. But since the brutal night-riding had begun, those un-friendly eyes had lost support. Men fighting men was one thing, but when men started killing women and kids, most people—no matter how strongly they felt about sheep or nesters—drew the line and backed off.

"Where do we start?" Sam asked, when they were out of town and alone on the road.

"What do you think about my idea?" Matt said.

"I think it's as good as any. It's farfetched, but the only way we'll know for sure is to check it out."

They rode for several miles, coming to a halt at a crossroads west of town.

Matt stuck out his hand and Sam took it. "Be careful, Sam."

"The same to you, brother."

Matt headed for Lightning range, Sam headed for a spot he'd picked out on Box H range. Both men rode cautiously, staying off the road and keeping to the timber whenever possible. They reached their pre-picked spots, stripped saddle and bridle from their horses, and with field glasses ready, began the long wait. They would, for the most part, keep a cold camp, only building a small fire in the mornings, for coffee. The fire would be in a pit, so the flames could not be seen; the wood would be dry and virtually smokeless.

The hours wore on slowly for the brothers. Through field glasses they watched hands at work, rounding up cattle and moving them to different pastures. They saw deer and an occasional bear foraging for food. They talked to themselves and to their horses to break the monotony. They ate hardtack and canned beans and watched and waited. They went to bed late and got up early, so they would not miss any sound or fail to spot any movement. But nothing suspicious came into view.

Matt was beginning to wonder if he'd made a mistake; truthfully, both men hoped Matt's theory was wrong.

On the second night out, both men heard gunfire coming from the south. Men riding hard and wearing long dusters came within a hundred yards of Sam's location about an hour after the shooting.

The night-riders had struck again.

They rode straight north, staying between the Box H and the Lightning ranches. Sam was not familiar with this area, but he'd been told by Jack Linwood that a heavily timbered area lay just north of his location, an area that could hide a small army for a long time . . . if they were careful.

Mid-morning of the third day, a lone rider rode east across Box H land. Sam watched the rider through long-lenses and smiled bitterly. At the same time, Matt was watching a lone rider lope across Lightning range. Both men quickly saddled their horses and broke camp, following their quarry. The brothers stayed well back and stopped often, being very careful not to alert those they followed.

The two riders disappeared into the timber that grew on each side of a creek. Matt and Sam circled the meeting place and joined up on a ridge above the creek.

"Good enough for you?" Matt asked.

"Unfortunately," Sam replied, uncasing his binoculars. "I hate this."

"No more than I do." Matt uncased his field glasses and the brothers settled in, well-concealed and high above the secret meeting place of the mysterious R. and D.

The brothers watched the timber, occasionally catching a glimpse of the pair. Finally, it got embarrassing and the brothers put their binoculars aside and were content to just wait the pair out.

After an hour had passed, two men rode in from the north. The brothers picked up their binoculars and studied the pair.

"Red Raley," Matt identified him. "I don't know the guy with him."

"Now we know who brought in the Raley gang," Sam said. "But are they in it alone?"

Matt laid his field glasses aside and stretched out on the cool grass, a very serious expression on his face. "Sam? I think we have two factions working here. I don't think one knows about the other."

"You want to explain that?"

He did, and at length, while Sam studied the timber below them.

Sam sat still for a moment, mentally digesting Matt's theory. After a time, he said, "I like it. It's disgusting, but it works. Talk about a power play on one side, and deception on the other—this takes it."

"Now that we know this much, what do we do with the information?"

"Are you familiar with the line about killing the messenger?"

"No. But I know what you mean. And you're right. But we can't just sit on it."

"True."

Matt sighed. "But I really don't want to be the one who delivers the message . . . to either side."

Sam said, "Let's get out of here. This makes me want to puke."

Fifteen

Jack's boots left the desktop and hit the office floor. "Are you serious?"

"We both saw it," Sam said.

But Dewey was the least surprised of them all. "Everybody thinks he's such a nice fellow," he said. "He never fooled me. He's always had a sneaky way about him. That's why we weren't friends. And as far as she's concerned . . . hell, she's a trollop, through and through. So was her mother."

"Was?" Matt asked.

"Oh, yeah. She ran off with the foreman years ago. No one knows where she is. Those two don't surprise me; but what are Dale and Chrisman up to?"

"We don't know," Sam said.

"That's just a guess on my part," Matt added.

"Who can we trust?" Charlie asked.

Sam shook his head. "We can trust ourselves. But who tells Pete Harris about his son and Hugo Raner about his daughter?"

"Man, don't look at me!" Jimmy Bryant said. "Pete's an easy-goin' fellow, but news of this . . . ?"

"If Red's gang is camped very far north of where you boys were today," Jack said, "that puts it in another county and out of my jurisdiction. And the sheriff up there is a damn crook. And that's bein' kind. But we got to do something about that outlaw camp. We can't have no more night ridin'. They struck out last night. They hit a farmer who was waitin' for them. Him and his two sons killed three and got lead in three or four others. That might put a damper on it for a time."

Jimmy had gotten up for more coffee and was looking out the window. "Oh, Lord," he muttered.

"What's the matter?" Jack asked.

"Look yonder. Here comes Pete Harris and some of his hands."

"Is Robert with them?" Sam asked.

Jimmy shook his head. "No."

"I imagine he's resting," Matt said. "He and Denise had quite a to-do today."

Jack laughed. "I've heard it called lots of things, but never that."

"Pete's headin' this way," Jimmy called. "And he's walkin' like a man with something on his mind." Jimmy left the window and headed for the back. "I just remembered something I forgot to do." He was gone out the back door, Dewey Vernon right behind him.

Sam leaned against the wall, Matt sat in a chair, Charlie leaned against a cell door, and Jack sat down behind his desk. Pete stepped in and closed the door behind him. He looked at Matt, then at Sam.

"Where you boys been? Millie's about to wear out the front porch waitin' on you two to show up."

"We've been up in the timber for three days, along

the ridges, waitin' for your son to disprove a theory of mine," Matt said.

"I . . . see," the rancher said, walking to the coffee-pot and pouring a cup. "And did he disprove your theory?"

"No, Pete, he didn't."

"Let me guess," Pete said. "He met with Denise Raner, didn't he?"

"Yes, he did, Pete, among others."

"I wish he had come to me. I wouldn't have disapproved of them sparkin' each other. I . . ." He paused in the lifting of coffee cup to mouth. "What did you say, Matt. Among others? What others?"

"I didn't know one of the men. But the other one was Red Raley."

"Red Raley! The outlaw gang leader?"

"Yeah. Sorry, Pete. There was no mistaking it. Sam was there. He saw it same as me."

"Damn!" Pete swore. "I knew something was wrong; I started to tell you when you were out at the ranch one time. Just couldn't bring myself to do it. Something turned the boy wrong. I don't know what it was. It wasn't Denise, although I'm sure she didn't help matters any. His mother hasn't noticed the change, neither has Millie. At least, I don't think so. Red Raley! You think my boy brought him in, Matt? Sam? Where would he get the money?"

"I don't know, Pete—to both your questions. I'll guess and say no, he didn't. Like you, I don't know where he'd get the money. How about Denise?"

"Oh, she has money of her own. Her mother saw to that before she run off with another man."

"Enough to buy Raley and his gang?" Sam asked.

"No," Pete replied. "But enough to pay a sniper."

Glad that Pete had not blown sky-high, Jack relaxed some. "So how did Robert meet up with Raley, then?"

"Through Chrisman and Dale," Matt said.

"How did you arrive at that, Matt?" Pete asked.

"Well, it's just theory. But who else has the money to hire a whole gang but Dale or Chrisman? A lot of folks say Dale has nothing to gain. But that might not be the case. How heavily in debt are Vernon and Raner to the bank?"

"Yeah," Pete said, after a moment. "That would do it. He's loaned them both a lot of money. But they manage to stay even with him." He frowned and shook his head. "No. No, that ain't it, boys. It's something else. Back when Hugo and me was at least speakin', he told me that Dale used to come out to his place all the time and just ride all over the place. Always by himself. Never wanted anybody to go with him. Said Dale told him it was the prettiest place he'd ever laid eyes on. He'd even camp out in the hills; said it was his vacation."

"How about Vernon's place south of here?" Sam asked.

"No, Dale never spent much time down there. Practically none at all. But say!" He snapped his fingers. "Back before the sheep came in and split this area up into factions, Chrisman used to prowl all over Vernon's place. Blake finally had to run him off. Both those men, Dale and Chrisman are strange men."

Matt met Sam's eyes. "You take it, brother."

"They're not too strange," Sam said. "Chrisman's found silver on the Circle V and Dale's found gold on the Lightning range. Bet on it."

"So the two men, Chrisman and Dale, working together, concocted this plan to create a range war," Jack mused aloud. "Then the sheep came in a few months back and that just made things better for them. But what part do Robert and Denise play in all this?"

"They found out and wanted in," Charlie said.

"Sure," Pete said. "That fits. I'll buy that. Even though it hurts my mouth to say it about my own flesh and blood." He sighed and said, "Robert and Denise hired that long-distance shooter to kill me. Then they came up with a better plan: use him to create fear in everybody and maybe we'd all kill each other."

"You don't know that, Pete," Sam said. "Don't torment yourself before you know all the facts."

"It fits too well," the rancher replied. "Robert has always been a good boy, but even as a child, he was sneaky. He's always had a ready grin and a joke and would go out of his way to help people, but then afterward, he never let them forget it. He liked people to owe him." He blew out air and set his coffee cup on the table. "I don't know what to do. I can't trust Robert; even with just suspicions, I can't afford to trust him. If my son wants me dead, how can I sleep under the same roof with him?"

Pete leaned back and propped his boots up on the table. Matt tensed. On the right sole of Pete's boot, there was a V-shaped cut. Just like the sign left by the sniper in the rocks.

"It doesn't make sense," Jack said.

"Nothing about this makes any sense," Charlie said. "But I seen the cut on Pete's boot, and it's a match with the boots the sniper is wearin'."

"It's enough to arrest him on," Jack reluctantly said. "But I don't know if it's enough for a conviction. Nobody around here would convict him. He's too well-liked."

"Could he be in on it with his son and the Raner girl?" Matt asked. "Is that possible?"

Jack rubbed his face and sighed. "Hell, Matt, the whole town might be in on this thing, for all I know. I feel like I'm bein' pulled in fifteen directions."

A boy stuck his head into the office. "Here comes the sheep!" he hollered. "Thousands of 'em."

The handlers did not push the sheep through town, but instead skirted it on the north side. Still, it was more sheep than anyone in town had ever seen. Louis Longmont rode in, accompanied by his bodyguard, Mike. They stood on the boardwalk in front of the sheriff's office while the sheep were being moved to the newly-leased range on the Box H.

"Will you be stayin' in the area long, Mister Longmont?" Jack asked.

"Long enough to see that my investment is properly cared for," the man said. "One way or the other," he added.

There was a very thinly-veiled threat there, and Jack Linwood knew it.

"I trust," Louis said, "that I will not have to pull in some, ah, associates of mine to protect my investment?"

"I sure hope not," Jack replied.

The men paused to watch Victoria drive by in a buggy, a picnic basket on the seat beside her. She waved and smiled at the men.

"Pretty girl," Louis remarked.

"She draws," Jack said. "Real good at it. She's goin' just outside of town, to that crick that runs into the Colorado. She'll spend all day there, drawin' pictures of trees and birds and the like. Them's her drawin's on the walls of the cafe."

Jack stepped off the boardwalk and walked to his horse, buckling the straps on a saddlebag. Sam looked down at the dirt. Each time Jack's right boot hit the earth, a V-shaped mark appeared.

"Now wait just a damn minute!" Sam said. "What's going on here?"

"What do you mean?" Jack asked, turning to face the men on the boardwalk.

Sam pointed to the ground. The men stared at the damning mark in the dirt. But it was Dewey who found the real culprit. He sat down on the edge of the boardwalk and got up a lot faster.

"Oww!" he yelled, grabbing at the seat of his jeans.

Matt knelt down and ran his hand over the boards. Two headless nails had been exposed as the boards had worn down over the years of foot-traffic, one set just behind the other. He put his boot over the nails and turned, feeling the drag as the nails cut into the sole. He sat down and pulled off his boot, holding it up for all to see.

A V had been gouged into the sole.

"Well, I'll be durned," Charlie said, kneeling down and carefully feeling the sharp nails. "And look where it is. Anybody steppin' up from tyin' their horse at that rail would step right on the nails."

"And the pressure from their weight would be enough to mark the sole," Jimmy said.

"That means that half the people in town might have those cuts on their boots," Sam said.

The sheriff took off his hat and scratched his head. Matt noticed the man was graying. "We're right back where we started from," Jack said. "A right-handed man, with a cut on his sole, and totin' a Springfield rifle."

Louis Longmont's fancy wagons came rolling through town and Louis and Mike got back into the saddle and followed them toward their new campsite.

"I pity anybody who tries to attack that bunch of sheep," Dewey said.

Charlie smiled. "Louis told me not too long ago that some ranchers up north of here tried to squeeze him out a couple of years ago. He just bought up all the land that surrounded their ranches, damned up all the creeks, fenced off the river, and blew down part of a mountain, blocking the only road for two, three miles. He sealed them in. Didn't take them long to come callin', hat in hand. Said he settled that situation without firin' a shot."

"I wish this one could be," Jack said wistfully. "But right about now, Pete's got his son by the throat, Hugo's yellin' at his daughter, Blake's probably gettin' drunk, Red Raley is plannin' more night raids, that damn sniper is layin' in wait to kill somebody, and Dale and Chrisman is plottin' and schemin' against everybody else. I wonder what else is gonna happen?"

In the middle of the afternoon, a farmer came rattling his wagon into town, galloping his team. He whoaed in front of the sheriffs office and started hollering.

"That Mexican girl is layin' out yonder by the crick," he yelled. "She's unconscious and ain't got a stitch on. I threw my coat over her and come into town as fast as my old team could pull."

"Dewey, run fetch the doc," Jack said. "Jimmy, go get Matt and Sam. Charlie, go get the girl's father while I beat it out to the crick. Move, boys!"

Doctor Lemmon was only seconds behind Jack. He covered Victoria with a blanket and used salts to bring her to consciousness. She had been beaten very badly, her face swollen and one eye closed. There was blood on her mouth. The inside of her thighs were bruised.

"Raped?" Jack asked, his face and eyes hard. One thing that was not done in the West was manhandling a good woman. Raping meant a sure rope or bullet.

"Yes," the doctor said. "Who did it, Victoria?"

"Lightning and Circle V riders," she whispered. "The cowboys called Burl and Dixon and Rusty and Tulsa. Ned from Lightning. I don't know the name of the other one." She closed her one good eye and began sobbing uncontrollably.

Matt and Sam galloped up. The brothers listened to Jack relate what Victoria had said. Jack grabbed Sam by the arm. "We do this by the book," he warned. "No losing control. You hear me?"

"I hear you," Sam said, his face dangerously hard. "But you know that those men will just alibi for each other. Nothing will be done. No one will be arrested. No one will stand trial. She's Mexican. I've seen what happened to men who raped and even killed Indian women. One and the same thing: nothing."

"That won't be the case here, Sam," Jack said, but everyone knew they were hollow words.

"Sure won't," Matt said, spinning the cylinder of one of his .44's and filling the empty sixth chamber. "Book justice doesn't always equal what's right." He held up the Colt. "But this does."

Sixteen

Sheriff Linwood told Matt and Sam to keep their butts in town and to stay the hell away from Lightning and Circle V range. If they didn't, he promised, he'd put them both in jail and their reputations as fast guns be damned, he'd still get lead in them both.

The brothers believed him.

They returned to the sheriff's office and sat with Dewey, drinking coffee and talking. Finally Sam stood up and walked out of the office, saying he was going to check on Victoria.

Juan and Anita were sitting in the doctor's small waiting room. Anita's eyes were red and puffy from crying and Juan's face was stony hard, dark and terrible Spanish vengeance plain in his black eyes.

"They will be brought to justice, Juan," Sam said, taking a seat.

"*Sí*," the man replied. "One way or the other."

"Have you spoken with the doctor?"

"*Sí*. Her physical wounds are not serious. But mentally . . . ?" He shook his head. "Those are terrible men to do something like this. I never dreamed I was capable of so much hate."

"Cold hate is better, Juan. You cannot think during hot hate."

The father cut his eyes and smiled at Sam. "Yes, I know. You perhaps have some Spanish blood in you as well, Sam?"

"My Cheyenne blood boils just the same as yours."

Doctor Lemmon stepped into the room, drying his hands on a towel. "She's sleeping now. I sedated her very heavily. She should sleep for hours. There is no need for any of you to stay. The ladies from the church are going to take turns staying with her during the night."

Sam stood up. "Come on. I'll walk with you back to the café."

"The café will be closed for this night," Juan said. "But the cantina will be open."

They passed people on their way; all stopped to express their horror at what had been done, and to wish Victoria well. The outpouring of sympathy seemed to make the father and mother feel better, just knowing the majority of the townspeople were with them in their grief.

Matt joined Sam in the cantina part of the establishment and both of them had a beer. Juan came back in with a long-bladed knife and a honing stone. He took very small sips of tequila while he honed the wicked-looking blade. The brothers had a pretty good idea what he intended doing with it.

If Juan got hold of any of the rapists, they were going to be very uncomfortable sitting a saddle for a long, long time.

At dusk, Jack and Charlie entered the cantina and ordered a pitcher of beer. Jack threw his hat down on the table in disgust. Juan had honed his knife to razor sharpness and sheathed it, putting it away. He sat quietly, waiting for the sheriff to speak the words he already knew would come out of his mouth.

"They alibied for each other," Jack said, after taking a big swallow of beer and wiping his mouth with the back of his hand. "The hands on both spreads all said the men had not left their sight all day."

"Blake and Hugo?" Sam said.

"They also gave their men alibis—and did so with real smirky, smart-alecky grins."

"Well, that cuts it as far as I'm concerned," Matt said. "Every man-jack on those spreads is trash. And that includes the owners. Did you see any of the men Victoria named?"

"Saw all of 'em," Charlie said, a bitter tone to his words. "They was all scratched up around the face. That gal must have fought 'em to a fare-thee-well. They said they all been brush-poppin' cattle and got their faces tore up. But they all grinned and pulled at theirselves whilst they was sayin' it. *The bastards!*"

Jack stood up, an angry look on his face. "I'm sorry, Juan. I'm truly sorry. I like Victoria. I like you and your wife. You've put up with me while I was blunderin' around actin' like a lapdog for Dale. And I apologize for that." He took a ragged breath to try and settle his nerves. "Maybe it's time to settle this with guns. I don't know. I don't know if I can keep my own temper in check. If I don't do something to cool down, I'm gonna blow my top." He tossed way too much money on the table. "That'll pay for the broken window."

"What broken window, señor?" Juan asked.

Jack picked up his beer mug, drained it, and threw it through a side window. "*That* broken window, Juan."

* * *

The next morning, after checking on Victoria, the brothers told Jack they were going to ride out to the Box H and they would stay clear of Lightning and Circle V range.

"And if you run into any of Blake or Hugo's hands on the way?"

"We won't draw first," Sam assured him.

"Hell, boys, don't neither one of you need to drag iron first." He smiled. "You got more nerve than I have, headin' out to Pete's place. Tell me if his boy can sit down, will you?"

Matt laughed. "Right!"

If Robert could get his aching bones out of bed, he probably couldn't stand up. The father had literally whipped the snot out of his son. Then he dumped a bucket of well-water on him, dragged him to his boots, and beat hell out of him again, just for good measure.

Millie said it was a terrible fight to behold.

"Did your mother see it?" Matt asked, while Sam was rummaging around in the kitchen, filling a sack with doughnuts.

"Yes. Robert confessed everything. He's really not a very brave person. Daddy's going to take him in to the sheriff this afternoon. In a wagon. Hands are filling it with hay now. Robert couldn't sit a saddle. Daddy broke several of his ribs. He's all taped up. That new hand we hired just about two months ago was really one of Red Raley's men. He left while Robert was getting his trashing from Daddy."

"Then taking him into town is no good, Millie," Matt said quickly.

"Why the hell not?" Pete demanded, slamming open the screen door and stepping out onto the porch.

" 'Cause that hand that pulled out went straight to

Raley and Raley went straight to Chrisman and Dale. You'll never get your son into town alive. At least here on the ranch, you have a chance of keeping him alive."

The rancher sat down. His big hands were bruised, swollen, and knuckle-cut. "I hadn't thought of that. I been so damn mad I'm not thinkin' straight. You're right."

"What we can do is have the sheriff come out here with two townspeople to act as witnesses. We write it all down and that should be enough." He then told them about Victoria.

"Good God!" Pete said, jumping to his feet. "And Blake and Hugo backed up their alibis?"

"To the hilt," Sam said.

"Those sorry . . ." He bit back an oath. "Well, that tears it for me, boys. I got no use for either of them. None of the hands would tell the truth?"

"Not a one of them."

"I better not catch one of them in gunsights," Millie said. "I got no use for men like that."

"No more ridin' alone, girl," her father told her. "And I mean that."

"I understand, Daddy. I won't. And that's a promise."

Pete looked at the sack in Sam's hands. "You get enough doughnuts, boy?"

"It's a long ride back to town," Sam replied.

"I'll let you borrow one of my packhorses," Pete said dryly.

Sheriff Jack Linwood and Jimmy left early the next morning with two townspeople, heading for the Box H to listen to and take down Robert's confession. Jack had wired the nearest judge to get an opinion on it and the judge had wired back that once the confession was taken in front of witnesses it would hold up in a court of law.

Of course the rumors were flying, and Chrisman and Dale had heard them; but they were going about their business as usual. Both looked a little strained around the mouth and the eyes.

One rumor had it that Hugo Raner had walloped the tar out of Denise's rear end and confined her to the house, under guard. Blake Vernon had sent his wife, Martha, off to visit relatives back east and was sending out wires to hire more hands, offering them fighting wages. Hugo had done the same.

"Who are they going to fight, each other?" Jack questioned. "Have we missed something here? Once we get Robert's confession, it's over, ain't it? If those two try to fight Louis Longmont, he'll hire a damn army."

"That confession of Robert Harris is not gonna be worth spit," Charlie opined. "It's just his word against Dale and Chrisman, and both of them are respected— more or less—businessmen. It'll never come to trial. I've toted a badge in too many places not to see that."

"But it will cast suspicion and bring a lot of things to light," Sam said.

"What it'll do is start some shootin'," Charlie said. "And maybe that's what it's gonna take to bust this situation wide open."

Sam walked down to the doctor's office to see about Victoria, and Matt lounged in front of the office. Dewey walked the town while Charlie cleaned the sheriff's department's weapons, loading them all up full. He was too old a hand and too wise to the ways of the world not to know that war was only a step away.

Some sheepmen were in town, buying supplies, and a few farmers had rattled up in wagons with their families. The town seemed serene. But Matt had sensed an undercurrent of tension, as if everyone was just waiting for the lid to blow off. And tomorrow was Saturday. Hands from Box H, Circle V, and Lightning, as well as the Spur, the Horseshoe, and several other smaller spreads, were going to be wanting to come into town for tobacco, a few drinks, and cards and conversation. And Matt would bet that the men who had assaulted Victoria would be among them.

In a way, he hoped they would come into town.

Jack returned, the confession in his pocket. He was not put off by Charlie's sourness that the confession was no good.

"It'll make Chrisman and Dale pull in their horns, Charlie," he told the grizzled old gunhandler.

"No, it won't," Charlie countered. "Not unless Denise Raner goes along with what Robert said. And I'll bet you she'll deny the whole damn thing."

"Matt and Sam saw them together and, uh . . . doin' what comes naturally," the sheriff stood his ground. "And saw them meet with Red Raley. Both of them will testify to that effect."

Charlie leaned back in his chair. "And you know what will happen if this comes to trial, Jack? That little Denise Raner gal will come into town with her hair all done up nice, gussied up in a white dress that'll make her look so pure it'd melt the heart of a snowman. She'll bat them eyes at the jury and when she speaks it'll be pure honey comin' out of her mouth. She'll say that she don't know why Matt and Sam is castin' them terrible aspersions agin' her character. And she'll cry a little bit, and that jury will play right into her pretty little hands. I've seen it done, Jack. More'un once.

"And Chrisman and Dale? Why, they'll deny the

whole damn thing. We got no hard proof, Jack. In the end, Robert Harris will be made to look like the damn fool he is; he'll be left way out on a limb, all alone, and them lawyers will tear him to pieces. It'll be his word against dozens of folks. We got nothin', Jack. Nothin' at all."

"I'm ridin' for the county seat in the mornin', Charlie," the sheriff told him, "to meet with the judge. You're in charge until I get back."

"Take the stage," Charlie told him. "You'll be safer against that damn sniper thataway. And take Jimmy with you. Matt and Sam will be around; we'll handle it. I got me an idea on how to shut down Saturday night."

"Play it your way, Charlie," Jack said.

"What?" Dale and Chrisman both hollered.

"I told you, the saloons are shut down tight," Charlie repeated.

Saturday morning in Dale, Colorado. A bright, sunshine-filled day. Peaceful so far, and Charlie intended to keep it that way. The sheriff and Jimmy had just left on the stage, heading for the county seat and a meeting with the district judge.

"But Saturday is our most profitable day," Dale protested.

"I don't give a damn *what* it is," Charlie told them. "If them doors ain't padlocked in fifteen minutes, I'll put you both in jail for disobeyin' the orders of a lawman. Now do it!"

Matt and Sam and Dewey had been busy painting huge signs and the signs were up on both ends of town. ALL GUNS MUST BE CHECKED AT THE SHERIFF'S OFFICE. ANYONE FAILING TO DO THIS

WILL BE FINED FIFTY DOLLARS AND SPEND THREE DAYS IN JAIL. ALL SALOONS ARE CLOSED UNTIL FURTHER NOTICE.

Charlie, Matt, Sam, and Dewey all carried sawed-off double-barreled shotguns. They stood highly visible on the boardwalks of the main street.

A group of hands from the Lightning spread were the first into town, coming in at mid-afternoon. A hand called Kid who fancied himself a real tough gunslick ripped the sign down and rode up to Charlie. He tossed the sign at Charlie's feet. It plopped on the dirt in front of the boardwalk.

"I'd like to see you take my guns, you old son-of-a-bitch!" Kid said.

"All right," Charlie said. "I'll just do that." He lifted the express gun and gave the kid both barrels in the chest. The double charge of buckshot blew the Kid slap out of the saddle and spread him all over the street.

"Jesus God!" Clint whispered.

Dewey pointed his greener at Clint. "Check your guns at the office," the young man told him. "And do it right now."

"You got it," Clint said. "Man, don't pull them triggers. We'll git us some tobacco and notions and we're gone from here."

"Somebody get a shovel and scrape up that mouthy one," Charlie said. He looked at Clint, who had unbuckled his gunbelt and handed it to Sam. "You wanna tote him back to the ranch for plantin' there?"

"Tote him back how?" the Lightning hand said. "In a tub?"

Seventeen

The hands from the Lightning spread must have ridden straight to the Circle V and warned the hands that to ride into Dale meant big trouble, for not one single puncher from either the Lightning or the Circle V came into town the rest of that day.

A few hands from the Box H came in, read the sign, and checked their guns without any hesitation. They had a few drinks in the cantina, and ate supper, and everybody behaved. The boardwalks were quiet and the town nearly asleep by ten o'clock.

At midnight, Sam came awake, wide-eyed and worried. He looked around the shack; Matt was snoring softly. He threw a boot at him, hitting him in the butt, and Matt rolled off the narrow bunk and landed on his belly on the floor.

"Grace in motion," Sam said, swinging his legs out of bed. "That's you."

Matt crawled to his knees. "I'm gonna stomp your . . ."

"You'll do no such thing and you know it. We settled

all that by the Crazy Woman a year ago. Get dressed. Something is very, very wrong."

"You just got lucky that day," Bodine said, pulling on his jeans and sticking his feet into his boots. "I'd been pinned down there for hours and was exhausted by the time you got there." He buttoned his shirt.

"Bah! I couldn't whip you and you couldn't whip me. That's the way it is, so fighting each other is foolish." He grinned. "Old Fat Bear really beat our backs and butts good with that stick, didn't he?"

Bodine laughed. "He sure did. Hurt me a lot worse than those puny punches you were throwing." He buckled on his gunbelt and found his hat.

"Wagh! You couldn't even walk to your horse when it was over. I had to half-carry you."

"Now that's a damn lie. If I hadn't been pulling my punches so I wouldn't hurt you too bad . . ."

"Oh, be quiet, you babble like a gossiping old squaw."

"Sam?"

"What is it now?"

"What the hell were we fighting over that day?"

Sam thought for a moment. "A woman, don't you remember Terri?"

"Oh, yeah. You ever think about her, Sam?"

"Not for many months, brother."

"Why did you wake me up? What's wrong?"

"I don't know. Get your rifle. Something's wrong."

"You just said you didn't know what it was!"

"I'm an Indian. I know things that you white people don't."

"You're half Cheyenne and you were educated back East. I look more Indian than you do."

"Then act it. Be quiet for a moment and sniff the air. Feel the tension."

Matt listened. The night was totally silent. He sniffed. "Dust," he said, picking up his rifle. "Let's go wake up those at the jail."

They ran hard and hammered on the office door. Charlie stumbled out, quite a sight to see in his long-handles. "What the devil's goin' on, boys?"

"Too much dust in the air, Charlie," Matt said. "Nothing's moving out there; not a cricket, not a bird, not an owl, nothing at all."

Charlie nodded and walked to the cold stove. He drank lukewarm coffee right out of the pot while Sam briefed Dewey. Dressed, Charlie passed out shotguns and the men checked their pistols and rifles.

"Dewey, you defend this office. I'm gonna be yonder in that alley. Matt, Sam, you boys pick your spots." The sounds of hard-ridden horses reached them. "We ain't got time to wake the town. Good luck, boys."

"Luck to you, too, Charlie," Matt yelled, running out the door and jumping off the boardwalk, heading for the alley that led to the café/cantina.

He just made it before the masked men, all wearing long dusters, opened fire, shooting out windows and wantonly firing, not giving a damn if women or children might catch one of their careless bullets.

Matt lifted the greener and gave a rider both barrels as he galloped past the alley. The charge lifted the man clear out of the saddle and tossed him to the street. Matt dropped the sawed-off and pulled his .44's and let 'em bang.

Charlie leveled his express gun and gave both barrels to a rider. Recognizing the night-rider was going to be difficult without a head. Dewey took aim with a rifle and emptied a saddle. Sam fired both barrels of his sawed-off into a knot of riders all bunched up and their screaming cut the night like a knife.

By this time, the citizens were awake and firing anything they could grab into the shadowy forms of the raiders. The raiders decided that attacking the town had been a really bad idea. They left their dead and wounded behind and galloped out of town.

"Do we chase them?" Dewey asked Charlie.

"New. Time we got saddled up they'd be three, four miles ahead of us and all scattered. Let's see what we got on the ground, boys."

"Hell," Simmons said, rolling over a body. "This here's Jigger from the Circle V."

"This one's called Boots. He rides—rode—for Hugo Raner," another citizen said.

"I don't know who this is," a man called. "He ain't got no face left on him. And not much head left, neither."

The raiders left four dead and six wounded behind them, all from either the Lightning or Circle V ranch.

"Patch them up best you can, Doc," Charlie said. "Them that can walk is goin' to jail."

"On what charge?" a puncher for Blake Vernon yelled.

"Four counts of attempted murder," Charlie told him.

"Who did we try to kill?" another hand hollered.

"Matt Bodine, Sam Two Wolves, Dewey Vernon, and me, that's who, you sorry piece of crap!"

"Oh, hell, we was just lettin' off steam!"

"Well, I got a dandy place for you to cool off," Charlie told them. "Three meals a day and lots of time to relax. Move, boys. You know the way to the jail."

"This one just died," Doc Lemmon said, standing up over the body of a Circle V rider. "Dear God, when is this killing going to end?"

"It ain't even started yet, Doc," Charlie said. "Raner

and Vernon won't sit still for this. They'll be comin' in the mornin'. You'd best stock up on medical supplies and get ready for it."

Hugo Raner and Blake Vernon rode into town that Sunday at mid-morning, bringing all their hands with them, and all the punchers heavily armed. Sixty-odd men thundered into town, their horses' hooves kicking up enough dust to put a cover on everything in town that wasn't protected. They reined up and dismounted, rifles in hand.

Every man in the town who could handle a rifle, pistol, or shotgun—that was the entire male population over fifteen—stood up from their positions on the rooftops, the muzzles of their Winchesters, Sharps, Springfield carbines, Spencers, Colts, and Remingtons pointed at the knot of riders on the street below them.

Matt, Sam, Charlie, and Dewey stood on the boardwalk in front of the sheriff's office, each of them carrying sawed-off shotguns.

"Howdy, boys," Charlie said. "Nice of you to come pay us a visit." He lifted his greener, the cavernous muzzles of the ten-gauge pointed right at Hugo's belly. "You seen the sign comin' into town, so shuck them weapons and let 'em hit the dirt."

"We can take you boys down with us," Hugo said hoarsely.

"But you'll be dead first off," Charlie said. "With your guts spread all over the street."

"And you'll be the second man to be blown in two," Matt told Blake Vernon. "Is that how you want it?"

"We're droppin' our guns," Hugo said. "You people just stand easy and ease off them triggers." He knew that four double-barreled shotguns, at a range of less than fifteen feet, could kill or maim twenty men during the first two seconds of any fight. Hugo dropped his rifle in the dirt, his gunbelt following that.

The fuse of war was jerked out of the charge . . . for the time being.

"Now back out in the street," Charlie told the men. "Away from them guns."

The riders complied and townspeople rushed out, collecting the guns and dumping them on the boardwalk. Half a dozen young boys began emptying the weapons of ammo; just the ammunition alone made quite a pile, the brass winking and twinkling in the sunlight.

"Good," Charlie said, lowering the express gun. "Now we can talk like civilized folks. What the hell were you boys plannin' on doin' in Dale on this fine Sunday mornin'? And don't give us no crap about attendin' church."

"Some of our men rode in last night, hoo-rahin' the town," Blake said. "You killed some and wounded others; put them behind bars. That's an outrage. They meant no harm. We want them out of jail."

Charlie got so mad Matt thought he was going to shoot the man. He quickly stepped in. "No harm?" he questioned. "Why, you dumb clod of dirt, look around you! Those are bulletholes in stores and homes. Two children were hit by bullets—none seriously, thank God—and three women were cut by flying glass. Sixty-five windows were shot out, merchandise in the stores and personal possessions in homes were damaged or destroyed. And you claim no harm was intended. You're ignorant, Blake, you and that big ox next to you." Raner flushed at that but was smart enough to keep his mouth shut.

Sam said, "Worse than being ignorant, you're dangerous. You and the men who work for you. You have no regard for others; none at all. You think the law doesn't apply to you. Well, you are very wrong. Your hands are going to be tried in a court of law and probably sentenced to long prison terms. And that's the way it's going to be."

Charlie and Matt began kicking the empty guns off the boardwalk, and they weren't gentle about it. Rifles and pistols went sailing and plopping into the dirt.

Charlie pointed to the guns. "Now pick 'em up and get the hell out of town. You want to come back in tomorrow and do some shoppin' or have a drink, that's fine. But your guns better be hangin' on the saddlehorn and your rifles booted. If they're not, I swear I'll kill you, and I won't give you no warnin' a-tall. I'll just blow you out of the saddle. Now *git!*"

Hugo, Blake, and hands mounted up, the ranch owners sending their men on ahead, except for their sons and the foremen. Hugo glared at the four lawmen on the boardwalk. "You know it isn't over, Starr. You're a man of the West; you know how things are done here. You know that we won't forget this."

"You best close your mouth and go home and tend to that sneakin', back-bitin', and treacherous daughter of yours, Raner," Charlie told him. "You got enough grief on your doorstep without askin' for more."

"I don't need you or anybody else tellin' me how to deal with my family!" the rancher snapped back.

"Git!" Charlie said, lifting the shotgun.

"You wouldn't shoot an unarmed man," Raner said.

Charlie jacked back both hammers. "I'd be doin' the world a favor, Raner. Open that big mouth of yours agin and I'll blow you out of the saddle."

Matt, Sam, and Dewey jacked back the hammers on their shotguns.

Their faces mottled and ugly with hate and rage, the men savagely spurred their horses and galloped out of town.

"Man who'd treat a good horse like that ought to be shot," Simmons called from the roof of his store.

Nobody disagreed.

Sheriff Linwood and deputy were back in town on the Monday afternoon stage. Jack tossed the judge's reply on the desk and looked at Charlie.

"You called it, Charlie. The judge said there wasn't enough to build a case on. He said it was regrettable, but he couldn't act on the evidence we had—or the lack of it."

Dewey stuck his head into the office. "Chrisman just hung a sign on his door," he announced. "No farmers or sheepmen allowed."

"What?" Jack said. "Well, that makes no sense."

"He done it," Dewey said. "And Reed and his boys are just comin' into town." The young man looked up toward the other end of the main street.

"Curiouser and curiouser," Sam muttered.

"And here comes some boys from the Circle V," Dewey said. "They're reining up at the Plowshare. And yonder's Chrisman and a fellow with a bucket of paint and a ladder."

The lawmen stepped outside just as a Circle V hand rode up, gunbelts hanging from his saddlehorn. He grinned, or smirked, Matt thought, and handed the weapons to Charlie. "There you are, Mister Badge-Toter. Just like you wanted. Now can I please go run along and have me a peaceful drink?"

"Yeah," Charlie said, wondering, like the others, what in the world was going on. "You do that."

"Oh, thank you so very much, your majesty," the hand said, his voice thick with sarcasm.

"Move," Matt told him.

The men walked up the boardwalk to stand watching as the Plowshare sign was removed and a clean board nailed up. The workman painted the words: CATTLE CLUB in bright red letters.

Chrisman looked over at the lawmen and grinned. "You like it, boys?" he called.

"Can't say that I do," Jack said. "But I guess we have to live with it."

"Or die over it," Sam muttered.

"You do have a point," Matt said.

Reed and two of his four sons, all big, rangy men, walked up to join the lawmen. The farmer and his sons pulled their weapons from behind their belts and handed over their pistols. "Jake and Joe," Reed said, pointing to his sons. "What does that sign say hangin' in the winder over there?"

Jake squinted. "Says we ain't welcome in there no more, Pa."

"Do tell," the father said. "Well, I bet Juan don't mind us comin' in for a drink. We'll just amble over there to the cantina and offer our sympathies for what happened to his girl and then have us a taste. How is Victoria?"

"Physically, she's fine," Sam told him. "But the shame is weighing heavy on her mind."

"I'll send my woman in to talk to her. Esther is good at comfortin' people in times of need. I'll do that. Come on, boys. We got things to tend to. By your leave, Sheriff."

"See you men around," Jack replied. When the farmer and his sons were out of earshot, Jack said, "Mountain people. Kentucky, Tennessee, somewhere back there.

Good people, but I'd sure hate to push them too hard. I've seen Reed and his boys back off and put a round into a knothole at five hundred yards. And they didn't like being banned from Chrisman's place. Did you notice their eyes?"

"Yeah," Matt said. "Boys, I got me a hunch that those Circle V hands are going to egg on a fight with some farmers this day. And since Reed and his boys are the only farmers in town, it's gonna be them."

"Those cowboys will be sorry they did it," Sam said. "I have a feeling that those mountain boys grew up on rough and tumble, kick, cut, and gouge fighting."

Jack smiled. "I think we'll just hang around the town today, boys. A good fight is a joy to behold sometimes. And them Circle V boys is sure deservin' of one."

"No one turned in their knives," Dewey said. "And all of my father's men carry knifes on their belts. And some of them are pretty good with them . . . so I've been told."

Jack chuckled. "My daddy come out here from the Blue Ridge Mountains. He toted him a long-bladed knife 'til the day he died. Momma buried it with him. Don't you worry none about them mountain boys and knifes. Them Reed boys is all carryin' Arkansas toothpicks—including the father."

"I'm going to walk over to the cantina and see Victoria," Sam said. "I'll see you boys over there directly."

The men split up, Dewey going with Matt and Jimmy walking along with Charlie.

"More hands coming in," Jimmy said.

"I see 'em," Charlie said. "Them's some of Hugo's hands. I don't like it, boy. Something's goin' on."

"Like what, Charlie?"

"I don't know."

The Lightning hands rode in with their gunbelts hanging on the saddlehorn. They reined up and smiled at Charlie, meekly handing over their weapons. Charlie didn't like the glint in their eyes, and neither did Jimmy.

This bunch headed for the Red Dog.

"You ever been an outlaw, Charlie?" Jimmy asked.

The question caught him by surprise. "Me? Hell, no. Why'd you ask?"

"Oh, just stories I've heard about you, is all."

Charlie watched Jack Linwood make his afternoon rounds, then enter the Red Dog. "I've been a lot of things, son. Drover, trail boss, marshal, I even farmed for two years to try to get away from my reputation. Over in Kansas. Sorriest two years I ever spent in my life. Horse got so he wouldn't even have nothin' to do with me. Widder lady got to makin' eyes at me and I knowed it was time to hit the trail. That woman must have weighed a good three hundred pounds and had a butt on her two ax handles wide. Whole house shook when she walked in. I was skired the damn roof was gonna fall in on me. I left in the dead of night and I ain't never gone back."

Matt and Dewey stopped directly across the street from them and Matt pointed. Charlie followed the direction of the point and grunted.

"More riders comin' in. Comin' from the east, so they're probably Lightning hands. I wish I could figure what's goin' on here."

Simmons of the general store and Walters of the saddle and gun shop walked up. "Charlie," Walters said, "them Circle V and Lightning hands all walk like they're bad stove up."

"I noticed it too," Simmons said. "What's goin' on here, Charlie?"

"Go get Sam, Jimmy. Move, boy! We got big trouble brewin'."

"But they don't have no guns!" Jimmy said.

"Yeah, they do, boy. 'Member you commented about how funny them hands was walkin'?"

"Yeah. So?"

"They got 'em stuck down in their boots!"

Eighteen

Matt noticed that the riders coming in from the east had stopped just shy of the warning sign. Tiny hairs bristled on the back of his neck. He watched Jimmy run across the street and duck into the alley, obviously heading for Juan's café and cantina. He looked at Charlie. The man lifted one Colt out of leather and then tapped the side of his boot.

"Damn!" Matt said.

"What's wrong?" Dewey asked.

"Get to the office and get a rifle. Get ready for some action if those Lightning hands come into town. If they come, they'll come fogging. Move."

Matt stepped into the newly-named Cattle Club and jerked both .44's out of leather. "First man who makes a move, I plug. So just stand easy, boys."

"What's up, Matt?" Jack asked, turning from the bar.

"They got six-guns in their boots, Jack. And a gang of Lightning hands have stopped just short of the warning sign. They're up to something."

A Lightning hand grabbed for his boot and came up

with a six-gun. Matt drilled him dead center in the chest; the room exploded in gunfire and the air was filled with smoke.

Across the street, Charlie and Sam had the hands in the Red Dog lying belly-down on the floor, while Jimmy collected the bootguns.

In the Cattle Club, Ned, seeing the battle was going against them, ran out the back door and headed straight for the cantina. It was the worst mistake he ever made, and for the rest of his life—which would not be all that lengthy—he would curse that decision. He ran through the dining area, cussing and hollering and waving his six-gun. He caught motion out of the corner of his eye and slid to a stop, leveling his pistol. A searing pain tore through him, beginning at his wrist. He heard something hit the floor and looked down. He started screaming.

What had hit the floor was his six-gun, with his hand still wrapped around the butt of the Remington. He lifted horror-filled eyes. Juan was smiling at him, a big, heavy, and bloody Bowie knife in his right hand.

"Now, señor," Juan said. "You will pay the ultimate price for violating my daughter." He swung the knife, the blunt edge hitting Ned on the side of the head and knocking him down.

"Juan's a-draggin' that no-good out the back door, Pa," Joe said.

"Yep," Reed said, turning the page in his Bible and taking a sip of tequila.

"Cut his hand off, too, Pa," Jake said.

"Yep. And something tells me Juan ain't through cuttin', neither."

"You reckon we ought to go fetch the doc, Pa?"

"Nope. Tell the blacksmith to git his bellows a-pumpin'. Git a iron white-hot. Move."

"Nothing is working," Dale said to Chrisman. The men sat in Dale's office at the bank.

"At least we got Robert and Denise out of the picture," Chrisman said with a sigh. He cursed. "And we were so close. So close."

"We're still close. Just stay calm. The gold and silver is still out there, and only we know where it is."

The shooting had stopped. A horrible scream ripped through the town.

"What in God's name was that?" Chrisman said, getting up and looking out the window.

But Dale wasn't terribly interested. "Perhaps I spoke too hastily. Actually, all this trouble is working for us, not against us. Sooner or later, Ramer and Blake will catch a bullet and that will be that. In the meantime, have Red and his boys start rustling their cattle. Drive them north and run them off cliffs. They've got notes coming due pretty soon. The sheriff up there can be bought. I'll see to that. What *are* you looking at?"

"Bodies bein' dragged out of my place."

"Either of you boys hurt?" Charlie asked, walking over to the Cattle Club.

"No," Matt told him. "What was that scream just a moment ago?"

"I don't know."

Ned came staggering out of an alley, lurching as he walked, his face white against the pain. "He gelded me!" Ned squalled. "He cut me like a horse!" He fell down in the dirt and passed out.

Doctor Lemmon took his time getting to the man. "Maybe there *is* justice in the world after all," the doctor was heard to mutter.

*   *   *

"You don't demand a damn thing!" Sheriff Linwood got all up in Hugo Raner's face. "And you sure don't tell me how to run this office."

"I want Juan Garcia arrested, by God."

Jack smiled and sat back down in his chair. Matt and Sam and Charlie sat in the office and smiled along with him. Dewey and Jimmy were checking the town.

It was the morning after the aborted attack on the town by Lightning and Circle V hands.

"On what charge, Hugo?" Jack asked.

"He castrated Ned!"

Jack shook his head. "We don't have any proof of that—only his word. Can't find the big knife Ned said he used. No sign of blood in the alley by his place. And you know what else, Raner? Must be eighty, ninety citizens of this town that's been in my office, yesterday and today, who will get up in a court of law and swear they were in his café bein' waited on—by Juan—when the incident took place." He smiled again. "It's like the Bible says, you reap what you sow."

"What the hell do you mean by that?"

"You alibied for Ned after Victoria was raped. And everybody in this town knew you were nothin' but a low-down liar when you said it. That's what I mean."

Raner opened his mouth. Jack closed it.

"Don't make threats. Not agin me, not agin this town, not agin the people in it. Do it, and I'll put you in jail."

Raner struggled to keep his temper in check. "I want to pay my hands' fines."

"Fine. Thousand dollars ought to cover it."

"A thousand dollars!" Raner squalled. "Are you out of your mind?"

"It just went up to fifteen hundred," Jack said calmly.

"Damn you!" Raner screamed, and leaned over the

desk, grabbing Jack by the shirt and hauling him out of the chair.

Charlie stepped over and laid a cosh on the back of Raner's head. The big man sank to the floor with a sigh. Put a terrible dent in Raner's expensive hat.

"Put him in a cell," Jack said. He picked up a pen and wrote in the jail register: *Hugo Raner, jailed for assaulting a peace officer. Fine, One hundred dollars.*

Pete Harris stepped into the office just as Hugo was being dragged into a cell. He chuckled at the sight. "Man, you are gonna have one irritated feller on your hands when he wakes up. What'd he do?"

He listened and shook his head. "I always thought Hugo had better sense than that. But I've been proved wrong so many times here lately, nothin' surprises me no more." He poured a cup of coffee and sat down. "How's Ned?"

"He'll live, Doc Lemmon says," Matt told him. "If you call that living."

Pete shuddered at the thought. "Juan ain't nearabouts through, boys. You all know that, don't you?"

"Do you blame him?" Jack asked.

"I wouldn't have waited this long," Pete replied.

When Hugo Raner woke up, he was killing mad. But he had enough sense to outwardly calm himself and pay his fine. Jack lowered the fines of his hands and cut them loose. Blake came in just before dusk and got his men out of jail.

Jack told him the same thing he'd told Hugo. "Blake, this has got to stop. Men died this day—and there wasn't no call for them to die. This ain't got nothin' to do with sheep no more. This is a personal thing that you and Hugo got goin'. You ain't got no support in this town. Maybe half a dozen people out of the entire population. The rest is hard agin you."

Blake, just as Hugo had done, stood facing the sheriff, his face hard and uncompromising.

Matt said, "Blake, you and Hugo are playing right into the hands of Dale and Chrisman; you're both doing exactly what they want you to do. Sam summed it up with divide and conquer . . ."

"I'm not interested in the opinions of a gunfighter and a damned half-breed," Blake said.

"Get out of this office," Jack said, shaking his head. "You're just like Hugo: stupid."

Dusk began settling over the town. The evening was warm and the men sat outside the office for a breath of air.

"Did Pete say anything about his son?" Sam asked.

"Said the boy was still in bed," Matt replied. "Said Robert hurt so bad it was hard for him to move. Doc Lemmon said the boy had about six busted ribs. Pete really stomped him."

"Should have killed him," Charlie said. "The boy won't forget this. You can bet that right now he's abed just plannin' and schemin' on how to get back at his pa. Has anybody heard anything about that Raner gal?"

No one had.

"Vicious," Jack said. "She was the brains behind their plans. Robert's not smart enough to figure out anything like that. We ain't heard the last from them two."

No one would argue that.

They looked up as a dozen men came riding slowly into town, most of the riders bearded and hard-looking and heavily armed. They reined up in front of the Red Dog and dismounted. The lawmen noticed that they slipped the hammer-thongs from their guns the instant their boots touched the ground.

Matt got up from the bench and walked to the end of the boardwalk to get a better look at the men in the rapidly fading light. He watched them enter the saloon, all of them glancing his way and giving him some dirty looks.

"The man in front is Del Monroe," Jack called from the bench. "Gunfighter from down Texas way. The big, fat, ugly one is Don Edison. The one behind him is Walker. I believe another one is called Bolinger. I don't know the others." He stood up. "Let's go collect some guns, boys."

Jimmy and Dewey stepped back into the office for a moment while the others walked up the street and pushed open the batwings of the Red Dog. The dozen men were lined up along the bar, being served beer and whiskey. They turned as one to stare at the lawmen.

"Jack," Del said. "Ain't seen you in a coon's age. You all re-formed now, totin' that star?"

"Don't insult me by sayin' I was ever as low as you, Monroe," Jack told him. "You boys saw the sign comin' in. Shuck them gunbelts."

"And if we don't?" a burly gunhand asked, dropping his right hand to his side.

"We'll take them," he was told.

"Old man," the gunhand said with a laugh, "I don't think you got the strength to pull that iron out of leather. You got a name, pops?"

"Charlie Starr."

The gunhand tensed, then slowly lifted his hand and placed it on the bar.

Jack cut his eyes first to the right. "That's Matt Bodine." To the left. "That's Sam Two Wolves. Anybody got anything else they'd like to say before them gunbelts is handed over?"

Jimmy and Dewey pushed through the batwings, each carrying a sawed-off shotgun.

Del chuckled, then downed his whiskey. "If you'll be so kind as to direct us to the Lightning range, we'll be movin' on, Jack. No need to get testy, now, is there?"

"Head north to the crossroads. Take the right fork. You can't miss it."

The men downed their drinks and walked out. Many a fight had been avoided by the sight of sawed-off shotguns. Del was the last one to leave the bar. Jack Linwood stopped him.

"You'd be smart to keep on ridin', Del. Louis Longmont is here, too."

"Longmont!" the gun-for-hire said. "Nobody told us nothin' about this gang of gunhawks bein' here and totin' badges. What the hell is goin' on, Jack?"

"That's a good question, Del. If I ever find out exactly, I'll tell you. Ride on out, Del. This ain't worth dyin' over."

"We agreed to ride for the brand, Del. That's the way it's gonna be."

"Then you're all gonna be buried here," Jack told him.

Del pushed him aside and stepped out into the night. The men waited until the sounds of their horses had faded away.

"I recognized a couple of them," Charlie said. "The one with the scar on his face is called Gant. The skinny one is called Woody."

Matt said, "Reno's the one with the fancy spurs, and the one wearing the black vest was Dean. I think the stocky one with the bullethole in his hat is known as Porter."

"Stakes just went up in this game," Sam said. "Porter is supposed to be a bad one."

Matt cut his eyes to his blood brother. "You seen any of his graveyards, brother?"

"Can't say that I have."

Charlie slipped the loop back on the hammer of his right-hand Colt. "All them boys that just left is scum. Bounty hunters and back-shooters. And there's something else you can all bet on." The others waited. "They'll be more just like 'em comin' in."

There was no trouble of any kind for several days. No night-riding was reported, and no hands from the Lightning or Circle V came into town. Both Hugo and Blake came into town to send telegrams, but they caused no trouble and their guns were hung on the saddlehorn. They left as soon as they had concluded their business at the telegraph office.

Robert was brought into town in the bed of a wagon and got a room at the hotel. A Box H hand drove another wagon in with all of Robert's possessions. Pete had kicked him out of the house and told him never to return.

When the young man did leave the hotel, he walked with the aid of two canes and moved very slowly. Mostly he stayed in his room and remained in a laudanum-induced stupor.

Toward the end of the first peaceful week the town of Dale had seen in months, Denise Raner was brought into town, accompanied by her brother, Carl, and two Lightning hands. A wagon followed the riders and the buggy. Denise's belongings were piled in the bed.

Carl hung his guns on his saddlehorn, but those watching him knew he didn't like it. He escorted his sister into the hotel lobby, checked her in, and left without saying a word to anybody, including his sister.

Matt and Sam strolled over to the hotel. For the second time since their arrival, the brothers had been banned from dining or staying at the hotel by Dale, who was not speaking to them because of the terrible and according to Dale untrue and libelous accusations brought against him by the brothers. But he couldn't prevent lawmen from asking questions. And the desk clerk was scared to death of the famed gunfighters.

"Their father is footin' the bills," the desk clerk said. "Accordin' to what I was told, as soon as Robert is able to get around on his own, he's to leave this country and not come back. Same with Miss Raner. I don't know nothin' else, boys."

They walked to Juan's café. Victoria was up and working again, but the sparkle was gone from her eyes and she seldom smiled. Not even at Sam.

"Her *madre* and I are sending her down to Arizona to stay with relatives there," Juan said. "We think it's the best for her."

"I agree," Sam said. "When's she leaving?"

"This afternoon."

Sam got up to say his goodbyes to the young woman.

Juan sat down at the table with Matt and poured them both a tequila. "I hear that Señor Vernon has brought in gunfighters."

"Yeah. I'm afraid so."

"Then no one has learned anything from all this tragedy and bloodshed?"

Matt shook his head. "I guess not, Juan." He watched the man drink his tequila and stand up. "Where are you going?"

"To sharpen my knife."

Nineteen

The fragile peace in the area was broken that night by another raid on a small farmer and his family. The man and teenage son were killed, the mother and ten-year-old-girl managed to run into the woods and hide before their men were cut down by a hail of bullets. The house and barn was burned to the ground, all the livestock was killed, and the family dog was trampled to death under the steel-shod hooves of the raiders' horses.

The little girl was still holding the little dog, wrapped up in a piece of sacking, when Reed and his sons found her and her mother.

"All right, boys," Reed told his sons. "This is all I'm a-fixin' to take. They want war, they'll get war. Anybody ridin' a Circle V or Lightning-branded horse, blow 'em out of the saddle."

The lanky mountain-bred man and three of his sons found shovels and started digging graves, while Joe Reed rode into town for the sheriff, and for some blankets to wrap the bullet-riddled bodies of the father and son in. The remaining family members had lost everything. They had nothing but the night clothing they were wearing when the raiders struck.

A rider from the Box H rode up and took a look, his face tight with anger. "I'll go tell Pete and Miss Becky and Millie. They'll get some blankets and clothin' and food over here pronto, Reed."

"I'm beholden to you," Reed said.

"It'll end someday," the Box H man said. "Keep your powder dry, man."

Reed nodded his head and the puncher rode off.

The cowboy crossed the road just as Matt and Sam and the sheriff were riding up. The Reed boy was behind them with blankets and food. "It's bad," the puncher said. "They shot them dead and then rode their horses back and forth over the bodies. Farmers is here, they're gonna stay, so we best live with it and try to get on. This has got to stop."

"All the Box H hands feel that way?" Matt asked, already sensing the reply.

"Damn sure do!" the hand said with considerable heat. "This killin' of wimmin and children and children's little pets has got to stop. It's got to!"

"It will," Jack said. "It will." He rode off, his back stiff with anger.

Matt and Sam lingered with the Box H hand. "Would you be willing to ride in a posse?" Sam asked him.

"You call the time and I'll have twenty-five men ready to ride."

"We might do that," Matt told him.

"Anytime, Bodine. Just anytime at all."

"They've got to be killed," Dale said. "They know too much."

Chrisman nodded his head in agreement. "I never expected that girl to have the nerve to march in your office and demand a share. I figured she'd got it through her head that nobody believed their story."

"Oh, the people believed it all right. The law couldn't *prove* none of it was all that saved our butts."

"It has to be an accident."

"I know. Anything else would point directly at us. Any ideas?"

"How do you feel about losing a hotel?"

Dale stared at him. "They might escape before the flames reached their rooms."

"Not if someone paid them a visit and conked them on the head before the flames were lit."

"A good point. But who?"

"I'll take care of it all."

"When?"

"Tonight. Be sound asleep at midnight."

"I plan on it."

Matt and Sam began tracking the night riders. They had provisions for several days, and this time they planned on taking the fight to outlaws—no matter whose land they might be on.

Back at his place, Reed and his sons were cleaning their Springfield long rifles, loading up shotgun shells, and checking their pistols. Their farm was only a few miles from the farm where they'd helped bury the father and son hours back, so there was a pretty good chance they'd be the next on the list to be attacked. If so, the night riders were going to be in for a very sudden and deadly surprise.

Chrisman went to the rear of his saloon and began collecting old rags and scraps of aprons and towels. He found some packing and stuffed it and the rags in a big bag; it was bulky, but light. He did not want to use kerosene; the smell might linger, and that would be a dead giveaway. Then he decided, What the hell? The lamps were all kerosene.

Chrisman filled two jugs with the flammable liquid and hid rags and kerosene behind his saloon. It was an easy stroll through the alley to the rear of the hotel. Denise and Robert had the only two rooms downstairs—because of Robert's injuries, he could not climb the stairs. Chrisman knew the back door to the hotel was never locked—sometimes local gentlemen took ladies into the hotel by that route. So getting into the hotel would be the easy part. He planned on people thinking that Robert, in a laudanum-induced stupor, knocked over a lamp and set the place on fire.

Chrisman planned on the fire starting in Robert's room; with the doors closed, his room and Denise's would be a blazing inferno within minutes.

Chrisman chuckled. It was a fine plan. He had keys to both rooms, given him by Dale, so getting in would be easy.

Chrisman found himself actually looking forward to the night.

"We're on Lightning range now," Matt said, as they stopped to water their horses at the creek.

"And the tracks are leading straight to the ranch-house."

"They're not even making any attempt to hide them. It's gonna be the same old alibi again."

"Do we ride right up to the ranch?"

"Being brave is one thing, being plumb stupid is another."

"The latter is something you should know well," Sam said smugly.

Matt knocked his hat off his head and rode on.

About a mile further, the raiders had stopped and rested their horses. Cigarette butts littered the ground and several empty whiskey bottles were found, along with a bloody bandage.

"The man or his son got at least one of them before they overpowered him," Sam remarked. "And that's a lot of blood being lost there."

"Tracks cut due north from here," Matt said, pointing to the ground. "Most of them. All they're going to say is that these tracks leading from here to the ranchhouse were made by cowboys doing a day's work."

"True."

"So let's follow the tracks leading north."

It soon became evident to the brothers that the raiders were a mixed bunch of Lightning hands and probably men from Red Raley's gang of trash. About a dozen horsemen, over a span of several miles, broke off from the main bunch and headed toward the Lightning Arrow ranchhouse. By late that afternoon they were out of the county and they reined up and made camp. They took their deputy sheriff's badges from their shirts and stowed them away. They would be no good in another county. And, according to both Jack Linwood and Pete Harris, whose land extended into two counties, the sheriff up here was not only a jerk, but a crook to boot. He and his men were on the take and would do anything and shield anybody for enough money. They ran a protection racket and forced the merchants to pay them. The elections were always rigged, and the people of the county were afraid.

"We going into the town?" Sam asked, already knowing what his brother's reply would be.

Matt looked at him and grinned.

* * *

Chrisman conducted business as usual that evening and closed up his saloon at ten. He stood on the boardwalk and smoked a cigar, as was his custom, making sure he was seen doing nothing out of the ordinary. He finished his cigar, tossed it into the dirt of the street, stretched and yawned, then went back into the Cattle Club and locked the door and put out the lamps. He went upstairs to his quarters, puttered around for a time, then put out the lamps at eleven. The town was quiet.

Dressed in dark clothing, Chrisman slipped out the back of his saloon and picked up his deadly bags. He made his way to the rear of the hotel and carefully eased into the darkened hallway. He stood silent for a moment, listening for any movement. The place was asleep. He moved to the door to Denise's room and closed his hand around the knob. It turned. The haughty young lady had not even bothered to lock her door.

Then it came to him: she wasn't in this room, she was with Robert in the next room. He opened the door and looked in. Her bed not been slept in. He quickly spread some kerosene-soaked rags around and moved to Robert's room. Locked. Chrisman unlocked the door and looked in. The lamp was off, but he could see the young couple was asleep, sprawled atop the covers. An empty whiskey bottle was on the floor by Denise's side of the bed, an empty bottle of laudanum stood on the nightstand at Robert's side of the bed.

Chrisman walked to the bed and pulled a blackjack from his back pocket and struck Denise savagely on the head. Robert did not move. Chrisman walked to the young man and bashed him on the side of the head with the heavy cosh. He poured kerosene onto the bed and the dusty carpet, threw kerosene on the walls. He lit the rags and quickly backed out, closing the door. He ignited the rags in Denise's room and left the hotel, moving silently and swiftly back to his own quarters. He dropped his odious clothing in a tub of soapy water he'd prepared before he'd left and washed himself quickly. He was just getting into his nightshirt when he heard the excited shout.

"Fire! The hotel's on fire! Everybody out. Get the pumper, boys."

Chrisman pulled a robe over his nightclothes, put his feet into slippers, and ran down the stairs, throwing open the front door to his saloon and running out into the flame-licked night.

"Buckets!" he shouted. "Form a line here and start them buckets moving!"

Most of those guests on the second floor never had a chance. Only a few managed to jump out, breaking bones when they hit the street. The others died as the hotel's second-story collapsed inward. The frantic screaming ceased abruptly.

The men working the town's only pumper and the men and women of the bucket brigade concentrated on saving the buildings left and right of the blazing hotel, which they managed to do.

"Those poor people in there," Dale said, shaking his head sorrowfully. He was covered with soot and burned in several places, having made a big show of running into the flames to save people. Several men had to restrain both him and Chrisman from entering the inferno.

"Quite an actor," Charlie muttered to Jack.

"Yeah," the sheriff agreed. "Its almost as good as that show Bodine and Two Wolves put on."

"Four got out," Jimmy said, after working the crowd and taking a head-count.

"Robert and Denise?" Jack asked.

"No sign of them."

"They were on the ground floor; they should have been the first out," Charlie said. "Unless somebody planned that they wouldn't make it."

"Denise was drinkin' heavy and Robert was developin' a need for laudanum," Dewey pointed out. "They may have been so addled they didn't even know what was goin' on."

"I guess we'll never know," Jack said. "But the fire sure happened at a good time for Chrisman and Dale."

"It's gonna be a mess, pullin' them bodies out of there come mornin'," Charlie said. "I've had to do it more times than I like to think about."

"Yeah," Jack agreed. "Me, too. Let's set up watches so's the flames won't bust out again. Rest of us should try to get some sleep. It's gonna be grim in the mornin'."

"And Pete and Hugo have to be notified," Jimmy reminded them.

"Yeah," Jack said. "I'll tell Hugo. Jimmy, you ride for the Box H as soon as we know for sure. Charlie, you take the first watch. Dewey, relieve him at four. I'll assign other townspeople to stay with you."

Jack Linwood stared at the smoldering jumble of wreckage. The hotel had been full with traveling drummers and several women travelers taking a break from a tiring stagecoach ride. If the fire had been set deliberately, somebody was as cold-blooded as anyone Jack had ever seen.

He cut his eyes to Dale and Chrisman, now standing together on the boardwalk across the street, in front of the Red Dog. There was no doubt in his mind that one or both of them had set the fire. But he also knew he'd probably never be able to prove it. Jack was also very much aware that if he had been able to sleep that night, instead of rolling and tossing and turning and pounding the pillow, finally dressing and walking the town, he would be dead cooked meat in those smoldering ashes.

That made it a very personal matter for the sheriff.

Matt and Sam rode slowly into the tiny town, their hat brims pulled down low and their eyes taking in everything there was to see, which wasn't very much. The town was not as large as Dale, and there were several boarded-up buildings, those merchants having had quite enough of crooked law enforcement and moving on to a more pleasant location.

The brothers reined up in front of the saloon and swung down, automatically freeing their guns in leather. That action did not escape the eyes of a so-called deputy sheriff lounging in front of the sheriff's office.

"I think we got us a couple of randy ones," he said, walking to the open doorway, for the morning was warm.

The sheriff, a big pus-gutted man rapidly going to fat, heaved his bulk out of the chair and lumbered outside. He stared at the brothers' backs as they entered the saloon.

"Lawmen?" he asked the deputy.

"They wasn't wearin' no badges. I'll amble on over there and check out their shirts for pin marks."

He wouldn't find any. Matt and Sam had changed shirts that morning for that very reason.

"Where's Red and his boys?"

"Out of town, 'ceptin' for four of his bunch. They're over yonder in the saloon, havin' 'em an early morning beer."

"I'll go with you. Something 'bout them two bothers me. I can't put my finger on it."

"They're gunfighters," the deputy said. "They got the mark stamped all over 'em."

Matt and Sam ordered drinks, although neither of them wanted beer this early, and took up positions along the bar, at the end of it, facing the batwings. They both were conscious of the four hard-eyed men sitting at a corner table. The men were really giving the brothers the once-over.

"That's the one who was with Red when they met with Robert and Denise," Matt whispered.

"Yeah. I recognized him right off," Matt returned the whisper.

"What's all that whisperin' about up there?" one of the men at the table demanded, raising his voice.

Matt looked at him. "Mind your own business." He looked back at Sam and winked.

The other three men at the table laughed at that. "I reckon he told you, huh, Nelson?"

"I bet that's Nelson Willis," Matt whispered. "He's supposed to be good."

"I don't like people whisperin' neither," another man at the table said. "You two knock that off."

Sam looked at him. "Go to hell."

Nelson slapped the table with his hand and laughed. "How about that, Miller?"

"Miller?" Matt whispered. "That name doesn't ring a bell."

The sheriff and his deputy stepped inside. They walked to a table and sat down, waving off the bartender.

Matt whispered, "That sheriff is a slob. Did you see the food stains on his shirt?"

"Yes," Sam whispered.

"Hey!" the deputy hollered at the brothers. "Are you two in love or something?"

Matt and Sam had a good laugh at that.

"My deputy asked you a question," the sheriff said. "You two drifters better answer him."

The brothers ignored the man. Sam whispered, "The sheriff surely must know about the Raley gang."

"Sure. That's what Jack thinks. As far as I'm concerned, that makes him no better than them."

"Didn't Jack say this sheriff has raped several women in this county and then killed their husbands after they confronted him?"

"Yes."

"All right, you two," the sheriff lumbered to his boots. "I think we'd all better have a talk. Over to the jail, the both of you."

"I really don't feel like walking," Sam said, straightening up and facing the big slob. "If you have something you'd care to discuss with us, this place will do just fine."

"Well, well, Les," another of the four outlaws said. "Ain't he the hoity-toity one?"

"The lard-butt's name must be Les," Matt said in a normal tone. "Les of what? His belly's hanging over his belt and his butt's so big he probably has a tent-maker sew his britches."

Matt and Sam cracked up laughing.

Sheriff Les cursed and lumbered across the room, the floor shaking each time a boot came crashing down. "I'll break your back, you damn lousy drifter!" Les bellowed.

Matt waited until the last second, then sidestepped and grabbed up a piano stool. Les had lumbered around to face him just as Matt swung the heavy stool. The stool hit the sheriff flush in the mouth and pearlies went flying as the big man's eyes rolled back in his head. He staggered back and his momentum sent him crashing into tables and chairs. He fell through the big front window of the saloon and landed on the boardwalk, out cold.

Matt turned to face the Raley gang. "All right, you baby-killing, worthless pieces of coyote crap. My name's Matt Bodine and this is my brother, Sam Two Wolves. Stand up, drag iron, and get ready to kiss the devil's butt!"

Twenty

Everybody in the room reached for their guns, all except the bartender. He hit the floor behind the bar and stayed down. As far as he was concerned, Bodine and Two Wolves could kill off every member of the sheriff's department—including the sheriff—and the world would be a better place by far.

Sam drilled the deputy through the shoulder, the .44 slug turning the small man around and depositing him on the barroom floor. He lay there groaning.

The four gunslicks yelled, jumped up cussing, and dragged iron.

Matt's first shot took one dead center in his forehead. The man sat back down in the chair he'd just vacated and put his dead head on the table, both hands dangling by his boots.

Sam drilled another in the brisket and doubled the man over. Matt shot the third one just as he was turning, the slug tearing through him and knocking him down, killing him. The fourth member tried for the shattered window. Matt and Sam fired together, their slugs striking true. The gang member cried out and landed on top of the sheriff, who was just struggling to get to his boots. Both men went crashing back to the boardwalk.

The brothers punched out empties and reloaded while the gunsmoke was still swirling around them. The bartender was peeping over the edge of the bar.

"I hear tell that sheriff's as crooked as a snake," Matt spoke to the wide-eyed man. "Is that right?"

"You got that right. Is the bum dead?"

"No. Not yet. But if he gets up with a gun in his hand he's gonna be."

"Good," the bartender said, and dropped back down to the floor.

"God bless you boys!" a man called out from the street. "But you'd better watch out for Les's deputies. They're all as bad as he is."

"Where are they?" Sam called.

He got his answer when a shot rang out and the citizen slumped to the street, a smoking hole in the back of his coat.

Matt walked to the batwings, pushed them open, and lifted his .44. He plugged the deputy who'd killed the citizen, the slug stopping the man in his tracks and sending him twisting to the street, the pistol dropping from his hands.

"The rooftops, boys!" a woman yelled.

A deputy lifted a rifle and took aim at the woman standing in the doorway of the general store. Matt and Sam fired as one. The rifle dropped to the awning, bounced, and fell to the street. The deputy fell right through the awning, his left boot catching on a rafter and holding him there head-down, dangling and dead.

The shoulder-shot deputy staggered out, a gun in his left hand and an oath on his lips. Matt stepped out of his lurching way and tripped the man, sending him stumbling out into the street. His own people filled full of lead.

"Jesus!" came the cry. "We kilt Benny."

Matt pulled the sheriff to his knees and stuck a gun under the man's chin and cocked it. "Tell your men to throw down their guns or you die right here, right now."

The sheriff's mouth was busted and bleeding, but he managed to get the words out, for all the good it did him.

"You go to hell, Les!" a deputy said. "Who cares if your brains gets blowed out? More money for us."

"Real loyal group of men you have, Sheriff," Sam said, after they dragged the sheriff back into the saloon. "Faithful and true right to the end, I'd say."

Matt dragged the barkeep to his feet. "Get some rope," he told him.

With the sheriff hog-tied, the brothers went head-hunting, leaving out the back door and walked through the alley. A woman held out a platter of hot buttered biscuits to them through an open window.

"It's little enough I can do if you boys clean out this den of thieves and murderers. There's not a decent man among those who call themselves lawmen."

"We'll do our best," Sam assured her, as the brothers partook generously of the treat. They walked on, guns in their right hands and their left hands filled with biscuits.

A hard-faced man with a Remington in each hand stepped around the corner of a building. His eyes widened with shock at the sight of the brothers, munching and chewing, melted butter dripping from their hands.

"What the hell . . . !" he said.

Matt laid the barrel of his .44 across the man's face

and knocked him reeling. He whacked him again for good measure and tossed his guns into the weeds.

The brothers slipped into the space between buildings where the deputy had popped out of and made their way to the street. A man with a rifle spotted them and yelled, "There they are!"

Matt winged him. The man yelped and dropped his rifle. It clattered on the boardwalk. His mistake was in reaching for it. Sam shot him clean and the lawless, on-the-take deputy sprawled on the boards. He would take no more.

"God damn you!" the shout came from a vacant store across the street. "Who are you people?"

"Matt Bodine and Sam Two Wolves!" the barkeep hollered.

All was quiet for several moments, then the sounds of galloping horses came to the brothers. The last two deputies had made the wisest of choices and were hauling their ashes.

They pulled the deputy with a knot on his noggin to his boots. "You want a biscuit?" Sam asked him. "I'm full."

The man cussed him. "I demand a trial!" he said. "I think it's going to be a very short one," Sam replied.

The citizens of the small town were tossing a rope around a tree limb when the brothers swung into the saddle. They had the mayor, the sheriff, and one deputy up on horses, their hands tied behind their backs. None of the men looked very happy. All of them gave Matt and Sam a thorough cussing.

"Bless you boys!" a man called. "You're welcome back anytime."

Matt and Sam waved at him and rode out of town. They had decided to return to Dale. The trail of the out-

laws was just too cold to follow. But they had cut the
size of the Raley gang down by four.

The stink of the remains of the charred hotel was
strong as the brothers reached the edge of town. They
rode slowly by the burned-out hotel. Clean-up had
begun, and bodies were still being pulled from the rubble. The brothers stepped down from the saddle and
handed the reins to the liveryman with instructions to
rub the horses down and feed them. The brothers walked
up the street to the sheriff's office.

Pete Harris, Hugo Raner, and some of their crews
were standing on the boardwalk across the street from
the ruins. The men were hard-faced and grim-appearing.
Deputies stood between them, so the men could not get
too close to one another. Pete spoke; Hugo did not.

"It was set deliberately," Charlie said. "I sniffed out
the kerosene. Real strong smell near the back of the
hotel. Some of the rags didn't burn. Looks like the fire
was set in the rooms of Robert and Denise."

"How many died?" Sam asked.

"We still don't know for sure," Jack said. "Only a
few made it out. They had to jump from the second
floor. One of them is in bad shape. Doc says it's a miracle the man is still alive. His back is broke."

Matt told the lawmen what had gone down in the
county north of them.

Jack smiled. "Ol' Les got hisself hung, huh? Good.
Couldn't have happened to a more deservin' person.
Them folks up yonder will elect them a sheriff proper
and Raley and his bunch will have to hunt a new place
to roost."

"And that'll be here in this county?" Sam asked.

"I 'magine. That'll make it some easier for us to find them and get rid of them."

Charlie had walked over to the ranch owners and joined Jimmy in keeping the two factions apart.

"What's goin' on over there?" Matt asked.

"Raner's blowin' off steam," Jack said. "Blamin' it all on Pete and the sheepmen and farmers."

"The fire?" Sam asked.

"Ever'thing," Jack replied. "I didn't try to enforce the gun law. Even Pete was actin' like he might bow up at that. I talked it over with the town council, and they said to hell with it. Ever'body in town is armed, so I couldn't very well set no double standard."

"That trash son of yours is responsible for this, too," Raner yelled at Pete. "He corrupted my good girl."

Pete said nothing in reply. His eyes were full of sorrow as he looked across the street at the rubble.

"Have they found Robert and Denise yet?" Sam asked.

"Not yet," Simmons said, taking a break from the clean-up work. "But they'll be pulling out what's left of them within the hour, I imagine. That's the last section."

As the charred boards and rafters were pulled away, they were watered down and then loaded into wagons, to be transported outside of town and dumped.

"Here they are!" a man shouted, then he staggered out of the ruins, sick to his stomach at what he'd just seen.

Raner walked across the street. Pete stayed away, not wanting to view the terrible sight. Their kids had given the men all sorts of grief; but they were still flesh and blood, no matter what they'd done.

"Where's Blake?" Matt asked, after looking around and not spotting any Circle V hands.

"Good question," Jack replied. "He ain't been seen in three days, and neither has any of his hands. Both Raner and Blake has hired on more men at fightin' wages. It's gonna blow wide open any hour and there ain't nothin' none of us can do about it except stand back and let her bang. Then we can go in and pick up the pieces."

"And help bury the dead," Sam added.

"Yeah."

Hugo Raner broke down and wept as what was left of his daughter was removed from the jumble of charred wood. He got control of himself and pointed a finger at Jack Linwood. "You want war?" he screamed. "By God, I'll give you war! There won't be a goddamn nester or sheepman left alive in this county. I swear on the bones of this dead girl of mine, I'll kill ever' damn one of them."

"No farmer or sheepman started this fire, Raner," the sheriff called across the expanse of street. "You know that."

"No, I don't know that!" Raner yelled. "What I *do* know is that we didn't have no trouble in this county 'til them damn nesters and sheepmen come in. *That's* when the trouble started. And *that's* who will pay!" He pointed at Pete. "And you'll pay with them, Pete. You sucked up to them and took their side. That makes you no friend of mine."

"I lost a child in there, too, Hugo," Pete called.

"Damn lousy no-good is what you lost!" Hugo yelled.

"Good, good," Dale said, a smile on his face as he sat listening through the open window of his bank office. "That's the kind of talk I like to hear."

"Now we just sit back and let them kill off each other," Chrisman said. "Then we go in and pick up the gold and silver and live like kings for the rest of our lives."

"Yes," said Hugo. One of us will, he thought.

Chrisman smiled. One of us will, he thought.

Raner continued cussing farmers, sheepmen, Bodine, Two Wolves, Pete Harris, and Jack Linwood as his daughter's charred body was wrapped in a blanket and placed in the bed of a wagon. He got his horse and swung into the saddle.

He rode over to where Matt and Sam were standing with a knot of men and women on the boardwalk. He opened his mouth to hurl more threats and Jack cut him off short.

"Don't say no more about what you're gonna do, Hugo. You're carryin' a load of grief now, and you're sayin' things that I just don't believe you mean. Take your daughter and go on back home. Get drunk. Shoot at rocks and trees and the sky. Get it out of your system. But don't threaten me no more this day. Get out of here."

Raner swung his horse's head and galloped out of town, his crew right behind him, the death wagon rolling slowly along.

"I'll go get my boy now," Pete said.

"Did you bring a wagon?" Matt asked.

The rancher shook his head. "We'll bury him here in the town cemetery. Now. Today. No big service. Get a box ready, Shorty. Then go fetch the preacher."

"Right, boss," the foreman said, and walked off toward the undertaker's place.

Matt and Sam walked across the street with the rancher, both men pulling on gloves. They helped Pete pull out the remains of his son—identified by a ring on his right hand—and place the body in a blanket. It was gruesome work and the men were relieved when it was over and done with.

Pete looked at them, and nodded his thanks, and the brothers walked to their shack to clean up.

The brothers bathed, shaved, and dressed in clean clothing, then strolled back up the street to the livery. They made sure their horses were getting all the grain they wanted, then walked to Juan's café for something to eat. Doc Lemmon walked in and joined them.

"There is a terribly cold-blooded killer in this town," the doctor said. "I agree with Charlie Starr: that fire was deliberately set . . . set knowing that innocent men and women would die a horrible death."

"Oh, it was either Chrisman or Dale or somebody they hired," Sam said. "They felt they had to get rid of Robert Harris and Denise Raner. Sooner or later those two would have become a thorn in their sides."

"Yeah, I've always believed that Robert was a little too quick to confess. He was holding something back. What, I don't know."

"Whatever it is, he's taking it to the grave," Doc Lemmon said.

"Yes," Sam said. "And that's the way Dale and Chrisman planned it."

"I wonder who else they want silenced forever?" the doctor mused aloud.

As before, something didn't add up in Matt's brain. Something was very wrong, and it was nagging at him. It was something that had happened this day, or something he'd seen or heard, but he couldn't pin it down. But it would come to him, he was sure of that.

The only thing that bothered him was that it might come too late to do any good. Or to save a life.

Maybe his or Sam's.

Twenty-one

Raner scarcely got his daughter in the ground before he struck and struck hard. He personally led an attack on a farmhouse and wiped out every person there. He and his men shot every hog, cow, horse, chicken, and dog, then burned the house and outbuildings. And Raner and his men made no effort to hide their tracks. They led straight back to the Lightning range.

"Yeah," Rusty the foreman told Matt and Sam the next morning. "We was all out for a ride last night. We seen that damn nester's place go up in flames, and then we rode over and seen what had happened. Then we come back to the spread."

"Why didn't you report it?" Matt asked.

" 'Cause I hope ever' damn hog-farmer and sheep-man in this county gets the same treatment, that's why, Bodine."

Matt and Sam could do little except stare at the man. The coldness in the foreman shocked them both. This was not some wild-eyed savage, not some person brought up in a totally different culture, but a man who, probably, was brought up much the same as any other western born-and-bred person. What had changed him into this child-killer? Neither man had a clue.

"I'll tell you this, Rusty," Matt said, his words hard as flint. "If I wasn't wearing this badge on my chest, I'd kill you right now."

Rusty paled under his tan. "I told you we rode by. That's all we done."

"Wrong, Rusty," Sam told him. "The boy you bastards trampled lived long enough to identify a half a dozen of you scum. He recognized Buck because of his missing front teeth. He recognized your mustang. He saw Hugo Raner in person. Oh, don't worry, Rusty. The little boy died. So his word won't go in a court of law. But you people won't kill off all the farmers and sheepmen. It's backfired on you, Rusty. Now, wherever you go, the word's gone out among the farmers. Any hand riding a Circle V- or Lightning-branded horse . . . they're going to shoot you out of the saddle. Or I will," he added softly.

"God damn it, we was here first!" Rusty flared. "We tamed this land. We fought Injuns and outlaws and storms and floods. The cattlemen *belong* here."

"But there's two things you didn't do, Rusty," Matt told him. "And that's where cattlemen like me and Sam here, and my dad and lots of others, got it on you. You didn't file on it, and you didn't buy it. Now you think you can keep it at the point of a gun. You might for a while; but not for long. Decent people are not going to put up with the killing of women and children. But you wouldn't know anything about that, Rusty, because you don't work for a decent man, and if you ever had a streak of decency in you, it's long gone."

"You get off Lightning range and you go to hell, Bodine!" Rusty turned his horse and rode away.

"I have a plan," Sam said, with a very wicked smile on his lips.

"Let's hear it, brother."

A moment later, both men rode back toward town, both of them laughing.

Nearly every citizen in town turned out for it—with the exception of two—and Pete Harris and all his family and crew rode in, as did Louis Longmont, all the sons and daughters of sheepmen and farmers, and all the hands from the Spur, Horseshoe, Bar K, and Double D. By the end of the day, three hundred and seventy people had filed on and now owned fifty-nine thousand, two hundred acres of Circle V and Lightning range.

"They done *what?*" Hugo screamed.

Blake Vernon repeated what he'd been told.

"They can't do that!" Hugo bellowed.

"Well, they done it," Blake told him. "Last week. And every man, woman, and child who can carry a board and swing a hammer is provin' up on it right this minute."

"You bring your hands with you?"

"No. Just a few."

"Well, hell, man! Go get them ready and let's go show them people who's boss." He jumped up and reached for his gunbelt, swinging around his waist.

"Sit down," Blake said softly. "Don't be a fool. This was planned out careful. There's two U. S. Marshals in this area out of the Denver office. We show any kind of force and we're in big trouble with the U. S. Government. They'll send troops in here. And that is something I sure don't want."

Hugo Raner picked up a whiskey bottle and hurled it across the room. Then he sat down in his chair and cussed.

"It's all coming apart!" Chrisman said, mopping his sweating face with a handkerchief. "It's out of control! Getting rid of two or three people on the land is one thing, but Jesus Christ, Dale, now we've got over three *hundred* people squatting."

"You're giving me a headache, Chrisman," Dale said. "Please shut up and sit down. We have to think."

Chrisman sat down, but he didn't shut up. "It was a dumb move on our part not to file with the rest of the town."

"I realize that now. But they haven't filed on the land where the vein runs—north or south of the river. Our plan can still work."

"On top of everything else, Dale, now we have a Pinkerton man in town from St. Louis."

"What the hell does *he* want?"

"The remains of two people who died in the fire, he says."

"But they were all shipped back by train. I personally gave money for that."

"Obviously, two weren't. Why else would he be here?"

"It's just a mix-up. The bodies are in some train depot somewhere. My God, they must be stinking by now."

"Well, he's sure asking a lot of questions."

"He's mistaken; he's looking in the wrong spot. Everybody who died in that fire was identified and either buried or shipped back to their families. Forget him. He'll soon move on."

"What do we do about the land-filing?"

Dale shrugged. "Nothing we can do, Chrisman. It's just a ploy, that's all. Most of those people won't prove up their sections. Conditions will settle down. We just have to wait and be careful."

The U. S. Marshals stayed for a few days, then pulled out when no trouble came from Blake Vernon or Hugo Raner. The two ranchers waited forty-eight hours and then hit a homesteader and his family hard. They burned the house and barn and thought they'd killed everyone there. But the father had put two of his younger kids down in the root cellar. Rescuers from the Box H heard their faint cries while digging through the rubble and frantically dug the boy and girl out.

After Pete got the kids calmed down, the boy said, "Pa said to tell anyone who come after us that it was Raner and Blake. Is our ma and pa dead?"

"Yes, son," Pete said gently. "I'm afraid so."

But the kids were cried out for this day. They took the news stoically.

Pete washed the girl's face with a wet cloth and smiled at her. "How'd you both like to come live with me and my wife?" he asked with a gentle smile. "We got a big house and plenty of room. How about it?"

The boy and girl nodded their heads, a solemn expression on their faces. The burly rancher swept them up in his arms and carried them to a wagon driven by one of his hands.

"Take them home, Don," he said. "Tell the wife we just got a brand new family. I'll be along directly."

"Right, boss," Don said with a grin. He handed the kids a sackful of Millie's doughnuts. "Little something to snack on," he told them, then clucked at the team.

Shorty walked up. "We got to stop this, boss. We got to do a little night-ridin' of our own and put an end to this misery and grief. Blake and Hugo have gone slap-dab crazy."

"If we do that, we can't let the sheriff in on it. Linwood's turned into a damn fine lawman and he'd put us in jail."

Shorty grinned. "I know two lawmen who wouldn't."

Pete smiled. "Yeah. I do, too. Send one of the boys for them. Tell them Millie's cookin' supper. That'll get them movin' for sure."

"Jack'll get word of it and hit the ceiling," Matt said, over coffee and cigars after supper.

They sat on the front porch, watching the last rays of sun dissolve into purple twilight.

"But if we do it right, we can hit them hard and get out fast and clean," Pete said. "We can hit Hugo first. I think the farmers will go for it, especially Reed and those sharpshooting sons of his."

"We can do it without losing a man, too," Sam said.

"Oh?" Pete looked at him. "You got a plan?"

"Yes. We lay siege against the ranch and put some terror into them. We lay back three, four hundred yards with rifles and snipe at anything that moves."

Pete nodded his head. "I got me a whole closet full of Springfield and Spencer rifles. But Lord, there ain't none of them been fired in two or three years."

"How about ammunition?" Matt asked.

"Two or three cases of it. We don't have any worries there, although some of it's so old we might have some misfires."

"Let's get to planning," Matt said. "We'll come out tomorrow about lunchtime and start drifting toward

Lightning a few at a time. Come late afternoon, we'll all be in place. Let's get those Springfields out and start cleaning them up."

One was gone from the rack.

Pete sighed. "I guess now we know who the sniper was," he said. "I apologize, boys. I never thought to look in here after the sniper struck. It just never dawned on me that it could be Robert. Come to think of it, the day Blake was grazed on the head, most of the hands were out with the herds. Robert could have used Coop's paint pony." He shook his head. "Well, that's past us. Come on, let's get to work."

On the ride back to town, Sam said, "Do you think the sniper was Robert?"

"I don't know. I think Robert would have been smarter than to use a rifle from his dad's gun closet. But the only one who knows is in the grave. Those Springfields were sure dirty."

"Two hours to clean them," Sam agreed. "But they'll be invaluable tomorrow. Hugo and his nightriders have nothing that will reach that far."

"We hope. We'll know tomorrow."

Charlie and Jack watched the brothers ride out the next morning. "They tell you where they were goin'?" Jack asked.

"Not a peep to me. And that's unusual for them two."

"They're up to something. Trail them, Charlie. See which way they go at the crossroads. Then get back to me."

"You think they might be plannin' on doin' some night-ridin' of their own agin Blake and Hugo?"

"It wouldn't surprise me none. And it wouldn't surprise me none to find Pete Harris right in the middle of it."

"And if it proves out to be?" Charlie asked.

"I don't know," Jack admitted. "I just don't know."

Twventy-two

Charlie reported back to the sheriff. "They're headin' for Box H range. Any hands from there been in today?"

"No. Not a one. You think it's about to pop tonight?"

Jack hesitated. The memory of dead farmers' kids and abused women and trampled farm families and sheepmen filled his head. Orphaned children, numb with shock over seeing their parents killed, drifted before his eyes. He took a deep breath. "No, Charlie. I think those boys are goin' out there to have supper and maybe Bodine is gonna spark that Millie some. That's what I think. I don't want any deputy outside of the town limits tonight. We'll just stay close here, in case we're needed."

Charlie chuckled. "That's what I was gonna suggest myself. Maybe play some checkers and hit the sack early."

"Sounds like a real fine idea to me. I think I'll eat early at Juan's and head on back to my new quarters; do a little work there. That new school teacher, Mary? She's comin' by tonight to help me hang some curtains.

And Charlie, I don't want to be bothered unless it's a real emergency. You know what I mean? Like if the President of the U-nited States comes to town, or something like that."

Charlie smiled. "Yeah. I know just what you mean, Jack."

"I think I'll go down to Simmons and see if them curtains Mary picked out come in."

"See you around, Jack."

Charlie sat down on the bench in front of the office. He had him a hunch that either Hugo Raner or Blake Vernon and their hands was gonna be in for a long night.

Hugo Raner stepped out on his front porch for an after-supper cup of coffee and a smoke. He sat down. Still had about two hours of light left. He reached for his cup, which sat on a small table by his chair, and the cup exploded into a hundred pieces; hot coffee lashed his hand. Hugo hit the porch floor belly-down.

Rifle fire from long-barreled Springfields slammed into and through the windows of the bunkhouse, sending hands to the floor, scrambling for their guns. Rusty was caught between his foreman's quarters and his personal outhouse; but the outhouse was much closer. He made a dash for the privy he'd just left.

Rusty made it just in time; a .45-caliber slug from a Springfield hissed wickedly past his head, so close he could feel the heat. Rusty flattened out on the cigarette-butt littered floor and cussed as slugs began slamming through the walls of the outhouse.

Hugo made it back inside his house and crawled to his gun closet. His Springfield was gone. "Damn it!" he yelled. "Who took my long-distance shooter?"

"Not me," his son Carl said. The boy was kneeling on the floor, his six-guns in his hands.

"Put them damn fool things up," father told son. "Hell's fire, boy, can't you hear the bark of them rifles? They're Springfield breech-loaders. They can shoot a damn mile!"

"Well, what the hell are we gonna do?" the young man asked.

"Do? Keep our heads down. That's Pete and his boys out there." A slug shattered a window and smashed into a lamp. The smell of kerosene became strong in the room. "Pete used to collect them things. Hell, the Army still uses 'em for their infantry."

"Pa? I know where that Springfield is. Hubby's got it."

"Hubby?"

"You 'member I told you I thought I seen him stealin' a broom from here a couple of months ago? That wasn't no broom; that was your old Springfield."

"But Hubby couldn't be the sniper. Blake nearly got shot right between the eyes hisself."

"Maybe he beat the fool again. You know how Hubby is. He just likes to kill."

"Could be you're right." Hugo got him a Winchester and levered a round into the chamber.

"That ain't gonna reach no half a mile either, Pa," the young man said. There was raw hatred toward his father in his eyes.

"It makes me feel better," Hugo grumbled.

"Maybe Red and his boys will hear the gunfire and come on the run?" *And maybe you'll catch a slug right between your eyes.*

"Maybe. Since they got run out of Les's county they move 'tween here and Blake's spread. I don't know for sure where they are right now."

A slug smashed through the front door and roared down the hall to the kitchen. It clanked into a hanging cookpot and went howling around and around inside the pot until it lost momentum.

"Pa? This could go on all night," son said to father.

"I know," Hugo said disgustedly.

"Good move, you getting Reed and his boys in on this," Matt said to Shorty. "They got one man pinned down in the outhouse and are slowly shooting the place to pieces."

"That's Rusty," the foreman said. "I was lookin' through field glasses when he made a run for the privy. There ain't no better place than an outhouse for him to meet his Maker, 'cause he's shore a real craphead."

Laughing, Matt took a Springfield and a bandolier of ammunition and slowly worked his way into a better position. He figured he was about five hundred yards from the main house. He'd be well in range if any of the hands and hired guns had Spencers. Matt loaded up and flipped up the rear sight, pulling the 1873 military model Springfield to his shoulder. Movement by the bunkhouse had alerted him.

He wasn't real sure, but it looked like somebody's foot was exposed. He'd soon find out. He sighted in and pulled the trigger. It was a narrow miss, but it was close enough to force the Lightning hand to get his foot out of the way and for Matt to adjust the rear sight.

To see how true the rifle was, Matt sighted in the bucket hanging over the well. He blew a hole right through the bucket. Satisfied, he squirmed around and made his nest more comfortable. He looked for targets.

In the outhouse, Rusty was getting desperate. He'd jerked the two-hole seat off to give him some better protection, but the slugs were punching right through the old wood. He'd soon be dead if he didn't do something. He sighed, knowing he had to get down in that pit so the earth would protect him.

The foreman wormed his way the short distance to the opening and slipped down into the pit, hanging onto the edge with all his might, and fighting the odor as he dangled. A slug plowed through the walls and very nearly took off one of Rusty's fingers. He yelped and lost his grip. Hollering, he fell the short distance into the very odious darkness. Rusty landed with a splash. He was now safe from bullets. He was also waist-deep.

On the floor in his fine house, Hugo looked around him at the damage the long-distance shooters were doing. His fine imported pendulum clock had taken a direct hit, the expensive works stopped forever by a slug. The china cabinet was a mess, the fine china shattered by lead.

"Carl!'" he said. "Get word to that bunch of gunslingers we brung in from Texas to start earnin' their pay. We can't wait for Red to show up." (Red wasn't going to show up. Red was not only taking money from Hugo, he was also on Mayor Dale's payroll and at the moment was busy rustling Hugo's cattle.) "Holler for 'em to make a run for the brush behind the bunkhouse and work their way into the timber where them snipers is hidin'. Do it, boy."

Carl passed the message and Del Monroe's bunch made a break for the brush. The first to try it got turned around and around like a top as several riflemen sighted him in and cut him down. The hired gun lay dead only a few yards from the back door of the bunkhouse.

"Halp!" Rusty hollered.

"Where's that comin' from, boy?" Hugo asked his son.

"I can't tell. Somewhere over yonder by the privy, I think."

"Get me outta here!" Rusty squalled.

Hugo raised his head and a slug from a Springfield just missed his noggin, the bullet tearing a gouge out of the expensive dining room table Hugo—at his wife's urgings—had brought in from Pennsylvania.

"Damn!" the rancher swore in helpless disgust, his nose buried in a rug.

A second gun-handler rushed from the bunkhouse, lead howling and popping and snapping all around him. He made the brush and went belly-down on the ground.

A third hired gun went down, a bullet in his leg. He crawled behind a tree and tried to shrink.

Two more guns that Hugo had brought in from Nevada made the brush.

Now the situation had changed slightly. But the men from the Box H still held the upper hand by far.

"Pa?" Carl called from the rear of the house.

"What is it now?"

"Come dark, they might try to burn the house."

Hugo hadn't thought of that. The boy was right—for a change. But the attackers would have to get real close for that, and Hugo doubted that Pete—and he was sure it was Pete and his hands, along with some nesters—would try that.

"Halp!" the faint shout overrode the firing.

"That man sounds desperate," Hugo said. "He must really be in a world of crap." At the time, Hugo had no idea how true his words were.

One of Pete's hands, with a wicked sense of humor, was concentrating his fire on the huge dinner bell mounted by the side of the house. Once a minute he rang the bell from a thousand yards away. It was beginning to get on Hugo's nerves.

"Halp!" Rusty hollered.

Clang!

"That's Rusty, Pa," Carl called. "He must be up to his knees in trouble."

Further than that.

"Damn it!" Hugo muttered.

Clang!

"Damn you, Pete!" Hugo screamed. He had worked his way to a window, but wisely stayed close to the wall. I'll kill you for this."

"And I'll kill you too!" Carl yelled.

Hugo shook his head. Sometimes he felt his son was about on a level with Hubby.

Clang!

The Nevada gunslinger on Hugo's payroll had worked his way deep into the timber in front of the ranchhouse. He was grinning as he made his way forward, his hands filled with Colts.

"Pphsst!" the sound came from behind him.

The gunslick turned just in time to catch the buttplate from a Springfield on the side of his jaw. He hit the earth out cold and with his jaw broken. Joe Reed took the man's gunbelt and guns. Then he worked his boots off and stripped him right down to bare skin. He left him naked on the ground. As an afterthought, Joe tossed the man's hat down beside him. It wasn't right to take a man's hat.

Sam was concentrating his fire on the gate to the corral. He was very careful not to hit a horse, but he had shattered the wooden gate latch with careful fire. Now he went to work on the hinges. At this distance he wasn't always sure he'd hit the hinges, but he was certain he was accurate about half the time. Sam carefully sighted in and pulled the trigger. The gate crashed open and the horses were off and running for anywhere that would get them away from the booming of guns and the snapping of flying lead.

The first gunfighter to make the brush from the bunkhouse bellied down in the tall grass and sparse timber and tried to locate a target. He caught movement out of the corner of one eye and rolled to one side.

Coop was about twenty-five feet away, both hands filled with guns. The gunslick lifted his rifle just as Coop cut loose. The gunhandler didn't know it, but Coop couldn't hit a mountain with a cannon at point-blank range. But what he *could* do was fill the air with lead flying in all directions.

"Jesus Christ!" the hired gun hollered, and began frantically rolling. He rolled off the edge of a slope and kept on rolling, losing his rifle, his six-guns, and his hat on the long roll down to where the cook dumped the garbage. He landed in a pile of fermenting boiled cabbage, rotting, fly-infested meat, and assorted odds and ends of discarded food. He was just about in as sad a shape as Rusty.

Clang!

Coop had reloaded and was lying on the crest of the ridge, firing at the weaponless gunslick slipping and sliding and cussing and falling down as he tried to extricate himself from the stinking piles of garbage. Everytime he thought he was free, Coop would accidentally come close with lead and he would have to belly down in the mess.

Another hired gun who had safely exited the bunkhouse found himself facing Pete Harris. Pete put two rounds of .45's in the gunfighter's belly and assured the good citizens of the West that the man would never again hire out his guns.

Quite by accident, all the men behind the Springfields fired at the ranchhouse, front and back. One slug sent splinters into Carl's face and another slug grazed Hugo's right buttocks, bringing a roar of pain from the man—more shock and anger than pain, for the wound was little more than a scratch.

The rifle fire was then directed at the bunkhouse, where most of Hugo's hands were still huddled, pinned down hard. One heavy slug struck the stovepipe and tore it loose, sending clouds of soot drifting all over the place. Another slug knocked a leg loose and sent the stove toppling over. The door opened and red-hot coals spilled onto the floor, igniting a pile of dirty clothes.

"Fire!" a Lightning hand yelled.

"Fire at what?" a hired gun snarled.

"No, you igit! The bunkhouse is on fire!"

A hand jumped up and a slug caught him in the shoulder and knocked him flat on the floor. The men crawled on their hands and knees to the smoking fire and beat at it with their hats until someone located a bucket of water and put out the flames.

"I'll be damned if I'll die like this!" a Lightning hand yelled, and ran for the door. He made it about ten feet before rifle fire spun him around and sent him to the unknown.

"Help!"

Clang!

"Start pulling back," Pete sent the word up and down the line of men. "I think we've made our point for this afternoon."

Hugo and son and hired guns and Lightning hands

stayed down for ten minutes after the firing had ceased. The first man to enter the clearing was the gunslick from the garbage pit. Coop had fired probably fifty rounds at him and missed all fifty times. But the gunhand was scared out of his wits and stinking like nothing anybody had ever smelled . . . however, all that was to change in about five minutes.

"Halp!" Rusty's cry was growing weaker. "Somebody get a rope and get me out of here."

"We got bad wounded over here," Tulsa yelled from the bunkhouse door.

The naked gunhand with the busted jaw came staggering into the clearing, holding his hat over his privates.

"Good God!" Hugo said from the bullet-pocked front porch. What the hell happened to you?"

"Halp!" Rusty hollered.

The naked gunhand mumbled his reply. His jaw was swollen so badly the words could not be understood.

"Somebody help me over here!" Buck called from the doorless and bullet-shattered privy. "We got to haul Rusty outta the pit. He's done fell in."

Carl appeared by his father's side, his face bleeding from the splinters. "You done been shot in the ass, Pa," he said.

"I know," Hugo said wearily.

Inside the house, the chandelier gave it up and fell crashing to land on the expensive dining room table.

"I'm gonna kill that goddamn Pete Harris," Hugo swore.

Rusty almost made it. But his hands were so slick and slimy just as he reached the lip of the privy floor he lost his grip on the rope and fell back whence he'd come. He surfaced, gasping for air.

Clint leaned over and lowered a fresh rope. "Tie this one around you, Rusty," he said. "We'll haul you out. Just give us time to back off about fifty feet."

"Pa?" Carl said.

"What do you want now?" Hugo asked.

"The bunkhouse is on fire."

Twenty-three

Blake Vernon stood gazing out into the darkness as he stood on his front porch, enjoying the coolness of the night. It was a pleasant night, but his mind was troubled. He had finally gotten it through his head that he and Hugo were fighting a losing battle. They weren't going to win against the nesters and the sheepmen. Not now, not ever. There would always be cattlemen fighting farmers and sheepmen, he reckoned, but as far as he was concerned, his part in the war was over.

He had told his hands that over supper and then fired all the gunhands he'd just hired and told them to git. They had packed up and were gone just after dark. He had also told Dixon, Jody, and Burl that if they'd had anything to do with raping that Mexican girl, they'd best get gone, too. They went right behind the gunhands.

Now he was down to sixteen hands. But roundup was over and he could easily get by with that number.

He sat down as the cook brought out a pot of coffee and cups and Frisco, his foreman, walked over and took a seat on the porch. "Boss, I've done some terrible things in my life, and I reckon I'll go to Hell for what we done to them nesters and sheepmen, but I'm glad it's over. I ain't got no use for nesters and I shore don't like sheep, but I am glad them gunhands is gone and this war is over for us."

"I am too, Frisco. Where did all the hands go?"

"Into town to celebrate. Don't worry, they'll behave. I told 'em that any who got in trouble with the law would lose their jobs."

Standing in the dark inside the house, listening, were Hubby and Lane. Lane wanted the ranch and Hubby just wanted to kill somebody, so Hubby agreed to go along with his brother's plan. They were just about ready.

"I'll ride into town in the morning," Blake was saying, "and put up a fund for the nesters to use to rebuild and such. It won't make what I done right, but it'll be a start."

"I'll ride with you," Frisco said. "It'll make me feel a damn sight better."

Lane looked at Hubby and he nodded his head and slobbered all down the front of his shirt.

The two brothers stepped out onto the porch and shot their father and the foreman. Then they shot them again to make sure they were dead. The cook came running to see what was the matter and Hubby plugged her twice, stopping the woman cold on the living room floor.

"Now, Hubby," Lane said, standing over the cooling body of his father, "we go nightherd, just like we planned. Let the hands find them when they come in from town."

"No," Hubby drooled.

"What'd mean, no? Damn it, Hubby. We agreed to do it this way."

"I don't wanna do it this way."

Exasperated, Lane said, "Well, how do you want to do it, you drooling igit?"

"This way," Hubby said. He lifted the Springfield rifle and blew a hole in his brother's forehead a silver dollar couldn't cover.

Grinning, Hubby took all the money in the men's pockets, then looted the house of cash and ammunition and food. He was mumbling as he filled sacks. "Call me stupid, will you? Call Hubby a fool all the time. Well, Hubby's not very stupid. You're dead and Hubby's alive." Hubby thought that was hysterically funny. Of course, Hubby thought all sorts of weird things were funny.

Hubby had him a real good plan all worked out in his head. He planned on taking a short trip . . . over to the Box H. And then he was going to take a long trip. Just him and Miss Millie.

Rocky switched saddles to a fresh horse and beat it back to town minutes after the hands had ridden in and discovered the bodies. The news shattered what had been the beginnings of peace in the area, at least on one side of the war.

Matt and Sam had just ridden in from the raid when Rocky came galloping in with the news. They listened with Jack and the others.

"But we couldn't find hide nor hair of Hubby." Rocky ended it with that.

"Hubby killed them," Dewey said, firm conviction in his voice. "I have always believed that he was responsible for the random killings over the years in this area. And those rapes."

"What rapes?" Jack asked.

"Before you got here last year. But Dad and Lane always alibied for him. Hubby's vicious, and he's not nearly as stupid as he'd like people to think. If it's possible, Hubby has conditioned himself to be stupid-acting. Either that, or he's one hell of an actor."

"You mean to tell me Hubby ain't addled?" Jack asked, buckling his gunbelt.

"He might be one spoke shy of a whole wheel," Dewey said. "But don't kid yourselves: he's plenty smart. And he's a killer of the worst kind. Hubby *likes* to kill."

"Regardless, I don't wanna have to be the one to put lead in a person that ain't totin' a full load," Jack said. "So what the hell are we gonna do when we catch up with him?"

"Knock a leg out from under him, I reckon," Charlie said, swinging into the saddle. "If we can. But I'll tell you all this: Hubby points a gun at me, ticked or not, it'll be the last time he ever points a gun at anybody."

"I talk to you boys?" the voice came out of the darkness behind them and both Sam and Matt spun in a crouch, their hands filled with .44's.

"Whoa, boys, whoa!" the stranger said quickly, holding his hands out wide. "I'm friendly. I'm a detective from the Pinkerton Agency."

The street was deserted and the town quiet. Matt clicked open his watch; it was near midnight. "You pick a strange time to want to talk, mister."

"I been trying to catch up with you. Shall we sit on the bench?"

They sat. "I hear tell you boys helped dig the bodies out of the rubble."

"One body," Sam corrected. "That of Robert Harris."

"You're sure it was him?"

Both brothers nodded their heads. "Yes," Matt said. "Same height, weight, ring on his hand. What was left of his boots and spurs was still by the bed."

The detective sighed. "Well, that's it, then. The damn railroad lost the bodies!" He explained that.

"I'm sorry we can't help you," Sam said. "But Robert Harris is buried right up there in the town's cemetery, and Denise Raner was taken back to the Lightning ranch for burial."

"Have you talked to Doctor Lemmon?" Matt asked.

"Yes. He said the same thing. Robert Harris was killed in the fire, sleeping by the side of Denise Raner. Several whiskey bottles—what was left of them—were found by the bed, as well as several bottles of laudanum. The poor wretches slept through the entire tragedy. And that was probably a blessing." He stood up and reached into his vest pocket. "Gentlemen, here is my card. Who knows, you may want to contact the agency about something in the future." He smiled. "If I do say so myself, we are known for doing fine work." He walked off into the night, back to his room at the boardinghouse.

"Let's hit the sack," Sam suggested.

"Yeah. I think tomorrow we'll be in the saddle early—looking for Hubby."

Dewey Vernon went back to the ranch to take charge of matters, and Charlie asked Louis Longmont to join Jimmy Byrant in town to help look after things. Jack and Charlie, Matt and Sam were in the saddle just after dawn, heading out to try and pick up Hubby's tracks. Hubby might have preferred to be known as a fool, but he was anything but when it came to throwing off his pursuers. Time and again, the men had to backtrack in order to pick up Hubby's tracks. But before long it became clear to the trackers where Hubby was going: straight north to the Box H ranch.

"Why?" Jack mused from the saddle as they walked their horses.

"Millie," Matt said. "Dewey said that he believed Hubby was responsible for the rapes that have occurred in this area over the years. Has to be."

The men quickened their pace. When they hit Box H range, they found a hand who was rounding up strays.

"Get back to the house, Boswell," Jack told the cowboy. "Get several of the boys and stay with Miss Millie and Becky. Don't let them out of your sight."

The cowboy had heard nothing about the killings of the previous night. He sat his saddle with his mouth hanging open as Jack explained.

"Jesus!" he said. "I'm gone."

The men resumed their tracking. An hour later, Matt shouted, "Over here!"

"What the devil . . . ?" Charlie said, looking down at the tracks.

"Hubby met with two other riders here," Matt said, getting down to inspect the bootprints. "One of them has a small foot and doesn't weigh very much. A woman or a child, I'd guess."

The men dismounted and studied the bootprints. The larger prints had that V-shaped cut on the sole, the smaller print was clean of the cut.

"They stood here for a long time," Jack said. "Even built them a little fire for coffee."

"They done their call to nature over here," Charlie said. "And one went over yonder behind them bushes," he said, pointing to the far side of the camp.

"So it's a woman with them," Sam said. "A woman. But who . . . ?"

Matt sat down on a log and took off his hat. He

scratched his head, trying to pin down that elusive little scrap of information that kept dodging around in the dark corners of his brain. He recalled the first time he and Sam had visited Pete Harris and his family at the ranch. They'd had fried chicken and mashed potatoes and gravy and pie that Millie had baked. Robert had passed Matt the gravy bowl with his right hand, Matt recalled. And . . . there had been no ring on that hand. The ring was on his *left* hand. The body he had helped pull from the charred tangle after the hotel fire had worn a ring on his *right* hand.

Matt stood up and plopped his hat back on his head. He startled everybody by saying, "Robert Harris and Denise Raner didn't die in that hotel fire the other night. That's who Hubby met right here."

"What?" Charlie said.

"This has been a triple-cross right down the line," Matt said, walking the camp and talking as much to himself as to the others. "I'll bet everyone a hundred dollars that Robert and Denise were in cahoots with Chrisman and Dale. After that so-called confession of Robert's, Chrisman and Dale backed out of their arrangement with Robert and Denise and left them swingin' alone in the breeze, taking the blame. Robert and Denise killed that man and woman who was staying at the hotel and burned it down."

"Why?" Jack asked.

"To assume the identities of the dead couple, maybe?" Sam offered.

"Could be," Charlie said. "Or maybe they was *plannin'* on burnin' it down and somebody beat them to it by minutes. Somebody hired by Chrisman and Dale to kill Robert and Denise and then burn the hotel down around them."

"Why are you so sure Robert is alive?" Jack asked.

"The ring on his hand. It was on the dead man's right hand."

"Yeah," Jack said thoughtfully. "Robert wore a ring on his *left* hand."

"Let's head for the ranch pronto," Charlie said. "The way this is workin' out, Red Raley and his bunch are probably takin' money from Hugo, Dale an' Chrisman, and just maybe they might be in cahoots with Robert and Denise, too."

"Takin' money from everybody and plannin' on gettin' the last laugh when all the gunsmoke and deception blows away," Jack said. "That works for me."

The hands of the Box H had taken their battle positions, ringing the house. They had all laid in a store of food and water and ammo and fortified their positions with logs, stones, and bales of hay. The horses were secure in the barn. The ranch appeared deserted. The children Pete and Becky had taken in to raise were in their rooms, safe from stray bullets.

"Blake and Frisco and Lane, dead," Pete muttered. "Killed by Hubby. Who is in cahoots with my son and Denise, who I thought were dead. And those are strangers buried in the grave in town and out at Hugo's ranch." He shook his head and took a sip of coffee. "You're right about the ring, Matt. I was so filled with grief I didn't . . . I didn't notice it. Grief and anger and disappointment," he added.

"Hubby gives me goosebumps," Millie said. "I never have liked the way he looks at me. And I'll tell you all something: Hubby isn't nearly as dumb as he makes out to be. Even when we were kids I saw that a lot of his so-called backward ways were nothing but an act. He figured out very young that if he acted goofy, he could get away with a lot more without punishment. He's just as smart as a lot of people."

"Here's something else," Sam said. "How many men on Hugo's payroll are actually working for Dale and Chrisman? Or working for Red Rally?"

"Interestin' thought," Charlie said. "Now let's think about this while we're playin' guessin' games: I'm wonderin' if Dale plans on killin' Chrisman, and if Chrisman plans on killin' Dale when this is near'bouts wrapped up."

"Good Lord!" Pete said. "This thing has more twists than a snake."

"If Red Raley is planning a real double-cross," Becky said, "is it possible that he has plans of attacking the town . . . perhaps after killing Hugo? If I'm reading your theories correctly, that is."

Pete looked at his wife. "It's damn sure something to think about."

"And whose side is Hugo's son, Carl on?" Jack tossed that into the hat.

"I got a headache," Pete said.

"I'm hungry," Matt said.

"Me, too," Sam said.

Pete looked at the brothers. "What else is new?"

Twenty-four

Robert and Denise and Hubby had seen the lawmen riding for the ranch and changed directions. They rode back for the town, nearing there at mid-afternoon. Robert wrote a short note and Hubby found a town boy playing in the dirt just outside town and gave him a dollar to take the note to Chrisman. The boy found Chrisman alone in the back of his saloon and handed it to him.

CHRISMAN, DALE IS PLANNING TO KILL YOU. MEET ME AT THE CRICK OUTSIDE OF TOWN AS SOON AS POSSIBLE. HURRY, YOUR LIFE IS IN DANGER.

It was signed, *Red*.

"That dirty . . ." Chrisman bit back the oath and walked to the livery, saddling his horse and riding out of town, staying on the back streets so Dale wouldn't spot him.

At the creek, he looked around him. He could see no one. "Red!" he softly called. "Red, where are you?"

"Over here," Robert called. "In the trees. Come on. Hurry, man."

Chrisman almost had a heart attack when he came face to face with Robert Harris and Denise. He sputtered and finally managed to gasp, "But . . . you two are *dead!*"

"No," Denise said. "But we were in that alley watching you slip into the hotel that night. Robert went to the back door and saw you go into the rooms we had rented. You did what we were planning to do. Thanks a lot, Chrisman."

"But the bodies . . . ?"

"They were already dead," Robert said. "I wasn't hurt nearly as bad as I let on. I was pouring the laudanum out, just like Denise was pouring the whiskey out. I killed them both and planted them in my bed."

Chrisman looked at Hubby. "You killed your own father."

"Big deal," Hubby said. "I've kilt lots of people."

"What . . . are you going to do with me?" Chrisman asked, although he had a pretty good idea.

"You're going to tell us where the gold and silver veins are," Denise said.

"No, I won't."

Hubby smiled and slobbered. "Oh, I bet you a dollar you will."

Louis Longmont was lounging in front of the sheriff's office when a farmer rattled up in a wagon. "It's Chrisman!" he yelled. "I found him in the road, back near the crick. Looks like Injuns got him. He's in a bad way."

Louis looked at the bloody mess that was left of Chrisman and shook his head. "No Indian did this. Get him down to the doctor's office."

The wagon rattled on. Louis waved to Jimmy, who was talking to a very pretty girl across the street. "Get Mayor Dale. Tell him to meet me at the doctor's office."

Stepping into the office, he could see Doctor Lemmon working on the man. The doctor had not even taken the time to close the door. He met Louis's eyes and shook his head. Louis stepped into the office and walked up to the bloody mess on the padded table.

"Is he conscious?"

"No," Doc Lemmon said. "It's amazing to me that he's still alive. And he won't be for long. Somebody with more pure viciousness in them than I thought possible did this. It's . . . inhuman."

Dale rushed in and gasped at the sight of his friend. "My God!" he said. "Who . . . ?"

"We don't know," the doctor said. "And we probably never will know."

"Put some salts under his nose," Louis ordered. "Get him conscious."

"Now see here!" the doctor protested.

"He's dying anyway, isn't he?" Louis' words were sharply spoken. "We've got to find out who did this to him so it won't be repeated. Now get him conscious."

When Chrisman was as conscious as he would ever be, he spoke with a labored whisper through his intense pain. "It was Robert Harris and . . . Denise Raner . . . and Hubby Vernon." He pushed a smile past bloody lips. They had smashed out all his teeth and gouged out his eyes. And that was only for starters. "I . . . didn't tell them anything, Dale. I . . . held on. I will take our . . . secret to . . . the grave." His head lolled to one side and he took one last rattling breath.

"Robert and Denise?" the doctor said. "But . . . they're *dead!*"

"Obviously, they are not," Louis said. "Jimmy, dispatch a rider out to find Jack and the others. Tell them of this new development. Move, lad." He fixed his hard eyes on Dale. "What secret, Dale?"

"I . . . don't know," the man lied.

"You're lying. But that's all right." Louis's smile was tight and hard. "Just remember what Chrisman said. He didn't tell them. So that means they'll be coming after you."

"I demand protection!" Dale hollered.

"Forget it," Louis replied. "I'm not going to ask someone to protect you without even knowing the reason why."

"You're a hard, cold, cruel man, Mister Longmont," the mayor said. He was so frightened he could hardly stand.

"Run along, Mayor," Louis told him. "And be sure to lock your door tonight. There are boogeymen among us."

The mayor scurried from the office, flapping his hands and squealing like a pig.

"He's right, you know," Doc Lemmon said to the millionaire adventurer. "You are a hard, cold man."

Louis smiled. But it did not touch his eyes. He said, "This man," pointing to the bloody mess that was Chrisman, "and that man," he pointed toward the open front door that Dale had just used, "are probably the reasons behind this range war and the hotel fire. They are responsible for *how* many needless and brutal deaths in this area over the past months?"

The doctor shook his head. "Too many."

"Precisely," Louis Longmont said, and walked out the door. Back on the street, he gathered a crowd of men around him and deputized them all en masse.

"I don't know what is going to happen next," he told them. "I'm not a soothsayer. But I am a wagering man. And I am betting that both this town and Pete Harris's Box H ranch are going to get hit and hit hard sometime within the next twenty-four hours. So let's get ready for it, shall we?" As he was speaking, Mayor Dale was leaving town in his buggy, whipping the matched team into a run. Louis smiled. He was heading for the crossroads, and Louis doubted he was going to take the fork toward the Box H.

"You stay here," Jack told the young rider from town. "These people are going to need all the guns they can use. Matt, Sam, you boys stay here. Me and Charlie will head on back to town. This here pot's just about to come to a boil."

"What are you sayin', man?" Hugo Raner grabbed Dale and shook him. "My Denise is *alive?*"

"Yes. She and Robert and Hubby tortured Chrisman to death, trying to get him to divulge something. I don't know what in the world it could have been. The three of them are mad, I tell you, mad!"

Hugo knocked the man to the floor with a big fist. He stood over him. "Now you tell me the truth, Dale. What in the hell is goin' on around here?"

Dale lay on his back and sobbed like a baby, both hands covering his bloody mouth. "Hugo, my God, man, I don't know! Why did you strike me? I came straight to you with this news. Why hit me? It's Pete Harris who is your enemy. Not me."

"All right, all right." Hugo hauled the man to his feet and dumped him into a chair. "Stay here and stay out of sight." He paused. "Blake and Lane . . . dead. Frisco dead. Denise and Robert alive and runnin' wild like crazy people. Hubby with them. What the hell does it all mean?" He asked the question as much to himself as to anyone else in the room. "None of this makes any sense."

"Don't you understand?" Dale almost shouted the words, thinking hard and fast. "We're alone in this, Hugo. Chrisman was in on it from the first. He and Robert and Denise and Pete Harris."

"Pete! What the hell are you talking about, you fool? Pete damn near killed his boy."

"Did anybody see it?"

"Doc Lemmon saw it."

"You don't think the young doctor could be bought?"

"Maybe he's right, Pa," Carl said. "Doc Lemmon's out there sparkin' Millie as often as he can. He'd go along with something like Mister Dale's talkin' about."

Hugo looked at Dale, dabbing at his mouth with a handkerchief. "Give me a motive."

Dale took a big gamble. "Gold," he said softly.

"Gold?" Hugo whispered. "On my spread?"

"Sure," Dale said. "Why do you think Pete backed all those nesters buyin' sections of your land?"

"He did?" Hugo asked.

"It certainly wasn't me or Blake. Who else could it have been?" Dale was really getting into the lie now. He was beginning to believe it himself.

"Now wait a minute, just wait a minute. I'm so damn confused my head hurts." The rancher poured himself a whiskey and sat down on the couch. He was silent for a moment. Then he looked at Dale. "You're a damn liar, Dale. I been believin' your lies all along. It's you and Chrisman that started all this trouble. Not the farmers, not the sheepmen, but you and Chrisman. And Robert and Denise was in on it too." He stopped at the sound of a Colt's hammer being jacked back. Father looked at son. "Oh, no, boy. Not you, too."

"Sorry, Pa," Carl said. "You should have taken the bait."

"My crew will tear you apart, Carl. You goddamn traitor."

Carl laughed. "*Your* crew, Pa? You ain't got no crew. You've surrounded yourself with hired guns, not punchers. I bought them off right after the raid out here."

"You don't have no money, boy," the father told the son.

"But I got gold, Pa. Denise told me all about it. This ranch is sittin' on tons and tons of gold. The hands was easy bought off with just the promise of that."

"You stinkin', sorry little pup!"

Carl shot him. Hugo lifted up and then fell backward, tipping the couch over when he did. Carl filled up his empty. "Couple of the boys will stay here with you, Dale. When I get back from burnin' out Pete, then you and me will have a talk. And you'll tell me where the vein is, won't you?"

"Oh, we'll work something out, Carl. You bet we will!" the banker said, sweat dripping from his face.

"I know we will," the young man said. He walked out the door, yelling for the hands.

Dale put his head in his hands. "Dear God," he whispered. "How did it get out of control?"

Two big, rough-looking guns-for-hire entered the room just as the hooves of forty horses thundered out. One of the men smiled at Dale. "Carl says we're to look after you, Dale. Then when he gets back, we're all gonna be rich."

"I doubt it," Hugo said, and shot both men. Dale scrambled out of the room on his hands and knees, the couch preventing Hugo from getting a clear shot at the man.

Hugo crawled to his boots. He was hit and hit hard. But he wasn't going to die before he did one more thing. Dale forgotten, Hugo staggered out of the gunsmoke-filled room and fell off the front porch. He crawled to his horse and managed to get into the saddle. "Let's go, feller," he said. "You got to get me to Pete's spread."

Dale found a rifle and a box of shells. His hands were shaking so badly he spilled half the box loading up the rifle. He shoved a pistol behind his belt. Only then was he aware of one of the gunhands looking at him.

"Help me," the man begged him. "I'm gut-shot and Lord, it hurts."

"Shut up, you vile, disgusting person," Dale told him, and rushed out the back door.

The gunslick had enough strength to lift and cock a pistol and pull the trigger. But the shot went wide, missing Dale. He fell back on the floor with a curse and began the slow and painful process of dying.

Dale left his tired team and saddled a horse. He cut across country, heading back to town. He'd be safe there. He had never been so frightened in all his life. He had gone only a few miles when he became aware that somebody was following him. He looked behind him. Three riders. And one was a small person. He was sure it was that horrible vicious Denise, Robert, and that nutty Hubby. He put his shoes to the flanks of the horse and took off at a gallop.

His horse was tired and faltering badly when he came up on a nester's place. He wasn't sure who lived there. But they'd take him in. He was sure of that.

"Rider comin', Pa," Jake Reed said.

"That's a Lightnin' hoss," Joe said. "I seen it a lot of times."

"And they's three more right behind him," John said.

"Jesse," Reed said. "Blow him out of the saddle. They're on our land."

Jesse lifted his Springfield and sighted in. He pulled the trigger. Dale went flying out of the saddle, the front of his white shirt stained with blood. He hit the ground, bounced once, and then was still. His horse loped on for a few yards, then stopped to rest. The three riders behind Dale reined up, turned around, and galloped off.

"That'll teach 'em, by God," Reed said.

Dale lay on his back on the earth and looked up at the sky. He was very cold, but he felt no pain. All in all, he thought, it was a grand plan. And it would have worked out just fine, if only . . .

Robert Harris, Denise Raner, and Hubby Vernon rode back to the Lightning spread and found it deserted.

"Two dead gunhands in here," Robert called from the porch. "And there's blood all over the couch."

Denise went into her study and worked the combination to the big safe. She dragged out all the greenbacks and took the several leather pouches of gold.

"What are you doing?" Robert asked.

"It's over," she told him. "Only Chrisman and Dale knew where the gold and silver was. They're dead. That was a .45 Springfield that took Dale out. He's sure dead. We got to have some runnin' money."

"I ain't runnin' nowheres, and neither are none of you," Hubby said, and lifted his rifle, aiming at the back of Denise's head. Robert slapped it away and laid his fist against Hubby's jaw, knocking him to the floor. Robert kicked the young man in the head, putting him out.

"Let's go," Denise said.

"Wait a minute," Robert said. "Denise, it's a fair bet

that your dad and Carl went to raid the Box H. If they get killed, this spread belongs to you. We've done nothing wrong. There are no charges against either of us. We'd be free to look for the gold then."

Denise thought about that. "Yeah. You're right." She smiled and lifted the sackful of money. "But I'll just hold onto this in case."

Robert and Denise saddled fresh horses and pulled out, leaving Hubby groaning on the floor. Hubby pulled himself to his knees, felt the knot on his head where Robert had kicked him, and got to his boots. He staggered around until he got his bearings and then stripped the dead gunhands of their pistols and gunbelts. He found his rifle and saddled a fresh horse, hanging the gunbelts from the saddlehorn. He studied the ground for a moment, riding in circles, until he found the tracks of two riders. He rode after Robert and Denise. He wasn't sure what he would do when he caught up with them. But he had a pretty good idea.

One of the Lightning hands—actually a plant from Red Raley's gang—didn't believe Carl Raner's story about gold. He didn't go on the raid. In the confusion, he slipped away and headed straight for Red's hideout, not very many miles from the ranch.

Red had to think on this for a moment. It was confusing to him. Hugo and Blake were dead. He'd heard from his man in town that Chrisman was dead. And Dale was held captive at the ranch. So who the hell was left to pay Red and his boys?

"Nobody," he said. "Saddle up, boys," he gave the orders. "We'll just ride to the ranch and take Dale ourselves. We'll torture the information from him."

They found the dead gunhands on the floor, and the

door to the safe was open, the safe empty of funds. Dale was nowhere in sight.

"Now what do we do?" Chavez asked.

"I don't know," Red admitted. "Shut up. I got to think."

He sat down by the bullet-scarred dinner table and poured him a whiskey. He began to smile. He had him a plan. A good one, he figured.

Reed and his boys tied Mayor Dale across his saddle and went to town, dropping off Mrs. Reed at a neighbor's house. It was late afternoon when they arrived.

"He was ridin' a Lightning horse with three other hands when he come a-foggin' acrost our land," Reed told Jack Linwood. "If they's penalties to be paid, I reckon we'll just have to pay them."

Jack shook his head. "No. No charges, Reed. Dale was in some sort of plot with Chrisman, and Chrisman's dead."

"Dead?" the head of the Reed clan said. "How'd that happen?"

Louis explained briefly.

"Pa," Jake said. "I bet you that was Robert and Denise and Hubby ridin' with Dale. I don't know no little-bitty puncher around here."

"You're probably right," Jack said. "Is your wife safe, Reed?"

"Oh, yeah. You want us to stay here in town with our rifles?"

"I'd be obliged."

"We'll sure do 'er."

* * *

"Here they come!" Shorty yelled from the loft of the Box H barn. "And there's a wad of 'em."

"Who's leadin' the pack?" Pete yelled.

"Looks like Carl from here," Shorty shouted, after peering through field glasses, trying to penetrate the murk of dusk.

Pete earred back the hammer on his Winchester as the thunder of hooves grew louder. "All right, people. Let's settle this once and for all."

Twenty-five

Stalemate.

Those entrenched on the Box H spread could not get out, but neither could Carl Raner and his bunch of no-counts get inside the compound.

The battle had raged all through the night. The bodies of four Lightning Arrow men lay in the dirt. No one on the Box H side had taken even a scratch. The men of the Box H had had the time to carefully prepare their positions and they had plenty of food and water and ammo. They were outnumbered three or four to one, but held the high ground, so to speak. And they weren't about to give it up.

Hugo Raner was less than a mile away, sitting on the ground, trying to regain strength enough to get in the saddle. He was in a world of pain and fever when he staggered to his boots and gripped the saddlehorn with both hands. He slowly pulled himself into the saddle.

"Let's go, boy," he said to his weary horse.

"I don't think so, Pa," Denise spoke from behind him.

Hugo turned his horse and faced his daughter, Robert standing beside her. "Looked like I sired a pack of cowardly hyenas," he told her. He faced her rifle without fear. He was dead and knew it and wasn't afraid of it. "Me and Blake and Pete. But at least they each had one apiece that turned out decent. You want to tell me the whole story before you shoot me, girl?"

"No," she said, and pulled the trigger.

Hugo felt the shock of the .44. He cursed his daughter and managed to stay in the saddle and pull his pistol from leather. Robert smiled cruelly and ended Hugo Raner's struggle. He shot the big bear of a man in the face with a .45. Hugo tumbled from the saddle.

"Now what?" Robert asked.

"We wait to see if Brother Carl comes back here to see what the shooting was about. Then we kill him," she said in a cold voice. "Once that's done, we're home free, baby. Let's get off this trail and into the timber."

"See what that shootin's all about back yonder," Carl told a hand.

The hand reported back. "Your pa. Somebody shot him twice. He's dead."

"Denise," Carl said without no hesitation. "And she and Robert will be after me next. With me out of the way, she's home *free* with everything. Find her and kill her," he ordered. "Take some men with you and kill her!"

But this hand had had enough of deceit and treachery. He nodded at three men he'd buddied with long enough to know they wanted no more of this. The four of them swung into the saddle and headed out. "Where are we goin'?" a gun-for-hire asked.

"I don't know," the ex-Lightning Arrow hand said. "But I figure to put some distance between us and them crazy people back yonder."

"Suits me."

"This ain't gettin' us nowhere," Rusty said to Carl. "We couldn't dig them people out over yonder with dynamite. And we can't get close enough to do no good. Too much cleared land around the buildings."

"All right," Carl said. "One thing's for certain: Dale got away; bet on that. Pa back yonder proves that. Dale's in town. So we gotta hit there."

"How about the bank?" the Texas gun-for-hire Del Monroe said, a grin on his ugly face.

"Damn good idea," Carl said. "Let's ride."

"Yeah," Reno said. "I want to get lead in that damned old Charlie Starr."

"I want Jack Linwood," Del said. "I got a personal matter to settle with him."

"Louis Longmont's in town," Carl said. "We could seize him and hold him for ransom."

"All right!" Rusty stood up. "Let's ride." The men ran for their horses, dreams of big money in their eyes.

"They're pullin' out!" Shorty called from the loft.

"All of 'em."

"Stay here, Pete," Matt said. "Just in case it's a trick. But I got a hunch they're heading for town. Come on, brother, let's ride."

"You boys be careful," Becky said. "And come back. Millie and I will start baking some doughnuts just as soon as we get this mess cleaned up."

Matt and Sam grinned. "Count on it!" they both said, then ran for the barn and their horses.

"Here they come!" Jimmy yelled from the rooftop of the bank. "Holy cow!" he shouted. "We got two big gangs comin'. They're gonna hit us from both ends of town."

"Let 'em come," Jack shouted. "They're after the bank."

"Matt and Sam comin' hard after 'em!" Jimmy yelled, looking through binoculars.

"Fire, boys!" Reed shouted, and he and his sons fired their long-barreled Springfields. Five saddles were emptied of Lightning riders.

The Lightning crew immediately laid on their horses' necks to offer less of a target and fanned out. Those men of the town who were stationed on the rooftops opened fire at the Raley gang and emptied several saddles.

Then the gangs were in the streets of the town and it was swirling dust, the eye-sting of gunsmoke, the screaming of frightened and rearing horses, and the boom of weapons.

Matt and Sam left their horses at the edge of the business district and hit the ground running, on opposite sides of the street, their hands filled with .44's. Matt came face to face with a Lightning hand and let the hammers fall on both .44's. The hand fell back under the impact of the hot lead and tried to lift his guns. Matt shot him again. The cowboy turned outlaw slumped to his knees on the boardwalk and toppled over.

Sam shot one of Red's men off his horse and ducked as a bullet lifted his hat off his head and sent it spinning into the street. Sam swore; he'd just bought that hat the past month. Sam stepped back into the mouth of an alley and began picking his targets, his guns roaring.

Dixon was thrown from his horse and went scrambling behind the Cattle Club. He burst into Juan's café, wild-eyed and both hands full of .45's. The café was empty. Dixon shoved tables and chairs out of his way, walking toward the cantina. Anita stepped out of the gloom, a smile on her face.

"What are you grinnin' about, greaser?" Dixon snarled at the woman.

"You are one of the men who violated my daughter." She spoke liltingly-accented English.

"Yeah? So what? Hey, you ain't a bad-lookin' old broad yourself. I think I'll just have me a taste of you so's I can compare." He laughed.

He stopped laughing when Anita lifted a sawed off double-barreled twelve-gauge shotgun and blew his legs out from under him. His guns went flying across the room. Dixon lay on the floor and screamed at the pain of his mangled legs. One of them lay several feet from him.

"I'll come back after a while to see if you need anything else, señor," Anita told him. She broke open the shotgun and shoved fresh loads into the chambers. She left Dixon screaming on the floor.

Louis Longmont stood in the door of the sheriff's office and emptied a saddle with each pull of the trigger; the famed adventurer was a dead shot with rifle or pistol. Louis stood calmly, with a tight smile on his lips.

Red Raley and Carl both had the same thought at approximately the same time: attacking the town had been a lousy idea.

"Let's get the hell out of here!" Carl yelled to his hands at the same time Red rallied his people.

They left a lot of men littering the streets, some of them dead, some of them badly wounded. Those still alive were looking at very long prison terms.

Dewey Vernon came riding in with some of his loyal crew.

Jack stepped through the swirling dust. "Dewey. Leave your crew here in case they double back and you come with me. Let's finish this today."

Seven men rode out of town on fresh horses— seven men with guns loaded up full and jaws set with determination. They rode to rid the land of human vermin, to make the West a safer place for all who wished to live on the land and become a part of a community, whatever their legal occupation, be it farmer, rancher, sheepmen, store clerk, or cowboy.

"They're splitting up!" Matt shouted, pointing at two plumes of dust just up ahead. "Carl's taking his bunch back to Lightning. Me and Sam'll follow them. Come on, Louis."

Jack, Charlie, Dewey, and Jimmy headed after Red Raley and his pack of hyenas.

The Lightning bunch were riding very tired horses. The brothers and Louis were nipping at their heels when they rode into the Lightning ranch compound. Buster Phelps jumped off his horse with an oath and pointed a gun at Louis Longmont. Louis shot him down, rode his horse right over the screaming man, and kept on riding.

Wes Fanin threw his guns down and threw his hands up into the air. "I yield!" he shouted.

Carl Raner shot him in the back from the front porch of the house.

Matt, Louis, and Sam jumped off their horses, rifles in hand, and fanned out across the yard, firing from the hip as they went. Bolinger took a .44 round in the guts and hit the ground, rolling and squalling.

Sam made the bunkhouse, dropped his rifle, and filled his hands with thundering iron. A bullet clipped his left leg, another burned his shoulder, yet another sent splinters into the face. He was still standing when the firing ceased. Woody, Porter, Dean, and Reno of the Del Monroe gang were dead or dying. Sam punched out the empties and reloaded. He walked to the stove and touched the coffeepot. Still hot. He lifted the hinged lid and looked inside. The coffee was black as sin and thick as homemade soup. He poured a cup and drank it down.

"Good," he muttered, then walked to the door and peeped out, checking to see what other mischief he could get into.

Don Edison was down on one knee, put there by two slugs from Louis Longmont's guns. Walker was stretched out on the ground, lying facedown. Scarface Gant was leaning against a corral rail, the front of his shirt soaked with blood.

Del Monroe was sitting on the ground, both hands empty and in the air.

Tony, Clint, and Buck had surrendered. They stood sullen-faced, their hands in the air.

Burl stood facing Louis Longmont. "Carl's done run off and you'll never catch him," Burl said. "So this is 'tween you and me. Draw, you two-bit gambler," Burl yelled.

"My pleasure," Louis said, and shot him before Burl could even grip the butts of his guns.

Burl sat down heavily on the ground, both hands to his bloody chest, a very peculiar look on his face. "I . . . reckon we all make mistakes, don't we?" he asked. Before anyone could reply, Burl toppled over, dead in the dirt.

"Drop your guns, boys," Matt told Tulsa, Rusty, and Jody. "And get ready for a good butt-kickin'."

"Oh, yeah?" Jody sneered. "From the likes of you, that fancy-pants gambler, and that goddamn Injun?"

"That is correct," Louis said. He jacked back the hammer on his short gun. "Or you can die right now."

Three gunbelts hit the dirt. The other prisoners were hog-tied and tossed on the ground. Buck had come wandering around the side of the house, his hands in the air, hollering that he didn't want no more of this mess. He was tied up with the rest.

Louis removed his coat and folded it neatly, laying it on top of his gunbelt. He rolled up his sleeves, exposing massive forearms. He slipped on a pair of thin riding gloves, as did Matt and Sam. With leather gloves, one can hit harder with less damage to the hands.

"You boys like to molest women and kill innocent children," Louis told the trio, stepping in close. "Let's see what you can do with men." Then he knocked the snot out of Tulsa, flattening the man.

Sam punched Jody in the mouth, Matt wound up and busted Rusty on the jaw, and the fight was on.

Twenty-six

The horses of the Raley gang just gave up and quit running. Some of them stalled flat out and stopped, sending riders flying over their heads. Some of the Raley gang elected to make a very short fight of it. Jack, Charlie, Jimmy, and Dewey brought those back to town tied belly-down across their saddles. The others surrendered meekly.

Meanwhile, back at the Lightning spread . . .

Tulsa got up off the ground cussing and stepped in to duke it out with Louis. But Louis was a skilled boxer. He hit Tulsa five savage blows, left, right, left, right, left, using the man's head as a punching bag, and then gave Tulsa a tremendous blow to the belly and the foreman was stretched out cold on the ground, blood pouring from his nose and mouth.

Sam had backed Jody up against a tree and was giving him what-for. The man's eyes were glassy and his mouth and nose bloody, both eyes swelling shut. Sam had taken some pretty good shots to the head, but they only served to make him mad and he was giving back ten for every one he'd received. Jody finally sank to his knees and fell over on his face.

Matt had been deliberately and coldly punishing Rusty with short, vicious jabs to the man's face, twisting his fists as he struck, the leather-covered fists tearing and ripping the flesh. Matt fought with the sight of dead and horror-filled children behind his eyes. He fought with a savagery he did not know he possessed.

"He's going to kill the man," Louis remarked.

"Yes," Sam said. "I know. It will take both of us to stop him."

"I'm not sure I want to do that," the man replied. "I saw the results of one of the raids Rusty went on. He dragged a young farmer's child to her death. He was positively identified."

"There is a coffeepot in the bunkhouse. I'll make a fresh pot."

"I'll help you."

The men buckled their gunbelts, slipped into their coats, and tied up Jody and Tulsa. They left Matt hammering at Rusty.

"You're gonna kill me!" Rusty gasped.

"Right," Matt said, and hit him a savage blow to the ribs.

But in the end he couldn't do it. He held Rusty off the ground, holding the man by what was left of his shirt. Matt's big right fist was poised to smash the man's face. Rusty's face was ruined, his jaw broken, one ear hanging, his mouth and nose pulped. Matt knew he had broken some of his ribs. The man was unconscious.

Matt dropped him to the earth. Rusty did not move.

"Lot of hate in you, Bodine," Clint said. "I doubt

Rusty will ever recover from that beatin'. You ruined the man."

"I hope so," Bodine said, after sticking his head and hands in a horse trough and sloshing them around. He ran fingers through his wet hair and found his hat. He buckled on his gunbelt and slipped into his short jacket.

Sam and Louis walked up, Sam holding out a cup of coffee for his brother. "Did you make this?" Matt asked.

"I certainly did!"

"You better not drink any of it, Louis. The last time Sam made coffee the horses took one sniff and ran off. Took us all day to catch them."

"I need a doctor!" Don Edison groaned. "I'm hurt."

"Shut up," Sam told him, "before I revert back to my Cheyenne heritage and stake you out over an anthill. I bet that would be *painful!*" he whispered to Bodine.

"You mean you've never seen it done?" Bodine whispered.

"Heavens. no. My father would never resort to such barbaric practices. You know that. You mooched off of us long enough."

"Mooched! Me, mooch? You couldn't wait to come spend summers at the ranch. Everytime mother baked a pie for supper, you stole it and ate it."

"Me, *steal?*" Sam said. "Cheyennes would never stoop to stealing."

"Wagghh! The Cheyennes were the biggest bunch of damn horse thieves on the plains. I know—remember? I went with you to steal those ponies from the Crow."

Louis leaned up against a wagon and lit one of his thin, very expensive imported cigars.

"And almost got us killed due to your clumsiness."

"Me? Clumsy? You're the one who tripped over your own big feet."

"I'm sittin' here on the damn ground bleedin' to death and them two is arguin' about stealin' Crow ponies years ago," Don Edison griped.

Louis placed the muzzle of his pistol against the man's head and jacked back the hammer. "How do you feel now?"

"It's a miracle, I reckon. I never felt better in all my life."

"That's nice. We want you all better for the hangman."

The district judge came over and held court. The courtroom was the Cattle Club. The judge handed out very long prison terms and the men were taken away in prison wagons; most would never live long enough to walk out of the shadows of those prison walls.

Dewey Vernon married Maggie and settled in at his ranch. Charlie Starr gave up deputy sheriffing and went to work for Pete Harris. Jack Linwood became engaged to the schoolteacher, Mary, and they planned on getting married in a couple of months. A special election was held in the county and Jack was elected sheriff.

Robert Harris, Denise Raner, Carl Raner, and Hubby dropped out of sight. Red Raley and some of the others involved in the conspiracy confessed and named Robert and Denise as the ringleaders. Warrants were issued for them and sent out over a three-state area. Martha Vernon never returned from the East, choosing instead to remain, as she put it, "In a more civilized part of the country."

Pete and Becky formally adopted the two kids they'd taken in to raise, and Millie was making eyes at Doc Lemmon, who planned to build a bigger office in the just-renamed town of Pleasant Valley, Colorado. Lemmon was all goo-goo-eyed.

Louis Longmont saw his sheep safely in pasture and pulled out. He had just bought more land in someplace called Australia. He was anxious to board ship and see his new ranch.

"It's near the bottom of the world," he told Matt and Sam.

"Don't fall off," Matt told him.

Sam gave his brother a disgusted look.

"So Dale originally had the plan, and Chrisman got wind of it and the two of them started plotting against the ranchers," Matt began summing it up.

"Then Denise and Robert wormed their way into it and Carl Raner found out about it and he became a player," Sam added.

"Red Raley and his bunch were cleaning up," Jack said. "Taking money from all sides."

"But only Dale and Chrisman knew where the veins of gold and silver were located," Matt said. "And they took the secret with them to their graves."

"Suits me fine," Jack said. "I don't want the hassle of this place becomin' a boomtown for a couple of years. The damn gold and silver can stay in the ground."

The mother lodes have never been found to this day.

"Robert and Denise killed those two travelers and planted them in their bed," Sam said. "They were going to burn down the hotel, but Chrisman beat them to it. But why were they going to burn it down?"

The families of the man and woman who were mistaken for Robert Harris and Denise Raner decided to let the bodies remain buried in Colorado.

"I guess to get back at Dale," Jack said. He tossed a telegram on the table. "From the U. S. Marshal Service.

Dale's real name was Hector Brandon. He was wanted back East for murder. That Pinkerton man got suspicious of him and did some checking. Guess it don't make no difference now, does it?"

Matt and Sam were packed up and ready to hit the trail. They were going to swing around and say goodbye to Dewey and Pete and Charlie on their way out.

They shook hands with Jack Linwood. "You boys ride easy," Jack told them. "Robert and Denise and Hubby and Carl are still in these parts, I'm bettin'. And they got a powerful grudge to settle up with the both of you."

Matt and Sam swung into the saddle and headed out of town, waving at the citizens as they rode toward the crossroads.

"Wonder what's going to happen to the Lightning Arrow spread?" Matt mused aloud.

"All that'll be tied up in courts of law for years," Sam opined. "The survivors of the homesteaders and sheepmen that Hugo had a hand in killing will sue. But lawyers will get most of the money, I'll bet."

Just for the heck of it, the blood brothers turned at the crossroads and rode over to the Lightning Arrow range. They rode up to the ranchhouse and sat their saddles for a moment, looking at the huge, deserted house.

Hugo Raner's grave was lonely, a mound of earth on a hill, shaded by a single tree.

"I guess when it comes down to it," Matt said softly, "that's what we all get, isn't it?"

They rode out of the yard, heading for the Box H. Miles south of them, brother faced brother.

"It's over, Hubby," Dewey told the man. They stood in the yard in front of the Circle V ranchhouse. Maggie stood on the porch, twisting her apron, her eyes filled with fear for her man.

"I was always better than you with a gun," Hubby told his brother. "Now I'm gonna kill you and then have my way with your wife."

"Don't make me pull on you, Hubby," Dewey told him. "Give yourself up."

"You go to hell!"

"Where's Robert and Denise and Carl?"

"That's for me to know."

"If you touch the butt of that gun, Hubby, you won't know it for long."

"Big words. I'm gonna have this ranch and your nester wife, Dewey."

They were alone. Dewey had fired many of the old hands and hired new cowboys. Those men were out with the cattle, riding fence, and doing the many other jobs that were required of punchers.

Dewey lost patience with his brother. He felt no pity for Hubby. He knew that Hubby was a mad dog, and while one might feel sorry for the animal, it had to be killed for safety's sake.

"Draw, Hubby!"

Hubby jerked iron. But he'd forgotten that Dewey had spent many hours with Charlie Starr. Dewey's draw was as smooth as velvet and as deadly as a striking rattler. A heartbeat later, Hubby lay dead on the ground.

A puncher came fogging into the yard and jumped from his horse.

"Get you a fresh horse and ride into town, Boone," Dewey told him. "Tell the sheriff that Hubby is dead."

"I fixed you a sackful of doughnuts," Millie told the brothers. "They should last you for several days."

"Not with him around," Sam said, jerking a thumb toward Matt. "He'll attack that sack like a bear to a honey tree."

"Where are you boys headin'?" Pete asked.

Matt shook his head. "Probably north to see my folks. After that . . . who knows?"

"You boys must be runnin' tryin' to forget something terrible," Pete said, coming alarmingly close to the truth. "You're welcome back here anytime, boys. Don't forget where we live, now."

They shook hands and walked to their horses. "I keep thinking that we're forgetting something," Sam said.

"We are," Matt replied in no more than a whisper. "Robert, Denise, and Carl."

A rider from the Circle V came busting into the yard. "I just talked to Boone down the road. He was on his way into town to fetch the sheriff. Hubby braced Dewey in the front yard of the ranchhouse. Said he was gonna have the ranch and Dewey's new wife. Dewey killed him. Couldn't have been no more than an hour ago."

"Light and sit," Pete told the rider. "Give your horse a chance to blow. You, there, Judy," he spoke to the little girl he'd adopted, "get some doughnuts and bring them to this puncher. And a mug of coffee."

"Obliged," the cowboy said. "I'm Augie. I come down from North Dakota way."

"Pete could never kill his own son," Sam said in a whisper. "I guess we'd better stick around for supper while we're at it. They're in the area."

"All right." Matt raised his voice. "Pete, my horse is startin' to limp. You mind if we sleep in the barn tonight and give this fellow a chance to rest?"

Pete smiled sadly. "Thanks, boys. But I can saddle my own horses and stomp on my own snakes."

"But could you kill your own son?" Sam asked gently.

"I don't know," Pete said, after a moment. "Mother, we'll have two more for supper."

Twenty-seven

The brothers ate lightly, not wanting to fill their bellies and sleep too soundly. They both knew that there was only a remote chance that Robert would show up; for all they knew, he could be five hundred miles away. But most of Pete's hands were out with the just-gathered herd, preparing to sell off a bunch to the Army. Only Shorty, Coop, and the cook were still on the ranch compound.

After supper, they rolled up in their blankets under a tree in the front yard. Matt would take the first two-hour watch, then awaken Sam, and they would do that throughout the night. Dawn came, and nothing else.

"You boys can't bodyguard me forever," Pete said, over breakfast. "I . . ."

"Somebody comin'!" Shorty shouted from the outside. "It's the sheriff."

Jack stepped inside and took off his hat. "Pete, your boy's in the area. He was spotted by a farmer not five miles from here. He was stealin' eggs from the henhouse about four o'clock this morning. Him and the farmer traded shots, but the man don't think he hit him. Carl and that girl was with him."

Pete nodded his head and motioned to the table. "Sit and eat, Jack. Got flapjacks and bacon and eggs, and Mother just made a fresh pot of coffee."

Jack pumped water and washed his hands at the sink and sat down. Millie filled his plate to overflowing and the sheriff dug in.

Pete said, "Stealin' eggs. He could have had a two-hundred-thousand-acre ranch. This one. I bought that little spread up north of here, that little ten thousand acres, just for him. With plenty more to add to it over the years. Lookin' back, it seemed to insult him. Now he's stealin' eggs in the dead of night. Lord God!"

"Pete," Charlie said, stepping in through the back door. He had come in during the night. There was a funny tone to his voice. "It's Robert and Carl and that girl. They're ridin' up to the front just as big as brass."

Pete reached down and jerked Jack's guns from the man. Jack didn't let up on his eating; it was almost as if he expected that. "You can put them back, Pete. I know you'd rather see your son dead now than see him swing. It's better that I don't even know he's in the yard until it's all over. And that's the way I'm gonna write it up."

Pete shoved his guns back in leather.

"I'll handle this," Charlie said.

"No!" Sam's voice was firm. "You've a good steady job for the first time in years, Charlie. You couldn't work for a man whose son you killed. There would always be a strain between the two of you. Matt and me? We're drifting. We won't be back. It's better that we face them."

"He's right, ol' hoss," Pete said gently. "But I aim to

see if my son dies well. Mother, you and Millie take the kids into the bedroom. Come on, Charlie."

They followed Matt and Sam out the front door. Jack Linwood refilled his coffee cup and calmly settled in to eat his breakfast. The West might be slowly taming, but it was still the West. Sometimes it was better to settle things outside of a court of law.

None of them saw Millie slip down the hall and exit the house through a side window, a rifle in her hands.

Matt and Sam stepped out into the yard. Robert and Carl faced them, Denise off to one side. The young men looked terrible. They were unshaven and unwashed. Their clothing was torn and dirty and stinking. Denise didn't look or smell a damn bit better.

"So you don't have the belly to face me, huh, Pa?" Robert called. "Well, it's better this way. After we put the Injun and his so-called gunfighter brother down, we'll take on you and that old fart beside you."

Pete and Charlie looked at one another and smiled grimly. They both nodded their heads and stepped off the porch.

"Now, wait a minute!" Sam said.

"Shut up and go inside and have a cup of coffee," Pete told them. "Or go to the porch and sit down. Just get the hell out of the way."

Matt opened his mouth. Charlie shut it. "Go stick a doughnut in that hole, boy."

Matt and Sam retired to the porch.

Pete faced his son, Charlie faced Carl Raner. Pete said, "I changed your diapers and wiped your butt when you were a baby. Me and your ma nursed you through sickness and worried and fretted about you. I built this ranch for you and your sister. I put in eighteen-hour days so you could . . ."

"Shut your goddamn mouth!" Robert screamed at his father. "I asked you to retire and give the place to me. You wouldn't do it."

"Retire! Hell, boy, I'm not yet fifty years old. What the devil would I do?"

"I'll tell you what you're gonna do," Robert told him. "You're gonna die. Right now!" The son began his pull.

The guns of Pete Harris and Charlie Starr roared. Robert and Carl stumbled back, both of them with a sick expression on their faces. Denise screamed as the young men fell to the earth, both of them mortally wounded. She cursed and leveled her rifle at Pete and a Winchester snarled, a small blue hole appearing in the center of Denise's forehead. She fell backward, dead before she hit the ground.

Millie walked out into the yard. "Since you talked so much to me and Robert about Charlie Starr when we were kids, Pa, he was always sort of an uncle-person to me," she said. "So I figured we'd best keep this in the family."

Twenty-eight

When the brothers forded the uppermost curve of the Little Snake, they knew they were back in Wyoming. They crossed the continental divide and rode toward the South Fork Powder. It would be good to see family and home country again, and check on their ranches.

The elder Bodine looked out the living room window one afternoon and smiled. "Mother," he called. "Put on a fresh pot of coffee. Our boys have come home for a spell."

AFTERWORD

Notes from the Old West

In the small town where I grew up, there were two movie theaters. The Pavilion was one of those old-timey movie show palaces, built in the heyday of Mary Pickford and Charlie Chaplin—the silent era of the 1920s. By the 1950s, when I was a kid, the Pavilion was a little worn around the edges, but it was still the premier theater in town. They played all those big Technicolor biblical Cecil B. DeMille epics and corny MGM musicals. In Cinemascope, of course.

On the other side of town was the Gem, a somewhat shabby and run-down grind house with sticky floors and torn seats. Admission was a quarter. The Gem booked low-budget "B" pictures (remember the Bowery Boys?), war movies, horror flicks, and Westerns. I liked the Westerns best. I could usually be found every Saturday at the Gem, along with my best friend, Newton Trout, watching Westerns from 10 A.M. until my father came looking for me around suppertime. (Sometimes Newton's dad was dispatched to come fetch us.) One time, my dad came to get me right in the middle of

Abilene Trail, which featured the now-forgotten Whip Wilson. My father became so engrossed in the action he sat down and watched the rest of it with us. We didn't get home until after dark, and my mother's meat loaf was a pan of gray ashes by the time we did. Though my father and I were both in the doghouse the next day, this remains one of my fondest childhood memories. There was Wild Bill Elliot, and Gene Autry, and Roy Rogers, and Tim Holt, and, a little later, Rod Cameron and Audie Murphy. Of these newcomers, I never missed an Audie Murphy Western, because Audie was sort of an antihero. Sure, he stood for law and order and was an honest man, but sometimes he had to go around the law to uphold it. If he didn't play fair, it was only because he felt hamstrung by the laws of the land. Whatever it took to get the bad guys, Audie did it. There were no finer points of law, no splitting of legal hairs. It was instant justice, devoid of long-winded lawyers, bored or biased jurors, or black-robed, often corrupt judges.

Steal a man's horse and you were the guest of honor at a necktie party.

Molest a good woman and you got a bullet in the heart or a rope around the gullet. Or at the very least, got the crap beat out of you. Rob a bank and face a hail of bullets or the hangman's noose.

Saved a lot of time and money, frontier justice.

That's all gone now, I'm sad to say. Now you hear, "Oh, but he had a bad childhood" or "His mother didn't give him enough love" or "The homecoming queen wouldn't give him a second look and he has an inferiority complex." Or "cultural rage," as the politically correct bright boys refer to it. How many times have you heard some self-important defense attorney moan,

"The poor kids were only venting their hostilities toward an uncaring society?"

Mule fritters, I say. Nowadays, you can't even call a punk a punk anymore. But don't get me started.

It was, "Howdy, ma'am" time too. The good guys, antihero or not, were always respectful to the ladies. They might shoot a bad guy five seconds after tipping their hat to a woman, but the code of the West demanded you be respectful to a lady.

Lots of things have changed since the heyday of the Wild West, haven't they? Some for the good, some for the bad.

I didn't have any idea at the time that I would someday write about the West. I just knew that I was captivated by the Old West.

When I first got the itch to write, back in the early 1970s, I didn't write Westerns. I started by writing horror and action adventure novels. After more than two dozen novels, I began thinking about developing a Western character. From those initial musings came the novel *The Last Mountain Man: Smoke Jensen*. That was followed by *Preacher: The First Mountain Man*. A few years later, I began developing the Last Gunfighter series. Frank Morgan is a legend in his own time, the fastest gun west of the Mississippi . . . a title and a reputation he never wanted, but can't get rid of.

For me, and for thousands—probably millions—of other people (although many will never publicly admit it), the old Wild West will always be a magical, mysterious place: a place we love to visit through the pages of books; characters we would like to know . . . from a safe distance; events we would love to take part in, again, from a safe distance. For the old Wild West was not a place for the faint of heart. It was a hard, tough, physically demanding time. There were no police to call if one faced adversity. One faced trouble alone, and handled it alone. It was rugged individualism: something that appeals to many of us.

I am certain that is something that appeals to most readers of Westerns.

I still do on-site research (whenever possible) before starting a Western novel. I have wandered over much of the West, prowling what is left of ghost towns. Stand in the midst of the ruins of these old towns, use a little bit of imagination, and one can conjure up life as it used to be in the Wild West. The rowdy Saturday nights, the tinkling of a piano in a saloon, the laughter of cowboys and miners letting off steam after a week of hard work. Use a little more imagination and one can envision two men standing in the street, facing one another, seconds before the hook and draw of a gunfight. A moment later, one is dead and the other rides away.

The old wild untamed West.

There are still some ghost towns to visit, but they are rapidly vanishing as time and the elements take their toll. If you want to see them, make plans to do so as soon as possible, for in a few years, they will all be gone.

And so will we.

Stand in what is left of the Big Thicket country of east Texas and try to imagine how in the world the pioneers managed to get through that wild tangle. I have wondered about that many times and marveled at the courage of the men and women who slowly pushed westward, facing dangers that we can only imagine.

Let me touch briefly on a subject that is very close to me: firearms. There are some so-called historians who are now claiming that firearms played only a very insignificant part in the settlers' lives. They claim that only a few were armed. What utter, stupid nonsense! What do these so-called historians think the pioneers did for food? Do they think the early settlers rode down to the nearest supermarket and bought their meat? Or maybe they think the settlers chased down deer or buffalo on foot and beat the animals to death with a club. I have a news flash for you so-called historians: The settlers used guns to shoot their game. They used guns to defend hearth and home against Indians on the warpath. They used guns to protect themselves from outlaws. Guns are a part of Americana. And always will be.

The mountains of the West and the remains of the ghost towns that dot those areas are some of my favorite subjects to write about. I have done extensive research on the various mountain ranges of the West and go back whenever time permits. I sometimes stand surrounded by the towering mountains and wonder how in the world the pioneers ever made it through. As hard as I try and as often as I try, I simply cannot imagine the hardships those men and women endured over the hard months of their incredible journey. None of us can. It is said that on the Oregon Trail alone, there are at least two bodies in lonely, unmarked graves for every mile of that journey. Some students of the West say the number of dead is at least twice that. And nobody knows the exact number of wagons that impatiently started out alone and simply vanished on the way, along with their occupants, never to be seen or heard from again.

Just vanished.

The one-hundred-and-fifty-year-old ruts of the wagon wheels can still be seen in various places along the Oregon Trail. But if you plan to visit those places, do so quickly, for they are slowly disappearing. And when they are gone, they will be lost forever, except in the words of Western writers.

The West will live on as long as there are writers willing to write about it, and publishers willing to publish it. Writing about the West is wide open, just like the old Wild West. Characters abound, as plentiful as the wide-open spaces, as colorful as a sunset on the Painted Desert, as restless as the ever-sighing winds. All one has to do is use a bit of imagination. Take a stroll through the cemetery at Tombstone, Arizona; read the inscriptions. Then walk the main street of that once-infamous town around midnight and you might catch a glimpse of the ghosts that still wander the town. They really do. Just ask anyone who lives there. But don't be afraid of the apparitions, they won't hurt you. They're just out for a quiet stroll.

The West lives on. And as long as I am alive, it always will.

Here's a preview for
Blood Bond: Devil Creek Crossfire,
coming in May 2006!

Prologue

"You boys got to settle down someday," the elder Bodine told the blood brothers. "You got to put what you seen on that ridge that day behind you."

"We know, Pa," Matt Bodine said, and Sam Two Wolves nodded his head in agreement.

"But it is not yet that time," Sam added.

"Where are you off to this trip, boys?"

"Who knows, Pa?" Matt said.

"You boys is gettin' the reputation of gunslicks," the older man said. "You don't want that rep hung on you."

"I'm afraid it's already there, Father," Sam said, for this man was almost as much a father to him as his blood father. "But we did not seek it out."

"I know you boys didn't. Well, did you tell your ma goodbye and give her a kiss?"

They had. And they both had a big sack of fried chicken hanging from the saddle horns. The elder Bodine stepped back and lifted a hand.

"You boys know where home is. Come back." He

turned and walked back into the house. The blood brothers rode slowly out the front gate.

The two young men were as much brothers of the blood as if they had the same mother and father, which they did not. Matt Bodine and Sam August Webster Two Wolves were brothers united by the knife and the fire and the blood bonding of the Cheyenne ritual that made them blood brothers forever.

Sam's father had been a great and highly respected chief of the Cheyenne, his mother a beautiful and highly educated white woman from the East who had fallen in love with the handsome Cheyenne chief and married him, both in the Indian way and the white man's so-called Christian way. Matt had saved Sam's life while both were young boys, and they had become close. Soon Matt was spending as much time in the Cheyenne camp as at his home on the ranch.

The two grew up together, and Matt was adopted into the Cheyenne tribe, thus becoming a Human Being in the eyes of the Cheyenne. Sam's father had been killed during the Battle of the Little Big Horn, after he charged Custer, alone, unarmed except for a coup stick. Matt and Sam had witnessed the slaughter, and had never told anyone about that day . . . but the elder Bodine had guessed. When the brothers rode down from the ridges to stand amid the carnage, it had affected them deeply. They decided to drift for a time, to try and erase the terrible memory of the battle.

Both were moderately wealthy men for the time. Sam's mother had come from a very rich family back East and had left him well-off. Both Matt and Sam owned very profitable cattle and horse ranches.

The brothers were handsome and muscular young

men, in excellent physical shape. Both were in their mid-twenties and both had a wild and reckless glint in their eyes. Sam's eyes were black; Matt's were blue. Sam's hair was black; Matt's was dark brown. They were big men for the time, well over six feet, and weighing a good two hundred pounds each. And they were very agile for men their size. They could pass for full brothers, and had, many times. Sam had inherited his mother's white features, with only his cold obsidian eyes—which often sparkled with high humor—giving away his Indian heritage.

When he knew war was coming and that he must fight, Sam's father, Medicine Horse, had ordered his son from their encampment and ordered him to adopt the white man's ways and to forever forget his Cheyenne blood. Medicine Horse made his son repeat the pledge, knowing that even after his death, his son would not disobey his wishes.

Both Matt and Sam wore identical bands around their necks, made up of three multi-colored stones pierced by rawhide.

Both men were highly respected when it came to gunslinging. It was not a title they sought or wanted, but they were called gunfighters, nevertheless. Of the two, Bodine was the swifter, but not by much. He was becoming a legend, although he didn't know it—yet. Sam was not far behind. It was just that Matt had been at it longer.

Matt had killed his first man when he was fourteen, defending his father's ranch against rustlers. The dead man's brothers came after him when he was fifteen and had the misfortune to find him. They were buried that same day. At sixteen, more rustlers came when Matt was night-herding. Two more graves were added. He lived with the Cheyenne during his seventeenth year and then went to work riding shotgun for gold shipments. Four men died trying to rob the shipments. Two more later made the mistake of calling Matt Bodine out into the street. Neither man cleared leather.

While Sam Two Wolves was back East at college (he hated every minute of it, so he claimed), Matt Bodine was a scout for the Army, when they asked him to and providing it was not a campaign to be waged against his adopted people.

Matt saved his money and bought land. His ranch was one of the largest in the state.

Sam Two Wolves was college-educated while Matt had been educated at home by his mother, a trained school teacher. Matt would be considered very well-educated for the time.

The brothers were not yet ready to settle down on their respective ranches. They were young and full of life, and they had a lot of country to see and a lot of life to live before thinking of settling down.

They now drifted into a small town for a drink and supplies. Matt and Sam ended up getting a hell of a lot more than they bargained for.

One

It was not a typical Western town, a fact that both young men picked up on real quick. There were two general stores, both with the same name painted on the front. Two like dress "shoppes," two barber shops, saddle shops, gunsmiths, and so on. Each store was directly across the wide dusty street from the other.

"Have I suddenly developed double-vision?" Sam asked, as they rode slowly down the street, aware of many eyes on them.

"If you have, so have I," Matt replied. "I have seen some strange sights, brother, but I believe this takes the prize."

Both sensed the tension in the air. And both sensed that they had ridden smack into trouble.

"Do you have any idea where we are?" Matt asked.

"Idaho, I think," Sam said. "Does it make any real difference?"

"I guess not." Matt took a second and longer look up and down the street. "Weird," he muttered. "Let's get our supplies and get gone from here."

"My sentiments, exactly," his blood replied. "I don't like the feel of this town."

Two men stepped out of one of the two saloons and stood on the boardwalk, watching the blood brothers. Matt and Sam noticed that the guns of the men were worn low and tied down. A lot of men wore their guns low and tied, and in a dozen other ways for that matter, so that in itself was not unusual. But it was more than the way these two wore their guns that caught the eyes of the brothers. The guns seemed to be a natural part of the men.

"Hired guns," Matt said softly.

"You know them?"

"I know one of them. That's Burl Golden in the black hat. The other one looks familiar, but I just can't place him right off."

"How about a beer?" Sam mused softly, his words just audible over the plop of horses' hooves and the creak of saddle leather.

"That sounds good. Which saloon? You remember the last time we picked a saloon."

Sam chuckled. "Brother, if we didn't constantly stay in trouble, life would be so boring."

They stepped down from their horses and looped the reins around the hitch rail. After they had used their hats to beat the trail dust from their clothing, the brothers looked up and down the street. The fact that they had automatically slipped the hammer thongs from their guns did not escape the eyes of the many loafers who sat in chairs or leaned against support posts on both sides of the street.

The brothers stepped up onto the boardwalk and covered the short distance to the saloon, pushing open the batwings and stepping into the beery-smelling semi-gloom. They stood for a moment, on either side of the batwings, assessing the unusually large crowd for this time of day and letting their eyes adjust to the dimness.

The men in the saloon had fallen silent, everybody staring at the strangers.

"I think they're both Injuns," a man broke the silence, his voice holding a taunting, ugly note.

Matt glanced at Sam and the other smiled. Together, they walked to the long bar. "Beer," Matt said. "For both of us."

The barkeep kept shifting his eyes from Matt to Sam. Both of them did sort of look like Injuns. Sort of. But so did a lot of other men. The barkeep couldn't be sure and didn't want to offend either of these big, rugged-looking hombres. Both of them looked like they'd been across the crick and over the mountains more than once. He finally shrugged his shoulders, drew two mugs of beer, and slid them down to the men.

"Hey, boy," the same loudmouth called. "You with the one gun. Are you a breed, or what?"

Sam took a sip of beer and carefully set the mug back on the scarred-up bar. He sighed, knowing what was coming. But he damn sure wasn't going to let it alone. "Or what," he said.

"Huh?" the loudmouth called.

Matt smiled and sipped his beer. The beer was cool and felt good after a long dusty day on the trail. Neither of the two young men were trouble-hunters, but neither were they known to back away from it.

"I ain't drinkin' with no damn Injuns," the bigmouth persisted.

"Then leave," Matt told him, his back to the man.

The batwings pushed open, and a man wearing a

star on his shirt stepped inside. He looked around, then walked to the bar and stood staring at Matt. "Connors, right?"

"Wrong," Matt told him.

The marshal waited for a few seconds, then said, "Well, if your name isn't Connors, what is it?"

Something in this town was all wrong, and both Sam and Matt could smell it like the odor of a dead skunk. There was too much tension in the air, and it was thick and ugly.

"I'm Matt and this is my brother, Sam."

"I still think that ugly one is a damn stinkin' Injun," the man with the big mouth said.

"You know that gentleman, Marshal?" Sam asked.

"I know him. Why?"

"Then I would suggest that you tell him to shut his face before he finds his mouth separated from it and on the other side of the room."

"He's got a right to an opinion," the marshal replied.

"That he does," Sam agreed evenly. "And so do I."

"What'd you say about me?" The mouth man shoved back his chair and stood up.

Sam turned and faced him. His eyes were hard and dangerous. "I'm half Cheyenne, Mister. Now if you don't like that, you're wearing a gun."

"Hold it!" the marshal raised his voice. "That's enough. You sit down, Eddie. And you boys drink your beer and then leave town."

"No," Matt said softly.

The marshal stiffened. "Cowboy, you can ride with anybody you like. That's your business. But this town is my business. And when I tell you to haul your ashes, you move. Don't play games with me."

Sam stood facing the man with the big mouth. Matt stood facing the bar, his back to the room, the beer mug in his left hand. "I'm not playing games, Marshal. We just came into town to have a beer and stock up on beans and bacon and coffee. When we've done that, we'll leave. And not before."

"I could put you in jail for refusing my orders to leave town."

The man facing Sam was getting angrier by the moment, his face red and his hand by the butt of his gun. "They're both wearin' necklaces, Marshal. That's pure Injun crap. Let's run 'em out of town."

"Settle down, Eddie," the marshal said. "Just settle down. There's something all wrong here. These two are just too calm to suit me. You boys got last names?"

"We're the Smith brothers," Matt said.

"Why couldn't it have been Callahan, or O'Malley, or Frankenhurt?" Sam asked. "Must you always be so unoriginal?"

"My name's Smith," Matt said with an easy grin. "He's Sam Frankenhurt." He gestured toward Sam.

"Couple of damn funny boys," Eddie said. "I'm callin' you out right now, Injun."

"I'm sorry, Eddie," Sam told him. "My dance card is all filled up for this evening."

A couple of the men in the room chuckled.

"Sit down, Eddie!" the marshal shouted. "I mean right now."

Eddie sat, but he wasn't happy about it.

"Who sent for you two?" the marshal asked softly.

"Nobody sent for us. I told you, we're just drifting."

"What are your real names?" The question was asked very low, so no one else in the room could hear.

"Bodine and Two Wolves," Matt whispered.

A nervous tic appeared at the corner of one of the marshal's eyes.

Before he could respond, a man blurted out, "Hell, I

know who them boys are. That's Matt Bodine and Sam Two Wolves."

Eddie sighed and placed both hands on the table top.

"I don't give a damn who they are," another said. "I don't like greasy Injuns."

"Shut up, Prince!" the marshal warned him. He cut his eyes back to Matt. "Nobody sent for you?"

"No one. We're just ridin' through. It looks like we picked the wrong town to light."

"I wouldn't suggest staying long," the marshal said drily.

"This Connors you mentioned," Matt said. "Ben Connors?"

"Yes. You know him?"

"I know of him. Gunfighter from over western Kansas way. He's a bad one. Mean clear through. Why would he be coming to . . . what is the name of this town?"

"Carlin-Sutton."

Sam looked at the marshal. "That's a strange name for a town."

"It's a strange town. And getting stranger. You're in the Carlin half now."

Matt blinked. "I beg your pardon?"

"You boys really weren't kidding, were you? You're just drifting."

"That's right."

"Get your beers and come on over to a table with me. Let's talk."

"What are you gonna do about that stinkin' Injun Marshal?" Prince hollered.

Sam walked over to the man and Prince stood up, ready to draw. Sam never gave him the chance. What he did give him was a combination of lefts and rights to the jaw, mouth, and nose. Prince flattened out on the floor and didn't move.

"That's one way to shut that flappin' trap of his," the bartender said.

"Bring me a beer, George," the marshal called. "And fresh ones for these boys."

"Comin' up, Tom."

Seated at a far table, the marshal said, "The name is Tom Riley."

"Pleased," Sam said. "Would you explain about the Carlin half of this town, Marshal?"

George set three full mugs of beer on the scarred table top and returned to his station.

"Long story," Tom said. "What maps there are of this area show this town as Crossville. It's been here about twelve years. Founded by two men. John Carlin and Bull Sutton. It used to be a nice place to live. Most folks got along well, and there was really very little trouble. Anyways, John and Bull never have got along well with one another. They both own big ranches, and they have big sons and pretty daughters. And they both think they're the cock of the walk. And so do their kids. Bull and John fought the Shoshoni and Bannock and pretty much settled this area. Give them credit for that. Now we got stagecoaches coming in regular, and it was shapin' up to be a right nice place to live and work and raise a family. That is until Daniel Carlin fell in love with Connie Sutton. It has all turned to road apples since then. Now, mind you, neither one of those kids is worth a tinker's damn for anything. It ain't proper to talk about a good woman, but Scarlett ain't no good woman. Not by a long shot. She's as mean as an angry puma and got her a temper and a bad mouth that'd cause any man to duck down and hide his head in shame. Bull has forbid Scarlett to see Johnny, and John has forbid Johnny to see Scarlett. Of course, they see each other every chance they get, which is often. Now Bull had accused John of settin' the whole thing up so's he can get his ranch, and John has accused Bull of the same thing. The kids of both men is eggin' things on 'cause none of them 'ceptin' Daniel Carlin and Connie Sutton has sense enough to come in out of a rainstorm."

"Both sides are hiring gunfighters?" Matt asked.

"You bet. A lot of them."

"Name fighters?"

"Some of them. Ned Kerry, J.B. Adams, Paul Brown, Dick Laurin have signed on with the Flyin' BS."

Sam almost spilled his beer. "The *what?*"

The marshal allowed himself a smile. "That is one hell of a brand, ain't it? Bull Sutton's brand. And he's full of it, too. Henry Rogers, Rod Hansen, Ramblin' Ed Clark, and Bill Lowry is on the Circle JC's payroll. And them's just the known guns. Every manjack on both spreads is now drawin' fightin' wages, and there don't seem to be no end in sight."

"You can add two more to the list," Sam said looking out the fly-specked window of the saloon to the street. "Simon Green and Peck Hill just rode up."

Tom clenched his hands into fists and quietly did some pretty fancy cussing for a moment.

"I hate to ask this, Marshal," Matt said, "and I hope you don't take it the wrong way, but which side are you on?"

Tom shook his head. "No offense taken, Matt. It's a fair question. I'm sittin' smack in the middle of this mess. No man, or no two men, own a Western town of this size. We have us a mayor and a town council, and they hired me. Only they can fire me. I'm paid to keep the peace in this town. I intend to do just that and to hell with what goes on outside it."

The batwings shoved open, and Simon Green and Peck Hill stomped in. They each wore two guns tied down low. Matt and Sam and the marshal were sitting in the semi-gloom at the far end of the saloon. They received a glance from the hired guns, but at that distance the faces of the trio were hard to make out. The gunfighters walked to the bar.

"Whiskey with a beer chaser," Simon said, in a voice too loud. "Both of us. And which way to the Flying BS?"

"Now you know, Marshal," Sam muttered low.

"Look there," Matt said, glancing out the nearest window. "Gene Baker and Norm Meeker riding up. It's getting real interesting around here."

"You boys best leave this saloon," George told the pair at the bar. "You're on the wrong side of town. Get on over to the Bull's Den." He had one hand under the bar, out of sight, and both gunslingers knew that in all likelihood, he was gripping a sawed-off shotgun. Some called them Greeners.

"Easy, now, friend," Simon said. "Just hold your water. We didn't know."

"Now you do," George told him.

"For a fact," Peck said.

Gene Baker and Norm Meeker walked in, and the four gunfighters stared at one another for a moment.

"Well, well," Simon broke the short silence. "Look who the tomcat done drug in. Baker and Meeker. I guess you boys signed on with the wrong side again."

"It damn shore ain't the side you're on, Green." Meeker scowled at him. "It never is. You and me, we'll end our quarrel this go around. Now get out of my way."

"I don't think so."

"That's it!" Marshal Riley said, standing up and stepping into the light from the window. His badge glinted brightly. He pointed at the gunslicks. "Take your difficulties outside of town. There will be no trouble in this town. You two," he said to Green and Hill, "take your butts across the street. Right now."

"Why, sure thing, Marshal," Peck said easily and with a smile. "We sure don't want no trouble with the law, now do we, Simon?"

"Oh, absolutely not," Simon added in a mocking tone. The two men grinned at each other and walked out onto the boardwalk, then across the wide street.

Baker and Meeker looked at the marshal, nodded their heads, and walked to the bar. Tom sat back down at the table. Two men were dabbing at Prince's face with wet towels. He was coming around, but slowly. Sam had really blown out his candle with that last punch on the button.

"What ran over me?" Prince mumbled. "A beer wagon?"

"No," one of those attending him said. "That half-breed Injun."

"I think I better make friends with him," Prince said. "I damn sure don't want him for no enemy."

"Marshal," Sam said, confusion in his eyes. "Do you mean that this country is about to explode in a shooting war because of a proposed *wedding?*"

Tom toyed with his beer mug for a moment. He sighed and shook his head. "That's the reason both men give. But this has been simmerin' on the back burner for a long time. The kids seein' each other is just an excuse."

"Lone rider coming in," Matt said.

Baker and Meeker left the bar and walked to the

batwings, looking out. "Ben Connors," Baker said. "Somebody is spendin' a lot of money gettin' him in here."

Connors reined up and swung down from the saddle in front of the Bull's Den.

"Seems like a whole lot of people arriving in this town in one day," Matt remarked.

"For a fact," Tom agreed. "And I hope the two I'm sitting with have decided to leave," he said hopefully.

Matt and Sam looked at each other and grinned.

"Oh, hell!" Tom said. "That's what I figured."

"Jesus!" Prince said with a groan. "I feel like I been kicked by a mule."

Two

The brothers got a room at the hotel, which was located at the end of the street in a fork of the road, and which had been declared neutral ground by both warring ranchers. That was because of the hotel's dining room. The chef had been brought in from New York City, and his food was praised by all.

Sam stood by the window of the room and looked up the wide street of the split-apart town. "I wonder what the real reason is behind this war? And I wonder why we don't just saddle up and ride away from this silly mess?"

"The real reason is probably a power struggle, and the reason we're staying is because of curiosity. You can't keep your nose out of other folk's business." Matt ducked his head to hide his smile.

"Me?" Sam said, turning from the window on the second floor. "You're the one who is the busybody."

Matt tried his best to look hurt. He couldn't pull it off. "You really want to ride out?"

Sam smiled and shook his head. "No. We've been on the trail for several weeks, and I'd like a few days sleeping in a real bed. Not to mention some time off from your lousy cooking."

"At least I can cook," Matt told him. "You have a tough time getting water to boil." He stretched out on the bed with a sigh. The brothers had taken baths in the tubs behind the barber shop, then had gotten a shave and a haircut while fresh clothing was being brushed and ironed and their trail-worn clothing was sent to the Chinese laundry, run by a pleasant enough fellow named Wo Fong.

"Whatever is going to happen must be close," Sam said, still standing by the open window. "Two more riders coming in, and they look like they've been on the trail for a time."

"Recognize them?"

"One of them does look familiar. The little man."

Matt heaved himself off the bed and took a look. "That's Little Jimmy Dexter. Texas gunhand. He's little but he's mean as a snake. I don't know that other fellow."

Dexter and his partner swung down in front of the Bull's Den and disappeared inside the barroom.

"I'm hungry," Sam said.

"I could use a bite myself."

The words had just left Matt's mouth when a dozen riders and two buggies came into view, racing down the street and kicking up a lot of unnecessary dust, sending people on foot scrambling for the safety of the boardwalks.

"Must be somebody terribly important," Matt said.

"Or somebody who thinks they are," Sam added. "More than likely, the latter."

"Let's go take a look."

At first, the blood brothers thought they were experiencing double-vision. The desk clerk cleared it all up.

"Identical twins," he told him, after smiling at the confused looks on their faces. "Bull Sutton's girls. Willa and Wanda. Don't get in their way, boys. They're pretty as all get out, but both as mean as snakes. And if you repeat that, I'll call you liars."

The twins sashayed across the boardwalk and wiggled into the lobby. One of them spotted Sam and pointed to him. "You there!" she hollered. "Water our teams and see to our buggies and be quick about it."

Sam looked at her, one eyebrow arched. "See to your own buggies," he told her.

"Oh, Lord," the desk clerk muttered. "And this started out to be such a nice afternoon."

The Flying BS riders who had crowded into the lobby stopped in their tracks and slowly turned, facing Matt and Sam, giving them hard looks. The desk clerk quickly dropped on all fours behind the counter.

"Boy, you don't talk to Miss Willa like that," a puncher said. "You better do like you're told and do it quick."

"I don't think so," Sam replied.

"Let's drag him," Wanda said, a wicked look in her eyes. "Somebody get a rope."

"What nice young ladies," Sam muttered.

"Yeah," Matt agreed. "They were at the top of their class in charm school, for sure."

Several of the Flying BS riders took a step toward the brothers, and Matt and Sam braced for trouble.

"Break it up!" Marshal Tom Riley spoke from the doorway. "Right now."

"Aw, hell, Tom," Willa said, and with those words, the brothers knew she was not a lady. "We were just gonna have some fun with this drifter."

"That drifter is Sam Two Wolves," the marshal quietly informed the crowd. "And that's his blood brother, Matt Bodine, standing to his right. If you people want to see blood all over this lobby, just crowd those two about one inch more and see what happens."

The punchers stood easy, being careful to keep their hands away from their guns. They weren't afraid of the blood brothers—they were all drawing fighting wages and rode for the brand—but they knew well the reputation of Bodine and Two Wolves, and this close in, confined to the lobby of the hotel, the brothers would get lead into a lot of punchers, and Willa and Wanda stood a very good chance of getting hurt or killed.

"Miss Willa asked that breed, or whatever he is, to see to her buggy," a puncher said. "The breed got lippy about it. Bull ain't gonna like that one bit."

"You think anybody who doesn't work for your brand is your servant?" Sam asked. "I have news for you."

Tom stepped between the men. "Well, Shorty, why don't you see to the buggies and then everything will work out?" the marshal suggested.

Shorty looked at Sam, an ugly expression on his ugly face. "We'll meet up again, Breed."

Sam smiled thinly at the man. "Anytime you feel lucky, Shorty. Just anytime at all."

"My daddy will hear of this," Wanda hollered. "You can bet on that."

"The people in the next county over probably heard it," Matt said, recklessness swelling up in him. "A pack of coyotes don't make as much racket as you."

"What?" Wanda shrieked. "What did you call me? Did you hear that man, boys? He called me a coyote. I've never been so insulted."

A big brute of a man stepped into the lobby. The man must have stood at least six-feet-six and carried the weight to go with it. He filled the whole doorway. "What's going on here?" he demanded.

Wanda pointed at Matt. "That saddle bum called me a coyote, Papa!" she bellered, rattling the wheel-spoke lamps overhead.

Bull Sutton cut his eyes to a puncher. "Is that right, Laredo?"

"Well . . . sort of," the man said, shuffling his boots. "But not rightly."

Bull sighed. "Laredo . . ."

"What I said was, she made more noise than a pack of coyotes," Matt explained.

A very small smile creased the big man's lips for an instant, and then was gone. "Well, now, she can do that for a fact," Bull said.

"Daddy!" Wanda hollered. "How can you say things like that in front of trash?" She threw her hands to her face in total mortification.

"Be that the truth," Bull said, "I can't let you insult a daughter of mine."

Matt shrugged his shoulders in total indifference. He stood with his hands by his side. Bull studied the young man. There was a flatness in the rider's eyes that he did not like. Then he realized what that flatness represented. Death. He cut his eyes to Sam. The same flatness and lack of emotion was in his eyes, too.

"That's Matt Bodine and Sam Two Wolves, boss," Laredo said quietly.

The big man's eyes narrowed. He cocked his head to one side and studied Matt, then Sam. His eyes shifted back to Matt. "So you're workin' for the Circle JC, now, huh?"

"Wrong. We're just passing through."

"Uh-huh. Well, you just keep right on passin'."

"Wrong," Sam stuck his mouth into it. His back was stiff with anger, and Matt could see it. And when Sam got mad, the odds were pretty good that somebody was going to get hurt—or dead. "We like it around here. So we think we'll stay for awhile. And that is with or without the permission from your lordship."

"That's the breed who insulted me," Willa hollered.

"Lordship," Bull said softly. He grunted and shook his head at the careless and flippant manner of the two young men. "You boys just stay in trouble, don't you?" He cut his eyes back to Sam. "You don't much look like an Injun."

"I really don't know how to respond to that, so I won't."

"You boys want to work for me?"

"No," they said together.

"I pay top dollar."

"Thanks, but we both own working ranches ourselves," Matt told him.

Bull's eyes narrowed at that. He nodded his head. "So I heard. All right, boys. The hotel is off-limits for trouble. But that's as far as the limits go. Outside, you're on your own."

Matt started to tell the man that they didn't need nursemaids, but wisely decided not to push his luck. Bull Sutton looked like he ate chuck wagons for lunch—wheels, rims, and all. And picked his teeth with the wagon tongue.

"Get your shoppin' done, girls," Bull said, turning his back to the brothers as a way of dismissal. "But stay on my side of the town."

Willa and Wanda looked at the brothers, both went, "Huumph!" and swished out the door, followed by several punchers who acted as bodyguards. Bull and several of his men went into the hotel dining room. Matt and Sam stepped out onto the long porch of the hotel.

Matt studied the town for a moment. "This is the craziest thing I've ever seen."

"Well, at least it makes the town look twice as big," Sam said cheerfully, his good mood fast returning.

Matt said, "You want to check out the Bull's Den?"

Sam grinned. "Why not? Might as well make both sides mad at us."

They angled across the dusty street and walked up the boardwalk, on the Flying BS side of the town, tipping their hats to the ladies and howdying the men. The ladies smiled, and the men frowned at them.

"Why are the citizens giving us such dark looks?" Sam questioned, just before they reached the entrance to the Bull's Den.

"They don't know what side we're on, I suppose. You ready for a beer?"

"I'd rather have something to eat. They probably have a free lunch in there."

"And we're probably going to get in a fight once inside. It's better to fight on an empty stomach. I keep telling you that, but you never listen."

"Thanks for reminding me," Sam said drily. "But I'm still hungry."

"I thought Indians could go for days without eating?"

"They do now," Sam popped right back. "After listening to the white man's lies and getting stuck on reservations."

Chuckling, the two men pushed open the batwings and stepped inside the Bull's Den.

Those seated at the tables and lined up along the bar turned and fell silent as the brothers walked in and stood for a moment on either side of the batwings.

"Paul Stewart," Matt muttered, his eyes shifting to a man standing at the long bar. "That's who rode in with Little Jimmy Dexter."

"I recognize him now. The beard fooled me. He probably grew it as a disguise because he's got warrants out on him."

"No doubt."

The brothers walked to the bar, spurs jingled softly in the silence, and leaned against it. The barkeep made no move to take their orders.

A lunch of meat and cheese and hard boiled eggs had been set up on a table near the far end of the bar. Sam walked over to it and began building a thick sandwich, spreading the mustard liberally on the bread.

"That's for regular customers," the barkeep told him, a sour note to his voice.

"I'm regular," Sam said with a smile. "A little rhubarb now and then sees to that."

The barkeep blinked and Matt laughed. "Two beers, please," he called.

The bartender ignored Matt's order. "Are you makin' light with me?" he asked Sam.

Sam finished building his sandwich, which now weighed about two pounds and was so thick a moose would have trouble getting its mouth around it. He stuck two hard-boiled eggs in his pocket and turned to the bartender. "Light of you? Oh, no. I thought you were inquiring about my health."

"I don't give a damn for your health! And you don't either, comin' in here."

"Hey, Breed," a gunhand called from a table. "Why don't you go on back to the reservation?"

"The general character and disposition of the immediate company would certainly improve dramatically if I did," Sam popped right back.

The gunny pushed back his chair and stood up, his hands by his guns. Pearl-handled, Sam noticed. "I think you just insulted me, Breed."

"Settle down, Chuckie," a man said.

"Settle down, hell!" Chuckie said, his face flushed. "That damn half-breed or whatever he is said something bad about me. I think."

Sam took a bite of his sandwich and chewed. Matt noticed that his brother held the sandwich in his left hand, his right hand close to the butt of his gun. Sam was proficient with either hand, but, as today, normally wore only one gun.

"What's your part in all this, Bodine?" another man called out.

"None, as long as it stays one on one."

"It ain't none of our affair," another said. "We're out of it."

"The bread could be a bit fresher," Sam said, after taking another bite. "But other than that, I have to say it's a pretty good sandwich."

"Damnit, man!" Chuckie hollered. "Will you pay attention to me and stop all that chompin'?"

Sam looked at the man, and Matt knew then that his brother was going to do something foolish. What, he didn't know. But Sam had a tendency to place more value on human life—even an outlaw's life—than Matt. Sometimes. "I seldom pay much attention to the braying of a jackass."

"Chuckie, man, back off!" J. B. Adams urged. "He ain't done you no hurt."

"He's part Injun, and I don't like Injuns." Chuckie made a half turn and faced Sam fully. "I hope you like that sandwich, Breed. 'Cause your belly's about to be full of lead."

"I really doubt it," Sam's words were softly spoken, but carried well to the man. "Why don't you take the advice of your friends and sit down? There is no need for a shooting."

"Sam Two Wolves," Chuckie sneered. "Big shot gunhand. Hell, you're yellow clean through."

The others in the room started watching Matt Bodine. They knew that if trouble started, and it was only a heartbeat away, if any of them took a hand in it, Bodine would fill both hands with iron and start shooting. At this close range, the barroom would be very quickly filled with dead and dying men. Bodine and Sam would take lead, but that wouldn't help those lying dead on the floor, and no one could be sure it wouldn't be them. All in all, it was a very bad situation, especially for Chuckie, for the most experienced gunhandlers knew that Sam Two Wolves was just a shade behind Matt Bodine when it came to skills as a pistolero. To a man, they wished Chuckie would shut his flappin' trap and sit back down.

The batwings pushed open, and Bull Sutton's bulk filled the space. The man quickly sized up the situation and immediately stepped to one side. Several of his hands went with him. He was not going to interfere. Matt read it right when he figured Bull wanted to see Sam in action, wanted to know just what he might be up against should the brothers decide to ride for the Circle JC. He moved to the bar, and Matt noted that for a big man, Bull Sutton was mighty light on his boots. That was something worth bearing in mind.

The barkeep quietly placed a bottle and several glasses in front of Bull.

"I said I wanted a beer," Matt reminded the man.

"Give him a beer," Bull told the barkeep. "Chuck

Babb is quick with a short gun, Bodine," Bull whispered.

"He's not quick enough."

"The breed that good?"

"He's that good."

Chuckie cussed Sam for a moment. Then he stood tense, his hands by his guns. Sam laid his half-eaten sandwich on a table and faced the man square, after pulling a hand on the back of a chair. "This doesn't have to be," Sam finally spoke.

"Yeah, Breed," Chuckie replied, his voice hoarse. "It has to be."

Sam arched an eyebrow and waited.

"Are you gonna grab iron?" Chuckie called.

"It's your play," Sam told him, his voice calm. "I never wanted this trouble."

Chuckie began to have doubts. Sam was just too calm and collected. But he made no move to wipe the perspiration from his face. Any move now would be taken as a move toward a gun. He silently cussed the situation. The damn breed was just too sure of himself. He just stood there, waiting, his face showing no emotion at all.

"A hundred dollars on Chuckie," Bull said softly.

"You're on," Matt took the bet.

"Chuckie killed that Utah gunhand, Rodman, down on the flats," Bull said.

Matt chose not to reply. He'd watched Sam put his left hand on the chair back and wondered what his brother had in mind. Matt lifted his beer mug with his left hand and took a sip, always keeping one eye on the men in the saloon. And the men knew it. Bull had placed both hands on the bar. They all were familiar with the unwritten rules of gunplay.

Chuckie lost his composure and began cussing Sam, the spittle flying from his lips. Sam waited, his face impassive.

"Now!" Chuckie screamed, and grabbed for his guns.